"THROW DOWN YOUR PHASER," LEONG SAID.

Trying to copy the air of cool defiance he'd seen Captain Kirk use so many times, Ensign Pavel Chekov locked his eyes on Leong's crooked smile and flicked his phaser away. It bounced with a soft *thump*, and Chekov didn't dare turn his head to see exactly where it landed.

But Leong glanced after the weapon and, quickly as he could, Chekov dove for his phaser.

Leong intercepted him less than halfway there. . . .

Look for STAR TREK Fiction from Pocket Books

Star Trek: The Original Series

Star Trek: The Next Generation

Star Trek: Deep Space Nine

STAR TREK®

TRAITOR WINDS

16699115

L.A. GRAF

POCKET BOOKS

New York   London   Toronto   Sydney   Tokyo   Singapore

This book is a work of fiction. Names, characters, places and incidents are products of the author's imagination or are used fictitiously. Any resemblance to actual events or locales or persons, living or dead, is entirely coincidental.

An *Original* Publication of POCKET BOOKS

POCKET BOOKS, a division of Simon & Schuster Inc. 1230 Avenue of the Americas, New York, NY 10020

This book is published by Pocket Books, a division of Simon & Schuster Inc., under exclusive license from Paramount Pictures.

ISBN: 0-671-86913-2

First Pocket Books printing June 1994

10 9 8 7 6 5 4 3 2 1

POCKET and colophon are registered trademarks of Simon & Schuster Inc.

Printed in the U.S.A.

For our favorite parents,
Domenick and Evelyn Cercone.
Thanks for adopting one of us,
and for letting the other
stay up late to watch *Star Trek*.

Historian's Note

This adventure takes place shortly after the end of the *Enterprise*'s first five-year mission, immediately following the events chronicled in *The Lost Years*.

TRAITOR WINDS

Prologue

U.S.S. DeGama
Donatu Sector, Coordinates Unknown
Terrestrial Date: December 25, 2269
2300 hours shiptime

"ALL HANDS, prepare for docking with enemy vessel in thirteen minutes, seven seconds."

Admiral James T. Kirk looked up from his coffee, tightening his hands around the warm mug in unconscious frustration. He wanted a window, or a viewscreen, or at least a place to stand on the high-speed courier's bridge. He wanted to know what *DeGama*'s commander was thinking, how the ship was feeling as they nosed up to the alien security buoys, how the crew would react when their communications officer hailed the alien commander and requested permission to board. He wanted to be something more than a passenger waiting in a blind mess hall for word of how the mission was going.

You want to be the captain, he told himself reprovingly. But wanting that now wasn't realistic, wasn't fair. He'd given up the right to stride the cosmos when he'd accepted the promotion to admiral all those months before.

Kirk glanced up at the chronometer above the replicator array. 2304 hours. What was taking so long?

"Admiral. I see that my son's characterization of your behavior was more accurate than I gave him credit for."

1

Kirk turned from the chronometer with no real surprise, fitting a polite smile to his features even though he got no reciprocal expression from his companion. He occasionally had to remind himself that prolonged close quarters with aliens who might not appreciate manners was no reason to forsake them. "Spock served with me for a long time, Ambassador Sarek. I would expect him to amass some fairly accurate data as to my demeanor."

"Indeed." Sarek passed from the open doorway with the smooth, silent grace Kirk had learned to expect from Vulcans, even those as tall and powerfully built as the ambassador. His feet treading whisper-light on the bare deck, his robes barely brushing one against the other, Sarek rounded the long mess table to seat himself directly across from Kirk. The admiral straightened ever so slightly and pulled his coffee a fraction of an arm's length closer, as if the strong smell might be offensive to Sarek.

"Spock often remarked upon the human propensity to expend emotional energy on events which have not yet occurred. It was a behavioral trait Spock found fascinating for its illogic." Sarek folded his hands within the pools of brown fabric that made up his sleeves, lifting one eyebrow at Kirk's coffee mug without interrupting his speech. Kirk had always assumed Spock was collecting auxiliary information whenever he glanced at something that way. He wondered what the well-stained coffee mug told Sarek now. "I informed Spock that you were an unusually intelligent human being, with a clear understanding of temporal relations and your own inability to influence them." The ambassador cocked his head. "Was my assessment in error?"

"Not really, Ambassador, no." Kirk smiled ruefully and took a mouthful of his coffee. It was only lukewarm, and tasted bitter and stale. "I think we humans view worrying as a way of planning for the future—of reminding ourselves of all the things that might happen because of what we do." *Or don't do.*

Something in the focus of Sarek's dark eyes shifted, constructing an echo of what Spock always displayed as a frown. "That is highly illogical. You cannot build models to any degree of accuracy based on . . ." Distaste tried but failed to turn down the corners of the ambassador's mouth. ". . . imaginary information."

Kirk smiled, then remembered that amusement might very well come across as rude, and concealed his humor in a sigh as he pushed away from the table. "Be that as it may, Ambassador, you'll never convince humanity of it. Besides . . ." He tipped the ruined coffee down the disposal bin. "It's not the future I'm worried about."

"The past is equally beyond your reach."

"Yes . . ." Kirk punched up a new mug of coffee, hotter and blacker than the last. "And so is the present."

Sarek said nothing while Kirk retrieved his mug, tasted it, and decided against adding sugar or cream. For some reason, anything approaching luxury seemed undeserved and sinful right now, considering the intergalactic war that might result from his failure here. He hadn't even let himself sleep since leaving Earth sixteen hours ago. It mattered to him that he be awake and aware for every moment of this last-minute gamble to prevent the galaxy from plunging into a conflict that none of them could survive. It also mattered that across the light-years of distance, Sulu and Chekov could have faith that their captain wouldn't abandon them to charges of treason and murder. Kirk sincerely hoped they knew that.

"Why do you persist in assuming responsibility for crimes other men have committed?"

Kirk snapped a startled look at the ambassador, then bit back the first angry words that filled his mouth. Sarek's face was as impassive as always, eyebrows lifted in the faintest indication of inquiry, head inclined as though listening intently for the most subtle meaning in every sound. Kirk's hostility guttered when confronted with the innocence of Vulcan curiosity.

"Because I'm their captain," he said, turning away

3

from the replicator to pace the narrow room. "Because they're my crew."

"You *were* their captain," Sarek stated gently, as though correcting an equation for a child. He pivoted in his seat to follow Kirk's progress. "They are no longer your crew."

Kirk felt a searing flash of pain and anger, then couldn't decide if his emotions were reacting to the ambassador's coldness or the subject of the ambassador's discussion. "It's about more than my crew now—it's about using my crew to try and destabilize the entire Federation. That makes it my concern." He stopped, matching his passionate stare to Sarek's stoic one, as if by sheer force of will he could make the Vulcan understand all the complicated feelings and beliefs that went into a human's convictions. "I won't stand by and let my crew be hurt. By anyone, for any reason."

"All hands, prepare for docking with enemy vessel in four minutes, four seconds."

An almost forgotten sense at the back of Kirk's brain confirmed the time estimate without his even being sure how he knew the *DeGama's* speed and direction. In contrast, Sarek glanced briefly at the intercom, then the chronometer, as if to verify the individual points in the data chain. "It is because of your service to my son and myself that I have made myself available for this negotiation," the ambassador said, bringing his eyes back to Kirk's. "However, I still fail to understand why you believe anything you do here—or with your colleagues from the other side of the Neutral Zone—can affect occurrences back on Earth."

"Because it has to." Because nothing Kirk could do on Earth would save everything, and he refused to choose between Sulu's and Chekov's lives and the Federation's future. Because taking daring risks had never failed him before, and he wouldn't accept that it would fail him now just because it wasn't his starship racing toward the rendezvous. Because if nothing he thought, or said, or did had any hope of setting right the horrible wrongs in motion back home, then everything he believed about life was a lie, and people really were nothing better than powerless flotsam on the mindless tides of circumstance. "It just *has* to," he said again, firmly enough to make it true.

"And if the war you seek to avert has already begun?"

Kirk swallowed more coffee and resumed his restless pacing, unwilling—and unable—to answer.

EARTH

Chapter One

New Harborplace
Baltimore, North America
Terrestrial Date: December 14, 2269
1730 hours EST

SMELLS.

That was what Uhura liked most about coming back to Earth between starship assignments—rediscovering the unique scent of every region and city on the planet. On board the *Enterprise,* life-support systems recirculated the air so efficiently that most smells got whisked away before they even reached your nose. Older ships and space stations tended to smell unpleasantly like chlorinated hydrocarbons, while the air on alien planets always held some note that jangled on human senses, subliminally warning you that you weren't really home.

But Earth . . . Uhura took a deep, happy breath of the Baltimore night. Earth smelled of the sea that ran in your blood, the trees that shared your DNA, the perfumes and musks of all the other human beings gathered with you in a city plaza on a crisp winter night. Not to mention the sweet smell of fresh-baked bread, the drift of smoke from char-grilled fish, the rich, dark fragrance of espresso—

"I'm starving." Sulu voiced the thought in Uhura's mind before she could say it. He leaned over the harbor rail to peer into the half-submerged geodesic domes of New Harborplace. The lights of the underwater mall

9

glittered through transparent aluminum panes, illuminating the night-dark water from below. "I hope Chekov gets us a table down there soon."

"Are you sure it was a good idea to send him into the restaurant?" Uhura stood on tiptoe, watching shadow schools of fish dart across the undersea lights. Her wool tapestry coat threw a fragmented glitter of rich colors across the water, with the reflection of Sulu's flight suit a thin silver slash beside her. As usual, the pilot had flown himself out for their weekly reunion dinner. "You know Chekov doesn't care if we *ever* eat. He probably wouldn't even come to have dinner with us here if it wasn't so close to Annapolis."

Sulu snorted. "That's true. But he's also been in photon-torpedo mode ever since he entered Security Academy—give him a job to do, and he'll do it, or explode trying."

Uhura turned away from the dark water to frown at him, troubled by the uneasy note beneath the usual mockery in his voice. It wasn't like Sulu to worry. "Is something wrong?"

Sulu opened his mouth to reply, but a familiar shout from farther down the dock interrupted him. Uhura saw a red-sleeved arm waving at them from the crowd around the mall entrance, and blinked in surprise. "Chekov *can't* have found us a table already—it's Friday night!"

Sulu laughed, and this time Uhura heard only merriment in his voice. "Let's hope he didn't have to stun someone to get it." He pulled Uhura's mittened hand through his arm and guided her through the press of people. His distinctive flight suit readily opened a path for them. It wasn't often that people in eastern North America saw a Starfleet test pilot, and a murmur of interested comment followed them down the enclosed stairs to the swinging glass doors. Chekov's head lifted to scan the crowd as they approached, as if the unusual ripple of sound had set off some new warning instinct inside him.

"Through here," he said curtly, holding the revolving door so Uhura could step in, then giving it a push that propelled her through and out into the aromatic warmth of the mall's eating plaza. Busy waiters threaded their way through crowded tables with grav-platters of seafood and steaming trays of Asian appetizers hovering over their shoulders. Uhura restrained an urge to hijack the nearest one. She hadn't eaten since she'd boarded the maglev from San Francisco earlier that afternoon.

Sulu emerged from the doors after another minute, Chekov on his heels. "We're over on the east side," the Russian informed them, not sounding too pleased about it. He led the way through the crowded geodesic dome and into the spiraling tube that led to the next one. "Right up against the east wall."

"Next to the aquarium tanks?" Uhura's eyes widened in startled delight. "Chekov, how on earth did you get us seated there?"

Sulu snorted again. "He must have bribed someone. Those tables are usually reserved months in advance."

"Security cadets don't make enough money to bribe anyone," Chekov retorted. "I ran into some friends, and they insisted that we join them."

"Friends?" Uhura scanned the eating plaza they had just emerged into. She didn't see anyone besides Chekov wearing the distinctive red and black singlet uniform of the Security Academy. "Old Starfleet Academy friends?"

Chekov's mouth curved into a reluctant smile. "No. Old *Enterprise* friends."

He swung her around to face the two men standing beside a table near the backlit aquarium wall. Uhura let out a delighted cry, and ran to hug the nearest one, a thin figure in civilian blue sweater and brown slacks. "Dr. McCoy! How are you?"

"Better now that I've seen you—I think." The ship's surgeon stepped back from Sulu's enthusiastic shoulder thumping and got his hand wrung by Chekov instead. He grinned at them, and Uhura found the sight of that familiar crooked smile inexplicably comforting. "I thought I was seeing ghosts in the aquarium tank when I caught sight of Chekov's reflection, but you people look pretty damn real to me," McCoy said.

"Real enough to treat you to dinner," Sulu assured him. Uhura saw Chekov wince, and shook her head at him reassuringly. Security cadets might not get paid much, but senior Starfleet Academy lecturers and experimental test pilots had no such problems. *Especially* the test pilots.

"What are you doing in Baltimore, sir?" Uhura asked, shrugging off her heavy wool coat while waiters scurried up with additional chairs. "I thought you had retired to Georgia."

"Oh, I have." McCoy tossed an amused look at his dinner companion. "I came up to do some guest lectures at Johns Hopkins, so I've been hanging out with some of the local medical riffraff. I think you know this one."

Uhura turned, eyes widening when she recognized the older man in Starfleet medical blues. "Is it—*Dr. Piper?*"

"Lieutenants Uhura and—and Sulu, isn't that right?" With a smile, the *Enterprise*'s former chief physician reached across the table to take the hand Uhura extended. He returned Sulu's polite handclasp, too, then glanced at Chekov and shook his head. "I'm afraid I don't recognize you, young man. Sorry about that."

Chekov gave him a restrained Russian nod. "Ensign Pavel Chekov, sir. I came aboard the *Enterprise* after you had gone."

"Chekov . . . hmm. Name sounds familiar to me for some reason. I'll recall it in a minute." Despite his fraying silver hair and stooped shoulders, Piper's eyes still snapped with the intellectual fire that had lifted him out of a field post and into the highest echelons of Starfleet research. He motioned them to take their seats at the round oak table, the gold braid on his uniform sleeve glinting in the light. "Can't say I expected to see any of my old crewmates again. Pleased to find out you're all still alive and in service." A tinge of teasing humor crept into his clipped New England accent. "Unlike Leonard here."

"Now, Mark, don't you start harping on my retirement again," McCoy growled. "After all, you only spent one year putting up with this crew's shenanigans. I was there for the other four—I deserve a rest!" He ran a hand across his thinning brown hair, looking rueful. "Unlike the *Enterprise,* I can't just put into an orbital station and get Scotty to repair the damage."

Uhura had been pressing her nose against the cold, blue-green wall of the aquarium tank, watching in delight as the dappled shadows of harbor seals blew sprays of bubbles against the transparent aluminum, then chased them back up toward the surface. The mention of the chief engineer's name pulled her attention abruptly back toward the table. "Have you seen Mr. Scott lately, sir?"

McCoy snorted. *"Seen* him? I had to take him to some horrible Scottish bar on his last shore leave. He said he was having the devil of a time getting a good haggis out of the new food replicators on board."

Sulu made a horrified face. "I didn't think there was such a thing as a *good* haggis."

"There isn't," McCoy agreed. "But Mr. Scott won't admit that until he's eaten at every place in the galaxy that serves one." He picked up his drink and swallowed a large mouthful, as if the mere mention of haggis had left a bad taste in his mouth. "He says the refitting's going as well as could be expected, given a planetful of engineers who don't know a blessed thing about designing for spaceflight at warp nine."

Chekov and Sulu exchanged amused looks. "Probably because the technical manual says you can't take a Constitution-class starship to those kinds of speeds," Sulu suggested with a ripple of laughter in his voice.

"No doubt." McCoy scrubbed a hand reflectively across his nose. "Now, who else have I run into on my lecture tour?" He lifted an eyebrow at Uhura. "Did you know Janice Rand has moved over to Communications? She's stationed at the Iceland Array."

Uhura's eyes widened. "At the main Communications Center? Good for her."

Dr. Piper smiled. "I always knew that young woman was too smart to stay a yeoman forever. And speaking of smart—where's Chris Chapel these days?"

"Back in medical school," McCoy said proudly. "Going for a joint M.D./Ph.D. in xenophysiology."

"At Stanford University," Uhura added, not without some pleasure. "Right down the coast from me. We see each other every few weeks."

Sulu chuckled. "Well, I can't say I *see* much of John Kyle, but I do get to talk to him every other day or so when I do the circumpolar test flights. He's stationed at the big transporter platform down in Tasmania. Says he likes the climate, but misses North American food."

"And speaking of food . . ." Uhura eyed one of the passing grav-trays with a wistful look. "Can we get something to eat?"

"Coming right up." Sulu waved, and the flash of silver in the darkness easily caught the attention of a passing waiter. "Bring us all the appetizers on your menu, to start with," he ordered, and tossed the woman his account card. "All of it billed to me."

Both Dr. Piper and Dr. McCoy objected vociferously to that, and even Chekov muttered a protest. Sulu merely grinned at all of them. "Hey, I've got to spend my hazardous-duty pay somewhere. What better use for it than a dinner with old friends?"

McCoy's expressive eyebrows arched into his furrowed brow. "Hazardous-duty pay, Sulu? On Earth?"

"Yes." The pilot ran a proud hand across the golden sun and mountain badge that glimmered on the shoulder of his flightsuit. "I told them I didn't really need it—not after five years on the *Enterprise*—but the base commander insisted. It's not like I'm doing anything really dangerous. . . ."

"Oh, of course not." Chekov made a skeptical Russian

noise. "Everyone knows that testing experimental landing shuttles is just like taking a vacation."

Sulu laughed. "Well, it *is* a vacation for me. All that New Mexican sun and sand and wilderness—it's better than a shore-leave port. And the work is easy."

Uhura and Chekov exchanged mutually exasperated glances. Despite weeks of argument, they had never been able to get Sulu to admit that his volunteer stint at the White Sands Experimental Flight Center was any more dangerous than a typical shift on the *Enterprise*. And the problem was, Uhura reflected wryly, Sulu was such a good pilot that, for all they knew, he was telling the truth when he said it was easy work.

"Let me get this straight." McCoy leaned back as the waiter lowered a huge platter of steaming crab cakes, oriental dumplings, and assorted other hors d'oeuvres onto their table. "You turned down an assignment as first officer on that deep-space research vessel . . . what was it, again?"

"The *Resolution*." Sulu eyed the grav-platter of appetizers with a quiet smile, then spun it so the pickled herring ended up in front of Chekov. The Russian gave him back an aggrieved look, but Uhura noticed he forked some onto his plate just the same. She hid a smile and reached for a roll of seaweed and flying-fish eggs. "Scheduled to explore out from Vulcan to Epsilon Eridani."

"Right—some of the most promising sectors in the Federation." McCoy pointed a barbecued chicken wing accusingly at the pilot. "And instead of doing that, you're out in the desert testing new landing shuttles to see if they'll explode?"

Dr. Piper steepled his fingers and regarded Sulu over them, brow furrowed. "That's not what I'd call a smart career move, son."

Sulu shrugged and speared his chopsticks through a second lobster dumpling. "No, but at least it's temporary." He pointed the chopsticks, dumpling and all, at Uhura. "Just like her teaching assignment at Starfleet Academy."

"Just like—" Understanding dawned in McCoy's blue eyes and his scowl slowly faded. "You two want to get back on the *Enterprise!*"

The astonishment—and hint of pity—Uhura heard in his voice made her duck her head and fiddle with her crab cake. "It's not like it's never been done before," she said, hearing the note of defensiveness in her own voice despite her effort to sound unconcerned. "A lot of line officers have transferred back onto their ships after refitting."

McCoy grunted. "A lot of *junior* line officers. Kids like Chekov here, who still need to climb a few ranks before they take a lateral transfer." He lifted an eyebrow at the Russian. "You're scheduled to be reassigned to the *Enterprise* when you finish security training, right?"

Chekov made a face that was neither acknowledgment nor denial. "I doubt the crew roster is finalized so far in advance, Doctor." His plans after training weren't something he talked about much around Sulu and Uhura.

"But you two," Piper took up the argument while McCoy wrestled with a rack of spareribs. "You should be ship-hopping for the next few years, getting all the experience you can before you put in for your own command."

Uhura shook her head definitively. She'd thought about this a lot on the long journey back to Earth, and she was sure about this part of her decision. "I don't want my own command. And I don't want to spend a lot of boring years touring the same old systems on some merchant patrolship or diplomatic envoy. I need new worlds—new communications problems, so I can learn new communications skills." She met McCoy's gaze calmly. "That means getting posted to a starship—and the next one due to be crewed is the *Enterprise.*"

"Hmmph." The doctor lowered his brows with an expression that meant he conceded her point but hadn't yet given up on the debate. "And what makes you think Starfleet is going to let you sign on her?"

Uhura shrugged. "They've got to have a few old-timers

on board to balance the ensigns they'll be assigning. I've got as good a shot at those posts as anyone."

"And it'll help to be stationed right here on Earth when the call goes out," Sulu said quietly.

McCoy glowered at him. "Don't *you* tell me you don't want a command post. Because I'm telling you right now, I won't believe you."

The pilot smiled. "Yes, I want one. Eventually." He swept the last lobster dumpling up with skilled chopsticks. "When I'm ready, and that won't be for a while." He held up a hand when McCoy would have spoken. "I'm not a Vulcan, Doctor, but I come from long-lived stock. I've got a lot of time yet."

"Hmmph." Stymied again, McCoy trained his frown on Chekov. "And how about you, young man? Why aren't you in Command School, instead of wasting yourself on the Security Academy?"

Chekov choked over a swallow of herring and reached for the nearest water glass. "I'm—not wasting myself," he said at last, his voice gruff from coughing. "Command officers can't command if their security department can't keep them alive."

"Sounds like security dogma to me," McCoy said bluntly. "You're too smart to get brainwashed by the kind of physical and mental indoctrination it takes to be a security guard." He gave the young Russian a searching look. "Aren't you?"

Chekov scowled and tore apart another herring without eating any. "I'm not being brainwashed." He looked up at McCoy with a sudden fierce directness. "And before you say anything else about security guards, Doctor—remember how many times one saved your life at the loss of his or her own."

McCoy had the grace to look abashed, and Dr. Piper grinned. "That's telling him, Mr. Chekov—*Chekov!*"

The unexpected shout made Uhura drop flying-fish eggs all over her plate, and brought the security cadet to his feet. "What?" he demanded, sounding startled.

"I just remembered where I've heard your name!"

Piper chortled and rubbed his hands together with what looked like sheer delight. *"You* were with the landing party that managed to capture the first Klingon disruptors, weren't you?"

Chekov blinked, then slowly subsided into his seat again. "I suppose I was, yes. I mean, I was on that landing party, sir, but we didn't actually get possession of the disruptors until after we evacuated the Klingons from their disabled ship."

"But you *have* seen a disruptor in use?" Piper pressed, eyes serious now and fire-bright. "Close up."

Uhura saw the puzzled look Chekov skated at her and Sulu, and shrugged back at him in baffled reply. "Yes, sir," the Russian replied at last. "We all have.

"Along with almost everyone else who's ever been stationed aboard a starship," Sulu pointed out.

The older physician spread his hands. "I don't doubt that, Lieutenant Sulu. But how many former starship crewmen are stationed within fifty kilometers of Baltimore?" He peered at them from under craggy silver brows. "I'll tell you how many: none. Except for your friend here, just down the bay at the Security Academy in Annapolis." He pointed a triumphant finger at Chekov. "With your starship background, I'll bet you already have a Class A security clearance, don't you?"

Chekov scowled. "Yes, sir. But why should that matter?"

Piper leaned forward and lowered his voice. "Because the research project I'm working on up at Johns Hopkins requires a Starfleet Class A security clearance." He dropped his voice further, to a murmur Uhura could barely hear over the swash of waves outside. "I'm doing a study on how to mitigate the medical effects of a disruptor blast. Starfleet's given me everything I need—disruptors and schematics, beam analysis, medical histories of victims—everything except someone who could show me how the Klingons actually used the damn weapon!"

"That matters?" Uhura asked, blinking in surprise.

"Of course it matters." It was McCoy who answered her. "Short, sweeping blasts will give you a completely different kind of trauma than a long, trained shot. That's one of the reasons it's so damned hard to build a tissue regenerator with the right capacity to undo disruptor damage."

Piper was staring intently across the table, ignoring their exchange. "So what do you say, Mr. Chekov? I'll only need you to come up twice a week or so, on days like this when you can get leave. Are you willing to help me out?"

Chekov paused for a long moment, frowning at the shreds of herring on his plate. "Willing, yes, sir," he said at last. "But I don't know if I'm able. I would have to ask for special leave from the Academy commander. . . ."

Piper nodded. "Commodore deCandido? I know him. He'll give it to you." A smile crinkled the lines around his eyes and melted their intellectual fire to a gentler warmth. "Don't worry, Mr. Chekov—I don't think you'll regret this."

Chapter Two

Starfleet Security Academy
Annapolis, North America
Terrestrial Date: December 14, 2269
2030 hours EST

WEATHER.

It was the one thing artificial environments couldn't begin to mimic, and the only thing Pavel Chekov had missed about planetary life. The *Enterprise* always knew what day it was. It reminded him of the change of seasons, or about the upcoming Earth-bound holidays, but there was never any character or wonder to those climate-controlled days. You couldn't watch the sky clear at dusk and feel your skin prickle in anticipation of a thirty-degree temperature plunge before dawn. You couldn't daydream out a window while watching leaves the colors of jewelry chase themselves in whirlwinds across an open road. You couldn't bask in the stroke of sun on your hair when a late-year thaw misted steam like silk curtains into the crisp and thirsty air. Compared with Earth, a starship was like an android when compared with a human—no personality, no passion, no soul.

The sidewalk beneath Chekov's feet rumbled faintly as the public transit rushed silently away beneath it, hurrying on for some other stop with barely a pause for Chekov's departure. He didn't mind. He liked the nighttime silence once the transit was gone, the way the slow, heavy snowflakes on the air made everything look somehow much brighter, and more real. Nothing in the physics texts could explain that mystical broadening of winter horizons. Where he was born, you either believed in the silent, absolute power of snow, or you huddled in the grip of a six-month darkness and failed to find the magic that preserved the land around you.

Stopping halfway up the hill from the transit stop, he crouched to splay one hand on the sidewalk and smile up through the treetops at a house light near the top of the rise. Snowflakes swirled in waves and rivers around the soft golden glow, flashing into brief, burning life just before the wind whisked them back into darkness again. It was like watching a tiny, silent melodrama with players who enjoyed a life span of only mere moments, displaying everything they had to offer in that tragically limited time frame. How could anyone not appreciate such splendor?

He'd made the mistake of slipping outside once during a winter shore leave to breathe crystal patterns onto a glass window as they passed. Sulu had thought he was crazy.

"You're gonna catch pneumonia!" the helmsman had declared, refusing to come any farther into the cold than leaning out an open doorway. "Get back in here!"

Chekov had scooped a handful of snow off the window ledge, then dropped it by the path when Uhura fixed him with a warning glare over Sulu's shoulder. She was almost as bad as having a big sister sometimes. "I *like* snow," he'd tried to explain to them while Sulu swept the melting flakes from his hair and Uhura scolded him about getting his feet wet in temperatures lower than zero degrees.

"Nobody likes snow," Sulu had avowed with the certainty of superior rank and years. "You just like winter sports. Skiing, ice hockey, that kind of thing."

Chekov only sighed and shook his head. *"You* like winter sports,"* he pointed out. *"I* like winter."*

"Bull hockey."

"No," Uhura chided the helmsman. "I can imagine what he means." Ever open-minded, she closed her eyes and smiled at whatever enchanting image she could conjure. "Sitting inside a warm bungalow with a mug of crème de mocha and a wool throw. There's nothing prettier than watching a snowfall in the mountains from behind a plate transparency."

Nobody maintained plate transparencies in Russia, and luxuries like crème de mocha were considered best appreciated beside the ice at Gorky Park where you could watch the steam climb up through the snowfall and crackle against the frozen sky. Maybe it was genetic, he'd decided at the time. He'd pitied them a little for their inherited cold-blooded metabolisms, then snuck away later, while they haggled over dinner, to build snowmen with the colony's schoolchildren.

Watching the delicate patterns of ice crystals build on the wool of his peacoat sleeves, Chekov felt a stab of regret that his friends were too far away now to argue with him about the weather. He stood and shoved his hands into his pockets, suddenly cognizant of the darkness and the lonely, late-evening chill.

The gates to the Annapolis Security Academy loomed like a fortress through the haze of blowing snow. A spray of powerful backlighting seared the sky behind it white, and the thermal conduits under the road ghosted steam up to mate with the overall brightness. There wasn't even a patina of frost to sparkle the wrought-iron gatework, or a dusting of crystals to lend color to the hollows and symmetry of the ancient stone wall. Confronted with such a symbol of man's defiance of the weather, winter lost a little of its supernatural charm.

Chekov stopped outside the tiny guardhouse, sweeping a hand back through his hair to dislodge the worst of the snowfall. "Ensign Pavel A. Chekov," he announced himself. "Cadet Grade One." The guard inside the kiosk keyed open the transparent window, and Chekov made an effort to look cold and in a hurry.

"Do you know what time it is, mister?"

At first, Chekov couldn't imagine why the lieutenant would need to ask such an obvious question. He nodded curtly at the chronometer on the wall of the kiosk beyond the guard. "Twenty hundred forty-four hours." He jogged for a moment in place, trying to keep his temperature up, then remembered to add, "Sir," before the lieutenant could say something critical.

Apparently, he didn't speak fast enough. "Are you aware that your grounds curfew goes into effect at twenty-one hundred hours, Ensign?" The lieutenant folded his hands on the counter as though planning to be there for quite some time. "You have left yourself only sixteen minutes in which to place yourself on this base. Did you know that, Ensign?"

"Yes, sir." Chekov ceased his fidgeting and slipped his hands out of the peacoat's pockets to stand a little straighter. "I know, sir." And it was his own damned fault for having forgotten.

Not about the curfew, really, but about the different world that lurked in wait for him behind these rough-cut walls. This wasn't like the regular Academy, where he'd been groomed and coached and encouraged right up to the moment he'd accepted his assignment as head navigator aboard the *Enterprise*. Annapolis was a place of bitter truth and hard reality; there wasn't room for insecurity or ego when you were trying to construct the finest human weapons. An evening with Sulu and Uhura —not to mention the doctors—had lulled him into believing that he could still occupy a place as any officer's intellectual equal. However true that might be anywhere else in the galaxy, though, it couldn't be part of his life as long as he answered to "Cadet" within the Security Academy's walls. Not for the first time, he found himself longing for the day he could officially take up his new position and turn his back on this place forever.

"You know, Ensign, if I kept you standing here for another seventeen minutes, I'd have to report you for violating regulations." He spoke in the tone all the upperclassmen used—diffident and condescending, and not because anything they said was personal. "That would not look very good on your record."

"No, sir," Chekov agreed flatly. He'd learned the Cadet One voice of stoic invulnerability pretty well himself. "It would not, sir."

"So what do you think matters more, Ensign? Your Academy record, or your social life?"

I haven't got a social life. The thought rose up in him unbidden, but at least made his next answer honest as well as easy. "My Academy record, sir."

"What?" The lieutenant's voice soared to that level of hateful sharpness that always made Chekov feel as if he'd been slapped at. He'd long ago given up flinching, but had never learned to quell the anger it inspired. "What did you say to me, Cadet?"

Chekov had to breathe deeply twice to keep his tone as cold and stiffly formal as required. "My Academy record," he said clearly, meeting the lieutenant's gaze and daring him to challenge the statement again. "Sir."

The lieutenant reached under the counter in front of him without taking his eyes off Chekov. Something inside the kiosk buzzed loudly, and a man-sized section of gate swung aside with a squeal. "You be careful what tone of voice you use with your superiors," the lieutenant warned the ensign grimly. "You're going to get yourself in trouble someday."

Chekov opted not to mention that there had once been a time when his superiors could hear what he said without forcing him to be sharp with them. It seemed like a small eternity ago.

"You've got nine minutes to get into your building. Move it."

He slipped through the gate with no more than an impassive nod, then broke into a trot where the lieutenant could still see him, just in case the guard felt like haranguing him for not taking orders seriously.

A tunnel carved of yellow light traced the sidewalk

leading along the edge of King George Street. Chekov cut into the road itself as soon as he was past the view of the gatehouse guard— he might be fond of snow, but no one jogged on a slush-wet sidewalk when the warm, clear street was available. He had entered the Academy at the Number Four Gate, as far from the Halsey Field House as he could get and still officially be on base. He'd never tried to cross the grounds in under nine minutes before. With luck, he'd never have to do it again.

Jogging down the middle of the deserted roadway, he tried to guess which instructor lived in which home by the pattern of lights and curtains and holiday decorations visible in the windows and front lawns. For just an instant, his heart swept back to the elaborate sand paintings that replaced most Muscovite windows in the winter. He used to help his mother pour the colored granules in between the panes of fragile glass, marveling at how the pigments swirled and curled around each other, but never truly mixed. An incredible spasm of homesickness pulsed through him at the thought. He shook his head with a snort of disgust that chased the melancholy away. It seemed all he was doing tonight was feeling homesick for one place or another. Sulu would have laughed at him.

He reached Halsey Field House with barely three minutes to spare. Punching in his logon while stripping out of his peacoat, he tossed the heavy bundle toward a locker before the computer had even accepted his access. He didn't like coming in to a workout this late. The bunkard called for lights-out at 2300, which meant not even two hours to go through his paces, shower, change, and ready himself for tomorrow's classes before having to be in his billet for inspection when the block commander made her rounds. At least tonight his unplanned run had upped his heart rate enough to register at the first level checkpoint. It passed him through to the training room without requiring a warm-up, and that saved him almost fifteen minutes right there. He'd learned to appreciate the value in such small blocks of time.

"If you want to come in now, after five years of riding a panel," his division commandant, Gloria Oberste, had told him disapprovingly at the beginning of the semester, "you've got a hell of a lot of catching up to do."

She'd made no secret of the fact that she didn't think he could do it. Nearly every other cadet at the Academy was a lieutenant—few of them had enjoyed starship service, but all of them had served at least three years in basic security before moving on to the upper-level courses. Only Chekov had made the lateral transfer from command. While he'd never burdened anyone at Annapolis with his reasons for that decision, he was more aware than anyone of the disadvantages he'd chosen for himself. Three years behind on the physical conditioning. Three years behind on the studying and practicing and handling of the most sophisticated Starfleet weaponry. Three years behind in learning the tempers and limits of his body and soul.

Chekov wasn't sure himself that he could ever make up the time. He paused at the top of an overhead press and studied his reflection in the mirror. This was the problem with growing too used to success in every endeavor you turned to. If he couldn't follow the path he'd originally signed on for, and security proved impossible to penetrate, he just didn't know what else he could turn to. The thought of being completely adrift at what should have been the beginning of his career made his insides cringe. He brought the weight back down more carefully than usual and seated it firmly on the holding pins. *Someone should make a rule about not thinking too much when you're trying to exercise.*

Morning tutorials and nightly workouts had gradually crept into his daily routine. An hour before the start of regular classes, he dashed to the library for curricula tutoring with one of the younger lieutenants. Marina Franz was only one year his senior, and the only other native Russian at the Academy. He enjoyed their forty-five-minute sessions more than anything else he'd encountered yet at Annapolis—partly because speaking Russian for a little while each day seemed to rest his brain after so many hours of listening to poor and hastily spoken English, and partly because Franz was so clever and pretty, a reminder of the days when he'd had time to appreciate a woman for something other than her ability to distill a day's worth of class notes into a comprehensible outline.

He left the training room less than thirty minutes later. Muscles warm and quivery, his whole body awake and light, he jogged back into the locker room to dig a sweatshirt out of the pile of rumpled clothes. The last thing he needed was to chill during his last hour of physical training. Wiping a towel across his face to clear his eyes, he dragged the sweatshirt over his head, then opened the toiletry case on the top shelf of the locker to retrieve the phaser pistol he'd hidden there among his gear.

It wasn't a functional phaser. He'd never even bothered to ask about keeping a working pistol outside the Academy armory; besides, it didn't matter if the gun could target or shoot. All he needed was the size, and weight, and shape exactly right, so he cajoled a broken model out of maintenance by promising the tech in charge a month's worth of ice hockey lessons. Thank God those weren't supposed to start until after the first of the year.

Hefting the smooth black pistol in the palm of his hand, he slammed the locker door and trotted into the open gym where he and a hundred other cadets practiced unarmed defense combat for two hours every single day. Standing in front of the floor-to-ceiling mirror with eternally repeated emptiness reflected in the other mirrored wall behind him, Chekov had to swallow a feeling of smallness as he reminded himself why he came here all alone.

During his first few months on board the *Enterprise,* he'd gotten turned around in the huge starship's gym complex, trying to find a vacant facility without having to actually admit to any of the resident officers that he didn't know where he was. He'd finally resorted to prowling the observation balcony, looking down on the gyms below, and was captured by the sight of the *Enterprise*'s captain working out in the training room all alone. Kirk confronted his own reflection in the mirror as if facing his direst enemy, a phaser held out before him as though holding his reflection at bay. When the captain first pitched his phaser toward the opposite end of the room, Chekov assumed Kirk had tired of whatever private game he played. Then the captain dove to retrieve the gun with grim determination, and Chekov found himself impressed at the speed and accuracy with which Kirk swept up the pistol and kept running.

Over and over again, Kirk enacted the same silent scenario. Sometimes farther, sometimes closer, sometimes rolling to put himself in reach of the gun, sometimes coming up onto his knees once he'd finally retrieved it, sometimes swearing into the bigness of the empty room and stalking about in frustration before positioning himself to start the sequence all over again.

Chekov didn't know when he realized exactly what Kirk was doing. When awareness came, though, the awe and respect that pulsed through him in response never really faded again. Kirk was practicing how far he could throw away his sidearm and still retrieve it before some unseen enemy could fire on him. He was actually *practicing* a strategy for getting out of what anyone else would consider an impossible situation. Sometime during that hour he spent observing his new captain, Chekov came to understand that the main thing separating exceptional commanders from the people who were merely in charge was the ability to get whatever they wanted out of everybody, including themselves.

As a navigator, he hadn't made any important decisions. It hadn't been his place to pass judgment on what course of action was taken during any given encounter, and he hadn't even been responsible for choosing his own role during a mission, much less anyone else's. Somewhere near the end of his first month at the Security Academy, though, he'd found himself awake most of a night with his heart pounding and his stomach clenched in anxiety because some now-forgotten nightmare had filled him with the knowledge that *he* would be the one in command when these two years of training were over. *He* would pick the guards for the planetary missions. *He* would decide who was good enough and who could be let go. *He* would make the subspace calls to the parents of crewmen who didn't return at the end of a mission.

He started practicing throwing away his phaser the very next day.

He initiated practice tonight the same way he had since the beginning—with a few easy tosses no more than an arm's length away, just to assure himself he could land the phaser wherever he wanted, and to remind his muscles how to stretch and tighten in an ongoing quest for speed. Even as a young man, playing intermural hockey in secondary school, his main advantage had been endurance, not speed. Unfortunately, endurance wasn't particularly helpful right now. The illusion of capability that rode on his postworkout endorphins shattered all too easily. His movements all seemed slow and awkward, as though he were trying to perform gymnastics in a two-gravity environment. He snatched up the phaser on every retrieval, meaning to bring it to bear on the same patch of the wall each time. But, every time, his unconscious expectation of where that target should be ended up frustratingly wide of where his eyes told him it was only an instant later. Chekov knew that an instant's delay in an emergency was just too long.

He threw the phaser behind him this time, closing his eyes so he would hear it land, rather than watch it in the mirror. Then, eyes still closed, he twisted to dive after it with an awkward shoulder roll. He almost lost his rhythm when his hand closed on the smooth metal first try, but momentum worked faster than thought. Coming to rest on one knee, he flashed his eyes open and instinctively swept the phaser toward a patch of dark movement on the opposite wall—

—and ended up with the phaser pointing at another cadet's smiling reflection in the floor-to-ceiling mirror.

Embarrassment seared Chekov's face like a slap. Lowering the phaser, he climbed slowly to his feet and turned to offer the lieutenant behind him a stiff but respectful nod. "Mr. Leong."

Jim Leong smiled, drifting into the open room as though he had nothing better to do than inspect the activities of his fellow students. It was an attitude Chekov had learned to despise in the last few months. He'd entertained illusions that he and Leong might be friends when he'd met the older lieutenant on his first day at the Academy. Leong had greeted him with a handshake and a smile, his exotic eyes and ready grin so reminiscent of Sulu that Chekov had wanted to believe that this slim, Canadian-born Asian would also share Sulu's kindness and playful patience. Instead, Leong had needed only an hour to prove himself a self-important braggart with a stripe of petty cruelty wide enough to strangle himself. Chekov only considered it too bad that Leong had never succeeded in doing so.

"Mr. Chekov." Somehow, Leong always managed to turn even the most innocuous of greetings into a thing of liquid insult. Chekov didn't know what made him angrier—the lieutenant's complete disrespect for anyone and anything that couldn't strong-arm him into behaving, or the way Leong succeeded in making Chekov feel stupid and small just in the way he smiled at him. "I'd think someone as far out of his league as you are would have better things to do than play around with this kind of hotshot crap."

"It's not . . ." Chekov tightened his grip on the phaser to remind himself he had more important goals in his life than subjugating Leong. "I'm not playing around," he said, trying to sound civil.

"Sure you are." Leong slowed to a leisurely stop in front of him, his head cocked speculatively as he eyed the gun at Chekov's side. "Because if you'd ever actually *worked* in security, you'd know that the A number one rule for any security guard is that you never"—one hand whipped out with stinging speed to slap the gun into the air between them—"ever"—Leong snatched the phaser one-handed and tucked it behind him before Chekov had even completely registered it was gone—"give up your weapon." He smiled and waggled the gun between two fingers. "To anyone."

Chekov brought his hands slowly back to his sides. He wasn't going to play this game. "It isn't always that easy."

"It isn't always that easy, *sir.*"

"It isn't always that easy," Chekov echoed formally. "Sir."

Leong acknowledged that small victory with a snort bordering on disgust. "Of course it is. Not that you would know."

It always came back to that with Leong. "Are you saying, sir, that if someone holds my landing party at gunpoint, I should let them shoot a crew member rather than throw down my phaser?"

"I'm saying that if you do your job right, no one should be able to take your landing party hostage."

The easy certainty of Leong's statement made Chekov want to slap him. In four years on board a starship, Chekov had seen more unpredictable circumstances and unfair situations than he'd ever dreamed of in Academy classroom discussions. Even promising yourself you would expect nothing and be prepared for everything wasn't the same as facing a decision no commander had ever exactly had to deal with before. So much of Kirk's dynamic style had stepped outside the rule of textbook teaching, but Chekov refused to believe that Kirk was simply an incompetent commander and that he was just too naive to realize it.

Still, the heartless taskmaster inside him reminded, *Kirk isn't here, and you have to put up with two more years of Leong. What's going to do you the most good here and now?*

Chekov almost had to grit his teeth before he could make himself hold out his hand in silent request for the gun. "Thank you for your input, Lieutenant Leong. I'll do my best to bear your advice in mind."

Leong glanced down at Chekov's waiting hand as though surprised to find it there. "You know, Ensign, somehow I get the impression you don't believe me. You want your phaser back?" He suspended the gun above Chekov's palm, then dropped it there and took two long steps backward. "Prove to me you deserve it." He made an L with thumb and forefinger and sighted along it like a weapon. "Throw down your phaser."

A real hostage situation could not have felt more immediate. Trying to copy the air of cool defiance he'd seen Kirk use so many times, Chekov locked his eyes on Leong's crooked smile and flicked the useless phaser away from himself. It bounced on the mat with a soft thump, but Chekov didn't dare turn his head to verify exactly where it landed.

Leong simplified matters slightly by tossing an amused glance after the weapon. "So is this where I keep talking to form my own distraction?" the lieutenant asked, turning his full attention back to Chekov. "Tell you my fiendish plan for taking over your ship, just in case the audience isn't clear yet on the details?"

It isn't like he'll really kill me. It was all just a matter of humiliation, anyway. Chekov assumed maybe he'd even get used to it by the end of this assignment. Diving for the gun, he told himself that he didn't expect to come up with it—he just wanted to get this confrontation over with so he could run back to his bunkard in time for curfew.

Leong intercepted him not even halfway to the phaser. In his heart, Chekov knew he couldn't twist aside and avoid the other cadet, but vanity made him have to try. He skipped just outside Leong's reach, dropping to dive for the phaser behind him, and slammed up hard against one of the many mirrored walls when Leong diverted his roll with a single, well-placed shove. The glass hummed with the force of his impact, and Chekov's attention refracted into a thought of breathless thanks that the whole wall hadn't shattered around him.

"Well, that was pretty pitiful, Ensign." Leong stepped back onto the mat and waved him to his feet with ruthless impatience. "Do it again."

This time, Chekov ended up beneath the other cadet's knee, not even sure how he got there, but breathless with anger at the grin of smug disdain bending over him. If Leong wasn't an officer, Chekov would have tried to beat that grin away with the same blunt force that had served him so well in more than one shore leave imbroglio and over a dozen schoolyard brawls. But trying to explain to a court-martial jury that he'd thrown his career out the lock because he couldn't stand to look at his classmate anymore didn't seem particularly preferable to where he found himself now. He snaked a hand behind Leong's bent leg and caught hold of that ankle in both hands.

The look of startled annoyance in Leong's eyes almost made their brief battle worth it. "Do you think I could break your knee if I twisted as hard as I can?" Chekov asked him matter-of-factly.

Leong's face closed down in a flush of anger. "I think I could break your jaw if you tried it. Want to go for it?"

"Gentlemen . . ."

The quiet interruption splashed Chekov with horror as blistering as molten copper. Freed suddenly from the weight of Leong's body, he scrambled back away from the other cadet, scooping up the abandoned phaser as Leong stiffened to attention. Somehow, even when presenting himself for a senior officer's discipline, Leong managed to do it with a swift efficiency that left Chekov feeling hopelessly outclassed. The young ensign snapped upright a full three seconds behind his companion, painfully aware of the delay.

Security Commander Gloria Oberste raked them both with a cool gray stare, her arms folded across the front of a black and red down jacket. Snow sprinkled the shoulders of her coat, clinging like bits of eiderdown to the braided knot of her blond hair. If she'd been taller or more slim, her measuring stare might not have seemed so keenly masculine and brutal. Being faced down by a woman who matched him well in both height and solid musculature, though, Chekov always got the impression Oberste had transcended the conventionalism of both human sexes, thus making herself more formidable than either.

She nodded shortly at the gun in Chekov's hand. "A mutually respectful training spar, of course," she remarked without a smile.

Leong kept his eyes dutifully trained on the hall behind her shoulder. "Of course, sir."

"Isn't that nice?" She tossed a glance at Chekov, neither asking for his input nor discouraging it. He felt a blush rise up into his cheeks, but opted to keep his own opinion silent. "I'd hate to think you were indulging in personal grudges at the expense of your Academy studies," Oberste continued, pacing slowly into the room. "After all, I'm sure you're both aware that a security officer's duty to protect and serve places him above such petty behavior as brawling with his classmates." She paused in front of Chekov just long enough to slip the phaser away from him and slide it into her jacket pocket. He let her take it with only the tiniest sigh.

"Mr. Leong." Pivoting neatly, she thumped the side of her fist against the lieutenant's outthrust chest. "Since you are not qualified to instruct underclassmen in unarmed combat, I'll have to ask that you not skirmish with Mr. Chekov anymore. Your skills far outmatch his at this point, making you a useless example and an unfair opponent. If I see or hear of you sparring with him again,

I'll be forced to take disciplinary action." She looked up sharply into Leong's staring eyes. "Am I understood?"

"Yes, sir." He flicked only the briefest glance aside at Chekov. "Perfectly, sir."

Oberste nodded and waved him toward the door. "Then you're dismissed."

Leong slipped out the door almost as quickly as he'd appeared. Chekov wondered if the lieutenant ever felt the humiliation and frustration he visited upon others, even while under a commanding officer's lash, and found himself more sure than ever that even Oberste's overt disapproval didn't register on Leong as anything more than inconvenience. How could someone put his life on the line for three years in a security squad and still have so little appreciation for the people he was trained to serve? And why couldn't there be another Security Academy on the other side of the world so Chekov could transfer his studies to someplace—anyplace—that didn't include Leong?

"Commodore deCandido tells me you'll be on special assignment to Johns Hopkins for the next several weeks. I'm not so sure that's a good idea, considering the special difficulties with your schedule."

Chekov jerked his attention back to Oberste, surprised that she had spoken. "It's important research, sir—work that could save many people's lives." He wasn't sure if she would value his qualifier, but added anyway, "I *want* to help with it, sir, if I may."

"You know that no one's going to grant you any special considerations if you can't keep up with your assigned work."

Chekov nodded. "I wouldn't expect that, sir."

"And you know that Mr. Leong is more likely to slow down your progress than help you."

He couldn't help smiling a little, then erased the expression before she could take offense at his wry amusement. "Yes, sir. I'm very much aware of that, sir."

Oberste surprised him by offering him a dry smile as

she underhanded the phaser to him. "Well, that said, then . . ." She unsealed the front of her jacket with a flourish, nodding at Chekov as though irritated with his obdurate lack of movement. "We can start by correcting some of the most obvious flaws in your defensive style. Show me a Tal defensive position five . . ."

Chapter Three

White Sands Flight Center
Alamogordo, North America
Terrestrial Date: December 15, 2269
0800 hours MST

GRAVITY.

Long before he actually set foot on Earth again, Sulu
knew what he missed most about it: the reassuring feel of
9.816 meters per second per second. No other planet in
the galaxy could tug at a landing shuttle with exactly that
gravitational force, or support it with precisely the same
air pressure as Earth's. Those constants engraved themselves so deeply into your neural pathways when you
learned to fly that no amount of experience on other
planets ever modified them.

Sulu hadn't even tried. Piloting the *Enterprise* through
the airless microgravity of outer space was so immensely
different from planetary flying that he'd simply
discarded all his innate assumptions about flight and
built new ones. And on other planets, he'd found that his
strength as a pilot was his ability to measure alien gravity
and air resistance against his Earth-schooled instincts,
and translate his maneuvers accordingly.

But now that he was back on Earth itself—Sulu
banked his shuttle over the night-dark bulk of the
Sacramento Mountains, orienting himself by the
spiderweb of lights to the south that he knew was El

Paso—the familiar gravity and air pressure felt like long-denied luxuries. His great-grandfather would probably say it was like being allowed to speak your native tongue after long years in an alien culture. To Sulu, it felt more like putting on a comfortable T-shirt, shorts, and sandals after a long day in an insulated flightsuit.

He left the bumpy air resistance of the mountain range behind, tearing a layer of cold winter cloud to tinsel as he did so, then rolled the shuttle into a dive that would have seemed dangerously steep to anyone who wasn't a Starfleet test pilot. A familiar blast of mountain-funneled wind met him when he pulled up a kilometer above the Alamogordo Valley floor, dancing the usual dry patter of sand across the shuttle's outer hull. After three months, Sulu was so used to the skeletal sound that it now seemed odd to land without it.

The rumpled landscape of White Sands unrolled itself below his shuttle's wings as he descended, its gypsum dunes glowing ghost-pale in the desert moonlight. Between the empty darkness of the Federation Wilderness Sanctuary to the south and the even emptier darkness of the Starfleet Experimental Flight Range to the north, Sulu caught the small sprinkle of lights that was Alamogordo. He toggled his chin-mike.

"Starfleet Shuttle *Serengeti*, requesting permission to land at White Sands Residential Shuttleport. Lieutenant Commander Hikaru Sulu, pilot and sole passenger."

There was a pause as the base computer checked his voiceprint, analyzing its stress levels to be sure he wasn't being held hostage and forced to lie. "Hikaru Sulu, cleared to land, residential lane five."

"Acknowledged." Sulu angled the *Serengeti* into the wind, increasing its speed slightly to compensate for the buffeting, then pointed the shuttle's blunt nose at the landing lights and cut its thrusters. Gravity promptly hauled the little aircraft toward the ground, counterbalanced just enough by forward momentum to produce a smooth, parabolic glide. Sulu grinned and kept his hand poised over the controls of the braking jets, waiting until the shuttle was a scant meter from its landing pad before he cut them in. Obedient as a leashed puppy, *Serengeti* settled into its assigned berth.

By the time his postflight check was done, the first rose-gray light of dawn had crept over the cloud-mantled Sacramentos and spilled into the valley below. Sulu lifted the shuttle's hatch and vaulted out, then simply stood and let the silent morning chill of the desert roll over him. The air smelled of mesquite smoke and ozone from his cooling thrusters. He took a deep breath, savoring the desert crispness after the miserably wet cold of Baltimore.

"Yaa' eh t'eeh, Sulu." An attention-getting slap rattled against the shuttle's hull as a stocky form in Starfleet coveralls ducked under it. Sulu barely restrained himself from groaning as he recognized his project design engineer. "Pushing the envelope again, eh?"

"Yaa' eh t'eeh, Dr. Nakai." The Navajo greeting still sounded halting on Sulu's lips, but it usually made the old man smile. Sulu hadn't found much else that did, aside from an occasional successful test result. Unfortunately, this time the tactic didn't work. "Uh . . . did we have a test flight scheduled for this morning?"

Hernan Nakai snorted, his flat-boned face creased with disapproval. "And if we did?" He poked an accusing finger at Sulu's rumpled flightsuit. "You in any condition to fly?"

Sulu blinked, then pulled on an impassive expression. When the old aeronautics professor was feeling querulous, the only defense was to play by strict Starfleet rules. "Yes, sir. Regulation eight-hour sleep, full breakfast, one hour of flight time logged on the day. No alcohol, stimulants, or depressants within the last forty-eight hours."

Nakai let out a bark that might—or might not—have been laughter. "Forty-eight hours? Heard you *never* use that stuff."

"Very rarely, sir," Sulu admitted. He eyed the project

engineer cautiously, trying to gauge his mood. "Did you want to run another test of the Wraith today, sir?"

"Hmmph." For a long moment, it seemed that was all the response Sulu was going to get. Nakai's gaze had gone beyond him, up to where the rising sun had kindled the snow-covered western peaks of the San Andres to molten gold. Around them, White Sands Experimental Flight Center was waking up in a hum of electric service vehicles and a rumble of warming shuttle engines. Six distant chimes echoed down the valley from the old Spanish church in Alamogordo, followed by the brief Starfleet whistle that meant the dining hall was open for breakfast.

"Time to go." Nakai jerked his chin at Sulu significantly, then swung around and started toward the low adobe shadow of the base administration building. Knowing better than to question the old man when he was in this mood, Sulu tucked his flight records under one arm and followed Nakai across the sunlit tarmac. He caught a sympathetic glance from two fellow pilots emerging from the officers quarters, and saw one of them make a zipping motion up her throat. Warned, Sulu began to fasten up the flapping collar of his flightsuit.

"We're going in to see the base commander?" he asked Nakai. The project engineer merely grunted, but his turn into the smaller of the building's two courtyards answered Sulu's question for him. He straightened his rumpled sleeves and ran a hand through his wind-ruffled hair, glad now that he'd taken the time for a shower before he'd left his hotel in Baltimore that morning. Commodore Willis liked his test pilots to look as precisely put together as the machines they flew.

The door on the far side of the leaf-dappled courtyard had been pushed slightly ajar, a clear indication that the base commander was expecting them. Sulu reached out to hold it open for Nakai, and got another wordless grunt in reply. Not a good sign. Usually, that act of generational respect would have earned him at least a contemptuous snort from the old man, if not a lecture on the insignificance of age. Sulu began to wonder how important this impromptu morning meeting was going to be.

He got his answer as soon as the military receptionist passed them into the commodore's office. For the first time that Sulu could remember, Commodore Adam Willis wasn't at his old-fashioned wooden desk. Instead, the tall, spare figure of the White Sands base commander stood silhouetted against the morning sun, his dark fingers resting on the transparent aluminum of a high-security crate that sat beside his east window. The sleek black device inside that crate was the heart—and the controversy—of the Wraith II project.

"Mr. Sulu." The commodore barely turned his head when they entered, but his deep voice filled the office with such resonance that he seemed to be giving them his full attention. "You've been flying the Wraith II shuttle for almost two months. Give me your assessment of its safety margin."

Sulu opened his mouth to answer, but Hernan Nakai put out a hand and stopped him. "The commodore is having second thoughts about approving the second phase of our project," he warned. "He thinks forty-five successful test runs still aren't enough."

Sulu eyed both men warily, weighing the project engineer's impatient scowl against the rigid set of their commanding officer's jaw. He guessed that this was the extension of an argument begun earlier that morning, or perhaps even the night before. The silence lengthened while he formulated his reply.

"Lieutenant Commander?" Willis turned to face him at last, his voice deepening with concern, although his lean, coffee-dark face remained impassive. "I asked you a question. I'd like to hear *your* answer, not Dr. Nakai's."

Sulu straightened to his full height, insignificant as he knew that was beside the towering base commander. He picked his words with the same meticulous care he would have used to pick a flight plan.

"Commodore Willis, the Wraith never was and never will be a shuttle safe enough for anyone to fly." He heard

Nakai's hissed breath and went on quickly before the old engineer could interrupt. "But in order to carry out the surveillance mission it was designed for, the Wraith can't fly any other way."

"If you can call what the Wraith does flying," Willis pointed out.

Sulu lifted a hand and dropped it again, realizing only after he saw Willis's lifted eyebrow that he'd unconsciously imitated the Wraith's flying style. "Sir, there's only so much you can do to automate an antigrav propulsion system. It's going to bounce a different way every time it bottoms out and reboots, and that bounce will always need a good pilot to control it. You can't expect that kind of system to hold the same safety margins we can build into the rest of Starfleet."

"But you think a good pilot can keep the safety margin within Starfleet minimum requirements?"

"Yes." This time, Sulu didn't have to hesitate. "Yes, sir. I do."

"Hmmm." The look of satisfaction that Sulu's initial words had kindled in the base commander's eyes slowly faded to grimness. Willis's fingers drummed on the edge of the transparent aluminum case, triggering interference ripples in the sunlight refracting through it. "So you think we should risk the second phase of testing?"

Sulu paused again, struck silent by the immensity of the decision Willis was asking from him. His gaze dropped to the gleaming black device inside the security crate. This was the critical decision, the one that had been haunting the Wraith II program ever since its inception—long before Sulu had been selected as the project's main test pilot. It was a decision Starfleet itself was still grappling with.

The Wraith shuttle had originally been designed to evade the primitive detection systems of precontact civilizations, with its combination of radiation-reflective hull and antigrav propulsion. Now, Starfleet's Aeronautical Division wanted to equip its planetary surveillance craft with Starfleet's newest evasive device: the cloaking mechanism whose Romulan prototype had been obtained by Admiral Kirk and Mr. Spock only a few short years before.

Hernan Nakai moved suddenly, crossing the room to drop his gnarled hands on the security crate's other edge, as if to assert his right to have a say in its future. The old man met Willis's hostile stare with one just as fierce, unintimidated by the difference in height between them.

"Stop vacillating!" the engineer said harshly. "It doesn't matter what Sulu thinks, or what I think either, for that matter! The bottom line is, if we don't use the cloaking device in the Wraith now, it will rot inside this crate forever."

Commodore Willis flinched slightly. "That's not true—"

"Yes, it damn well *is* true!" Nakai overrode him with a Starfleet engineer's usual disregard of rank in a technical discussion. "In the two years we've had this thing, no one in Starfleet has ever found a way to feed it enough power to cover a full-size starship, much less figured out how to eliminate the subspace radiation it spits out when it's used. The only chance we'll *ever* get to use it is on a short-excursion vessel like the Wraith, where we can protect the crew with antiradiation suits."

Willis frowned at him. "The Romulans don't use antiradiation suits. They must have some kind of protective system that you haven't been able to duplicate yet."

Nakai snorted. "Maybe. Or maybe they're just lucky and their bodies don't react to subspace radiation as badly as ours do."

"As badly as most species do," Willis reminded him sharply. "Do you really want to risk this device getting into the hands of a precontact civilization?"

"Hah!" Nakai waved that objection away as if it were a fly. "It's no worse than the risk we already take with the dilithium in the damn antigrav systems. I've got self-destruct circuits plugged into both systems, in case a Wraith is ever captured intact." He pointed a finger at Willis. "Admit it. It's not precontact cultures that you're worried about—it's the Klingons. With all the recent skirmishes they've had along their border with the Romulans, they'd love to get their paws on this device. *That's* why you hate the idea of risking the cloaking device on any unarmed vessel. You're afraid it'll fall into their hands."

The base commander's expression didn't alter, but Sulu saw the effort it took. Muscles tightened beneath the lean, dark cheeks, and for a moment the dark lashes dropped, shielding whatever emotion roiled in the senior officer's eyes. "That's certainly a factor in my decision," he admitted.

Silence fell over the office, broken only by the roar of a shuttle taking off across the valley. After a moment, Willis's gaze lifted again, sweeping past the tense figure of the project engineer to rest on Sulu. His deep voice had turned very sober.

"Lieutenant Commander, I believe you were briefed about the levels of radiation you might be exposed to in testing the cloaking device on the Wraith II. Are you still willing to participate in the project if I approve it?"

"Yes," Sulu said, again without hesitation. He saw the surprise in Willis's dark eyes and added, "I know there are a lot of officials who think we should ban use of the cloaking device within Federation space—by ourselves or anyone else. But I saw what Admiral Kirk and Mr. Spock went through to obtain the device for the Federation, Commodore. I'd hate to see that effort wasted because of conservative political fears."

"Ah." Willis nodded slowly, then his broad chest rose and fell with the force of his sigh. "Well, I've made my decision. You can install the cloaking device on the Wraith II prototype shuttle, Dr. Nakai."

The engineer nodded once in silent response, but Sulu saw his fingers splay triumphantly over the security crate. Willis rapped sharply against the aluminum to draw Nakai's attention back from the gleaming black metal inside.

"We'll have to go off base to test the Wraith's evasive

capabilities," the commodore reminded him curtly. "That means keeping this project wrapped in the highest level of security we can muster. Only you and Mr. Sulu should know what you're doing and why you're doing it. Understood?"

Nakai grumbled something to himself in Navajo, then nodded reluctant assent. "Aye, sir. Whatever it takes to get this damned project up and flying."

"Good." Willis gave the crated cloaking device a last impassive look, then stepped back from it. "Be very careful, gentlemen. The security problems involved here could be enormous, and those officials you mentioned will be watching for any opportunity to sweep this all under the rug." His gaze shifted to Sulu, and this time the compassion in his dark eyes was easy to read. "I'm usually jealous of my test pilots, but I don't envy you this task, Mr. Sulu. I don't envy you at all."

Chapter Four

Johns Hopkins University
Baltimore, North America
Terrestrial Date: December 17, 2269
0900 hours EST

THE TEMPERATURE that Monday reached a high of minus five at sunrise. By 0900, the guards at the Starfleet Research Center seemed more concerned about that record low than verifying Chekov's security clearance as they all huddled together at the fringe of the university's restricted grounds.

"We're supposed to get a windchill of minus fifteen tonight," the older guard informed Chekov through chattering teeth and a cloud of steam. He had his shoulders hunched up almost to his earmuffs, both hands shoved into a peacoat the same black-blue as Chekov's, if a good deal more weathered and worn. From the way he carried on, you would have thought he was standing naked in the town square of Ulan Bator and not on a relatively balmy North American street in the best everyday thermal gear Starfleet had to offer.

The younger guard flipped Chekov's access card over and over in his hands with a frown that said he was clearly skeptical of its authenticity. "I'm not familiar with any"—he peered at the front of the datacard again—"Dr. Piper at this facility. Are you sure you've got the clearance to be here?"

For a fleeting moment, Chekov thought about pointing out that he wore the same Starfleet black and red they did, but decided that probably wouldn't help him much in the long run. "He's a medical researcher," Chekov volunteered with helpful patience. "Dr. Mark Piper. If you have a trauma treatment center, or an alien technology division, he's probably associated with one of them."

The older guard continued to hop frigidly from foot to foot while his younger counterpart tapped the datacard against his hand reader set as though considering. Chekov quelled an urge to snatch the device away from him and run the card through the reader.

"He requested I report to his project here this morning. I'm sure if you scan my card against your main list, you'll find verification of my clearance."

The younger guard sighed, as if he had a half dozen better things to do than waste his time on Chekov's security claims. Then, pushing the datacard into the reader, he flipped the little device in his hand and thrust it out in front of him. "Put your hand on the pad, please."

Chekov pulled off his glove to comply. The clear reader panel felt cold and impossibly smooth in the subzero weather; his hand left an instant's misty ghostprint behind when he finally withdrew it to stuff it back into his pocket. As the young guard bore the reader off into the enclosed security booth, the older officer flapped the hem of his peacoat and remarked, "I sure hope the weather's not like this on Christmas Day—my kid and me, we're supposed to go ice fishing. I'd *hate* doing that in this weather!"

It didn't seem the sort of comment that required a reaction, so Chekov just turned a slow circle to survey the university that surrounded them and waited for the younger guard to return.

He read most of the historic landmark plaques in sight by the time a hush of released air caught his attention from the field beyond the guard outpost. A Spartan glass turbolift rose up from a grassy knoll several meters away, and the doors whisked aside to release a white-coated lab tech into the chill morning air. Until that moment, Chekov hadn't realized that the glass-covered stretch of park behind the hospital was the facility he'd been assigned to. Some bright engineer at Starfleet must have decided that underground was the only place they could build the Research Center without disturbing the quaint nineteenth-century campus around it.

The coatless lab tech scampered with as much dignity as anyone could manage with their chin tucked to their chest and their hands jammed under their arms. Her curly salt-and-pepper hair tangled in the wind despite an attempt to ponytail it at the back of her neck, and her broad, scholarly face looked white and pinched in the cold. As she waved a shivery acknowledgment to the guard inside the kiosk, Chekov was overwhelmed with an urge to strip out of his coat and give it to her so she wouldn't have to suffer the cold.

"I've got him," she chattered to the older guard still keeping Chekov company. She returned his nod with an amiable head bob of her own, then flashed Chekov a miserable but charming grin. He was beginning to feel guilty about being the only one not incapacitated by this weather.

"I'm sorry no one was out here to meet you—we thought there were still some arrangements to be made before we got you." Tugging one hand from out of her armpit, she extended a hand already shivering with cold. "I'm Yolande Stern, National Science Institute. And you're Lieutenant . . . ?"

He took her hand for the barest minimum shake, not wanting to keep her exposed any longer than necessary. *"Ensign* Pavel Chekov, Starfleet Security." It was the first time he'd addressed himself that way, and he couldn't help feeling a little twinge of peculiarity at the sound. "I'm here about the disruptor research. Dr. Piper said you'd be expecting me."

"Yes." Stern beckoned with her shoulder as she turned to start trotting back toward the waiting turbolift. "Well, *no,"* she amended, "not *you,* specifically. Mark just told us he'd be arranging for a weapons expert from Starfleet.

I thought . . ." She shook her head as though deciding not to enter that part of the conversation, and danced into the turbolift without the benefit of such social niceties as haggling over who should enter first. "I guess I was just expecting someone older."

Chekov squeezed in as best he could without crowding her in the confined space. "I'm not a weapons expert, precisely. I'm just familiar enough with disruptor technology to suit Dr. Piper's requirements." Then, because some explanation seemed appropriate once the turbolift had started its descent and they were alone without even the wind to fill the silences, "I was with the planetary landing party who first captured the disruptors you're using here."

"Ah." Stern nodded broadly, smiling. "Starship duty. No wonder Mark pushed to get you." The lift discharged them at a security door with no humans left to guard it. Stern processed her card and retina scan with the easy familiarity of someone who'd worked at too many labs to acknowledge the precautions anymore. "He's a little snobbish about preferring the 'caliber' of starship people," she went on as they pushed through the door onto a long, skylit stairwell. Doors to what could only be other labs branched off at every landing, until Chekov gave up wondering what could possibly be studied at them all. "Mark served on board a starship for a while, you know."

Chekov guessed that it wouldn't be politic to point out that he and Dr. Piper had served on board the same vessel.

"Well, I'm sure you'll be just as useful as whoever else they might have sent us." The final door swung open without the benefit of her touch, and three other technicians bobbed heads up from their computer screens and 3-D schematics like some shy native species of wildlife. "Guess what, guys? We finally got our guinea pig!" Stern lifted an apologetic smile toward Chekov. "Sorry," she said more quietly. "We had to have something to call you till you got here."

Chekov shrugged, amused by her apology. "That's all right. I've already been called worse."

Squeezing his arm in silent appreciation, Stern pointed out her colleagues as she introduced them. "Ensign Chekov, I'd like you to meet the rest of our technical staff. Robin Wood, our engineering designer. Peter Broad, our molecular physiologist. And Tim Anthony, our particle physicist."

They all nodded briefly, Anthony ducking his head back over his work the instant his social commitment was finished.

"I'm the token audiologist," Stern continued. "After all, this *is* supposed to be a sonic weapon." Wood and Broad replied with groans of tired laughter. Some private joke among them, Chekov assumed. It had never occurred to him that disruptor research could be funny. "Everybody, this is Ensign Pavel Chekov from the Security Academy. Mark was impressed with his starship experience."

Chekov shook hands all around, even disturbing Anthony briefly, at Stern's indelicate insistence. "Is Dr. Piper here?" he asked when the introductions were finished. He hadn't yet been able to shake the need to report to someone whenever he was given a new place to be.

Anthony snorted without looking up from the hologram in front of him. "I hope you didn't have your heart set on talking to him this morning."

"He doesn't come in until well after lunch," Wood volunteered, somewhat more civilly, the sharp glare she cast at Anthony going essentially unnoticed. "He keeps a later schedule than most of us."

"He's an old fart who can't be bothered to get out of bed."

Broad added his own castigation as he stood to carry a rack of test tubes across to another table. "Tim . . ."

"Well, excuse me if I don't appreciate not being told when to expect our consultant when *I'm* the one who first bitched about wanting someone." Anthony slapped both hands peevishly to his desktop, and the model whirling and spinning there vanished as if chased into hiding by the noise. "There were things I wanted to take care of before we started this stage of the testing—questions I wanted to answer before Piper started bringing up new ones. As it is, none of my data's even ready to crunch at this point!"

"That's right, Tim." Broad tipped his head back in appeal to the heavens, his voice and stance betraying how many million times he'd heard this refrain before. "Everything Piper does without your knowledge is just part of some grand conspiracy to keep you from completing your graduate thesis! In fact, he told me only yesterday that he plans to put an end to civilization as we know it just in case you have some chance of graduating this semester."

"I resent your tone, Peter—"

Stern slipped an arm around Chekov's shoulders and turned him away before he'd had a chance to witness too much of the men's argument. "As you might have guessed," she sighed, leading him back out of the lab and into an adjoining chamber, "Peter and Tim don't always play well with others."

"This works to our advantage, really." Wood hurried in behind them, pulling the door closed with a mischievous twinkle in her green eyes. "I wanted to run some pretty specific trials pertaining to the gun's mechanical design, and I know Yolande's been waiting for a chance to cycle the sonics through their full range." She grinned prettily at Chekov and ran a hand through her bob of bright red hair. "You wouldn't mind, would you?"

Chekov slipped out of his peacoat, shrugging, as Stern collected equipment from some other part of the room. "That's what I was brought here for."

"Great!" Stern waved him over to a squat duranium-alloy weapons locker in the farthest corner of the room. "You're already cleared for accessing the safe and handling the gun—the only one cleared, actually, except for Mark." She handed him a notebook with the locker's security sequence displayed on its tiny screen. "Is that going to be a problem?"

"Not if Dr. Piper doesn't come in until noon." If nothing else, Chekov couldn't afford to waste half a day waiting for Piper when he only had clearance to come to Johns Hopkins two, maybe three times a week. "Besides, I'm the one they're training to watch over things like this." He smiled as he tapped in the code, then swung wide the weapons locker door. "It's not like I'm going to steal it or anything."

"—and so, what do you suppose became the primary mode of communication among the A'Ila'Mos culture?"

Uhura paused after posing the question, trying to hide the twinkle in her eyes as she scanned her audience of Starfleet cadets. Only the very best of the senior communications majors had been given permission to enroll in her special-topics seminar at the Academy, and she could see them racking their brains, each trying to think past the obvious answer and come up with something no one else would have thought of. It was the way Starfleet trained its best cadets to reason. But if there was one thing Uhura had learned from her years aboard the *Enterprise*, it was that sometimes the obvious answer was the correct one.

"Remember—the A'Ila'Mos had no written language before they were colonized by the neighboring postcontact planet in their solar system," she reminded the silent classroom. "All of their public decrees had been in the form of long, alliterative poems recited in their markets."

One cadet in the front row raised her hand. "Did they adopt the alphabet the colonists brought with them, sir? The way our Japanese adopted Chinese pictographs?"

Uhura shook her head. "No, although the Naiilati colonists did try to teach the A'Ila'Mos their own alphabet. Unfortunately, it didn't work. You see, the word that meant 'writing' in Naiilati meant 'excrement' in Ila'Mos."

The roomful of cadets erupted into stifled chuckles,

and Uhura didn't reprove them, remembering how young they were, despite their serious faces.

"It really wasn't funny, though," she told them after the wave of amusement subsided. "By the time the *Enterprise* arrived in their system, the A'Ila'Mos were on the verge of a bloody revolution, simply because the Naiilati colonists refused to honor their tribal decrees unless they had some written version to keep track of." She spread her hands outward gracefully. "Put yourselves in my place, gentlemen. What would your solution have been?"

There was another long, mystified pause. Finally, in the back row, a hand went up. Unlike the others, it was wrinkled and dusted with age spots, but it waved as energetically as a first-year cadet's.

Uhura smiled again, recognizing the octogenarian who was permitted to audit her class as part of his Starfleet retirement. "Yes, Mr. Kahle?"

Despite his age, Jackson Kahle's voice boomed easily across the auditorium. "I'd say, give 'em all audio recorders."

"Exactly." Uhura swept the startled faces of the young cadets. "The Naiilati colonists had already violated the Prime Directive by settling on A'Mos to begin with. By giving the A'Ila'Mos a simple technology they could use to record their laws in a manner compatible with their oral culture, the Naiilati could keep track of tribal legislation and honor it. The two species were then able to coexist in harmony." She paused to let the lesson sink in. "And that, gentlemen, is why a good communications officer should always *listen* to an alien language as well as translate it. Dismissed."

The class dispersed in its usual scatter, some cadets bolting to make their next scheduled class while others lingered to talk to each other or clarify some point of the lecture with Uhura. She finished giving the last one a reference to the A'Ila'Mos recordings she had deposited in Starfleet's Culture Library, then began to gather up her notes and datacards.

"Now *that* was a good lecture, ma'am."

Uhura looked up, smiling a little at the old-fashioned title with which Jackson Kahle insisted on honoring her. The tall, stoop-shouldered retiree was a familiar sight at the end of her classes, but he usually came down to argue some detailed point of military history or alien contact procedure with her. Today, his steel-blue eyes glinted with distinct approval. Since the admiration was clearly intellectual, Uhura laughed and accepted it.

"Thank you, sir. I must admit, though, that I didn't come up with the A'Ila'Mos solution all by myself. I had some help from my colleague, Mr. Spock."

Kahle thumped his slim black cane dismissively. "Yes, of course. But it won't hurt those young ones you're teaching to think they might have to solve a problem like that on their own." He politely held the auditorium door for her to pass through. "Make 'em realize their job is more than just memorizing a jumble of languages."

Uhura nodded as she followed him outside, pleased by his perception. "Yes, that's what I'm trying to do."

She took a deep breath of the Academy's redwood-scented air while they emerged into the bright winter sunlight. Through the big trees, she could see the gleam of the Golden Gate Bridge over the clean blue waters of San Francisco Bay, the forested slopes of the Tiburon Peninsula rising like green-gray mist beyond it. This was the view the Presidio had been famous for long before it became Starfleet's headquarters and training center, the view Uhura woke up to every morning in her small apartment above the bay. It was another of the many reasons she'd accepted this temporary teaching assignment.

"Been meaning to ask you, ma'am," Kahle was saying as he followed her up the stone-flagged path, vigorous despite his advanced age. "Do you generally have lunch plans after this class?"

Uhura blinked in surprise. "Occasionally," she admitted. "But not always."

"Good." Kahle nodded once with satisfaction. "Like

to ask you for more details on this A'Ila'Mos affair, and some of the other *Enterprise* missions you took part in. Pay you for your time with a nice lunch down in Monterey. Sound acceptable?"

Uhura scanned Kahle's thin, Nordic face, seeing the fire-bright intelligence and roving curiosity of a former ship's captain, but nothing more than that. She allowed herself a slight smile, and a nod of acceptance. "Perhaps the first of next week?"

"Ideal, ma'am." Kahle switched his cane to his left hand and shook hers gravely. "See you then."

Uhura watched in amazement as the octogenarian strode away, then jumped when someone cleared his throat behind her. She turned to find a familiar wiry figure regarding her with ironic hazel eyes, as fire-bright and curious as Kahle's.

"Admiral Kirk!" This time, Uhura didn't have to censor her brilliant smile. "How are you, sir? I haven't seen you on campus for a long time."

"Diplomatic missions," Kirk said ruefully, and Uhura nodded, knowing he couldn't explain further. The admiral looked at her questioningly. "So, Uhura, how do you know Jackson Kahle?"

She laughed and fell into step beside him, heading for the Academy cafeteria. "He's auditing my special-topics course. And believe it or not, he's one of the best students in it!"

"Oh, I believe it." Kirk's voice held the same ironic note she'd seen in his eyes. "Did I just hear him ask you out to lunch?" He raised an eyebrow at her when she nodded. "Well, be careful he doesn't seduce you."

"Admiral Kirk!" Uhura threw him an indignant glance. "He's eighty-five years old!"

Kirk grinned, the expression momentarily erasing some of the lines of strain on his face. "Into working for him, I meant."

"Work for him?" Uhura cocked her head at him, puzzled. "I thought he had retired from Starfleet."

"Oh, he did. Over forty years ago." Kirk held the

cafeteria door for her, his grin widening wickedly. "And then he went out and founded UniPhase Incorporated. You've heard of them?"

Uhura came to a dead stop in the middle of the cafeteria entrance, staring up at her former captain. "Not the company that builds all of Starfleet's ship's phaser banks?"

"That's the one." Kirk steered her toward the stack of lunch trays. "Worth about half the gross planetary product of Vulcan on the present Federation market. And all still privately owned by Jackson B. Kahle II."

"Oh, my God!" Uhura was so stunned by the thought of a multibillionaire auditing her class that she almost accepted the meat loaf platter the cafeteria cook held out to her. Kirk's quizzical look brought her back to her senses, and she passed the dish on to him, then reached for her usual yogurt and fruit plate. "What on earth is he doing at the Academy?"

Kirk smiled and headed for the coffee urns. "Oh, he's mostly retired from UniPhase these days, too." He waited until Uhura had poured a cup of tea for herself, then led the way into the main dining hall. The room swarmed with its usual lunchtime crowd, but a table was respectfully vacated for them by a pair of second-year cadets who wolfed down the last of their meals. Uhura hid a grin. There were definite advantages to having occasional lunches with an admiral.

"I think Kahle just likes to keep his finger on the pulse of Starfleet," Kirk continued, stirring his coffee thoughtfully. "His Peace Foundation supports a lot of our cultural and medical research programs, you know. And they were instrumental in arranging the preliminary territorial conference we're going to hold with the Romulans this month."

"I knew that." Uhura shook her head in amazement. "I mean, I knew the Peace Foundation did that, but I didn't know it belonged to *him.*"

"Kahle likes to keep a low profile," Kirk said. He pointed a warning finger at her. "The better to recruit our cadets and senior officers to go work at his foundation. Just keep that in mind when you have lunch with him."

"Lunch!" Uhura had almost forgotten her casual acceptance of Kahle's offer. She dropped her fork, staring at Kirk in half-humorous dismay. "Oh, my God! I've arranged to eat lunch with the richest man in San Francisco. What am I going to do?"

Kirk's eyes lit with sudden laughter. "Order something expensive," he suggested helpfully.

Chapter Five

Starfleet Security Academy
Annapolis, North America
Terrestrial Date: December 19, 2269
1100 hours EST

A SILENT FLASH of phaser fire slammed him in the chest, kicking the wind from his lungs and knocking him back down below the barrier as efficiently as if he'd been struck by a shuttle. Not the most elegant method of obtaining data, perhaps, but the only one Chekov could think of in the artificial darkness of the crowded simulation chamber. By the time the waspish whine of the enemy phaser's report whistled over him, he had already backed himself against the barrier for protection as he caught his breath and checked the time.

Compared to some of the other Academy scenarios, this one was deceptively simple. A band of terrorists (cleverly disguised as Security upperclassmen) had ensconced themselves in a Federation embassy, complete with optic weapons and hostages. Chekov's class was expected to make some sort of contact with the criminals, free the hostages (preferably while all were still alive), and come away from the encounter with minimal casualties and damages. Chekov privately thanked whoever staffed such scenarios that he hadn't been picked as squad commander for this one.

They'd lost seven security officers already. "Death," in

58

this case, amounted to nothing more than a sensor-detected hit from one of the enemy's phaser rifles—the computer disconnected your weapon, you were informed of your ill fortune, and you slunk out of the scenario in defeat to face the harassment of your classmates when the test was finally over. Even the assumption that the members of Chekov's team would be outfitted with body armor—giving them four separate opportunities to be shot before the computer was forced to admit they were "dead"—hadn't done much to salvage their scores.

Chekov had even seen one unfortunate classmate take a phaser bolt in the face while they were still deploying to their positions. He'd made the mistake of scrabbling over to help her, and took a hit to his body in the process, but didn't gain anything for his heroics. A face shot was a face shot, whether in real life or a scenario—even in Starfleet's best body armor, after one shot to the face, you were simply dead, and the computer knew it. Chekov had watched that latest "cadaver" stumble from the scenario in silent surprise, scrubbing at her eyes as if still blinded by the light that had taken her down.

Since then, he'd tried to be more jealous about his exposure. Lieutenant Franz, as squad commander, had tapped Chekov to scout for enemy snipers, abandoning him to find his own way around the barriers and into enemy territory. Chekov had accepted the assignment as expected, without complaint, but he couldn't help feeling just a little betrayed that she would single him out for such a hazardous mission. As his tutor, Franz knew his tactical abilities better than anyone else in his peer group. She also knew that his marksmanship scores hardly made him a good choice to send sniper hunting.

Chekov didn't need four years of security experience to recognize that he was being sacrificed to preserve the lives of more valuable members of the team. It was the kind of command decision he could understand quite well when presented with it on paper—he just hated being on the receiving end of it, that was all.

Snapping his thoughts back to the present, Chekov

noted the .06 second time lapse between the sniper's phaser flash and its report, then plugged that into a wavelength/distance equation that he hoped would help him pinpoint the sniper's position. Maybe utilizing knowledge he'd picked up as a starship's navigator would give him an edge the upperclassmen terrorists didn't expect.

"What's the matter? Worried you won't get out in time?"

Chekov jerked his head up, startled, as Leong sidled into the shelter beside him. "What?" For some reason, knowing that Leong and he were supposed to be fighting on the same side didn't make Chekov feel any easier about the lieutenant's proximity.

Leong sank into an easy crouch at his end of the wall. "I hear you're leaving for San Francisco this afternoon."

"Oh." Blinking to clear his thoughts again, Chekov rose up on his knees to peek back over the barrier and continue his figuring.

"First Johns Hopkins, now guest lectures at the main Academy. Your dance ticket must look like the Who's Who of Starfleet by now."

He flicked a scowl over his shoulder at the lieutenant. "Don't you have anything better to do than keep track of my extracurricular activities?" he whispered.

Leong barked an acrid laugh. "You bet I do. I have classes. I have tests and labs and physicals to worry about." He crawled forward to grab at Chekov's elbow, yanking the ensign back down to his level. "Some of us actually have to work to earn our grades—we don't have the world handed to us just because we were important enough to spend four years doing nothing on a starship."

Chekov wrenched his arm from the other cadet's grip. "Maybe it just looks that way to someone who's never even spent four *minutes* on a starship," he snarled. "Even doing nothing."

He wasn't sure what hit him first—Leong's hand or the butt of Leong's rifle. The barrier wall thundered with the force of his slamming into it, and another shot from the unseen sniper splattered against the floor a half meter away as Leong pinned him, knee and elbow, to the flimsy structure. Chekov froze with both hands splayed flat against the wall behind him, momentarily stunned at the thought of what Leong could have done to him if he'd intended more damage than just knocking him back.

"You know what your problem is, Chekov?" The lieutenant shoved at him, then flushed with anger when the barrier behind Chekov didn't back up any farther. "You don't respect the position. You think being a security chief is all about flying all over the continent at a whim, and getting invited to tell Academy classes whatever stupid things you think about. You don't understand about the discipline, or the danger, or just how much power you'll hold. Does it even matter to you that someone without your exalted background might have needed the Johns Hopkins merit credits more than you did? It mattered to me! I didn't have a string of admirals and crewmates to help me along, and I *wanted* that position!"

Chekov lifted one hand to try and ease the lieutenant's arm away from his throat. "No one said anything about you when they offered me the assignment."

Leong's lip curled in disgust, but he didn't pull his arm away. "Would it have mattered to you if they did?"

"No." He wished he was able to lie, although he couldn't see what difference it would make here if he did. "A senior officer made a reasonable request. I did my duty and obeyed." Chekov tugged at Leong's arm again. "Isn't obeying orders what we're being trained to do?"

Anger moved like a cold viper through the depths of Leong's eyes. "You're right." He pushed back away from Chekov as though suddenly appalled with himself for the contact. "You're right," he said again. "You have nothing but the Federation's best interests at heart. And here we are, keeping you from your duty in San Francisco by tying you up in this silly war game! By all means, Ensign Chekov, let me help you set things right." The phaser rifle was suddenly at Leong's shoulder, as swiftly deployed as the lieutenant's hands. "You don't want to be accused of shirking your duty."

Chekov didn't even have time to open his mouth in protest before Leong squeezed the rifle's trigger and banished him from the scenario in a single, searing flash of light.

"Chekov, can you at least *try* to look like you want to be here?"

Chekov glanced up from his study notebook, momentarily unsure what Uhura's plaintive question had to do with the ethical ramifications of nonpeer judicial review.

"Oh, he's been in a mood ever since I picked him up out East." Sulu hadn't sat down since they arrived at the San Francisco Academy, wandering happily up and down the corridor outside Uhura's classroom as though expecting to find something exciting at one or the other end. "I tried cheering him up by showing him where I work, but he wasn't impressed."

A forty-minute detour over the windy Alamogordo Basin while trying to reread last night's ethics assignment was hardly something Chekov considered particularly mood-lifting. He marked his place in the notebook and looked up as Sulu wandered past again. "I'm just not sure that I really have anything to add to this discussion. This is a first-contact seminar. What do I know about first contacts?" He stopped himself just shy of adding, "I'm just a security guard."

"Don't underestimate your value." Uhura bobbed up on tiptoes to sneak a look through the window in her classroom door. "You've been in on a couple first contacts, haven't you?"

Shutting down his notebook, Chekov came to stand behind her. On the monitor just inside the doorway, an edited ship's log displayed the events and results of a recent alien encounter with some species that looked distressingly like milling herds of tattooed pigs. The notation at the bottom of the screen identified the origination ship as the *U.S.S. Resolution*. Maybe that was why Sulu didn't seem particularly interested in watching.

Chekov winced as some junior officer on the screen was swarmed with squealing piglets. "All I ever did on contact missions was what the captain told me."

"So?" Sulu peeked over Uhura's shoulder only long enough to verify that the log was still running, then resumed his explorations. "For the first ten years or so, that's all any of these kids are going to do."

"I just want you both to talk about your experiences," Uhura explained. "The things you remember, the things you noticed first, the things that ended up mattering." She turned to lean back against the door and grasped Chekov by the shoulders. "This isn't a test!" She shook him gently three times, and he finally had to smile at her teasing. "I just want the class to see someone else's viewpoint for a change. They get to hear only from me all the time."

"There must be a hundred exstarship personnel on the West Coast you could have brought in." Chekov pointed beyond her to indicate that the log had reached completion. "Why single out us?"

Sulu pushed open the door with one arm and grandly waved Uhura through. "Because we're the only ones who'll do it for free."

The communications officer aimed a prim scowl up at him on her way past. "Not for free," she scolded in a quieter tone. "You're both getting a lunch out of it."

Chekov exchanged a shrug with Sulu. "So what? I get lunch every night."

Uhura rewarded him with a swat on the shoulder, and Sulu murmured as they followed her to stand at the front of the room, "One of these days, Pavel, we have got to civilize you." Chekov had yet to figure out what civilization had to do with food.

Hurriedly finishing whatever notes or questions they'd been scribbling, Uhura's class responded to her arrival with quiet attention, their faces eager with interest, their eyes tracking her every expression and mood. When she smiled a greeting to them, more than half the students smiled back. A semester's worth of lectures at Annapolis had reminded Chekov how incapable classes were of masking their affections. These students truly enjoyed Uhura, he realized. Suddenly able to view her in the context of something other than a fellow bridge officer and a friend, he experienced an unexpected moment of jealousy that these cadets had such a good teacher when he was saddled with some of the instructors he sat through back home.

I'm turning into an academician, he thought dismally. If he kept this up, he'd never be fit to serve field duty again.

Mounting the podium at the front of the lecture hall, Uhura motioned back toward the viewing screen behind her. "A little scary, isn't it?"

A murmur of uneasy agreement ran through the big room.

"No matter how many classes, seminars, or lectures you attend, nothing can completely prepare you for the experience of first contact. The whole reason it's *called* first contact is because it's not like anything else you've ever encountered. First contacts are one of the rare privileges of serving on a starship, but even those aren't the orderly, well-structured affairs your textbooks sometimes lead you to believe.

"Today, I've brought in two special guest speakers with some firsthand experience in initiating alien contact. Ensign Chekov and Lieutenant Commander Sulu served as navigator and helmsman on board the *Enterprise* during her last five-year mission, and during that time . . ."

Chekov noticed the slight realignment of Uhura's focus just as the doors at the top of the hall swung open and a string of grim security personnel ghosted into the room to fan out along the perimeter. Students stood away from their chairs, shifting unhappily and muttering questions to the silent guards, to each other. "Everyone stay in your seats," Uhura ordered calmly. Whoever could hear her obeyed. Chekov motioned the other students down, trying to look as though he'd brook no argument, while a second squad swarmed in the lower doors and eddied around him. His new scarlet tunic must have put him in good stead as far as disciplining classes—Uhura and Sulu were the only non-security personnel still standing by the time the plainclothes operative displayed himself inside the main entrance and started his arrogant stride down the room's center aisle.

Uhura intercepted him at the foot of the lecture hall. "Can I help you, Mister . . . ?"

The plainclothesman darted measuring frowns to left and right, stepping neatly around Uhura as he did so. "Lieutenant Commander Hikaru Sulu?" He clearly aimed the question at the pilot in front of him, although his eyes never stilled to make actual contact with Sulu.

Sulu nodded doubtfully. "Yes?"

"I'm from Starfleet Divisional Security, sir." He flashed his identification too quickly for anyone to read it, but Chekov glimpsed the metallic sheen of the Judicial System's emblem and knew with sick certainty that this was for real. "I'm afraid you'll have to come with me, sir."

"Why?" Sulu jerked his arm sharply away from the guard who reached for his elbow. "What's all this about?"

Four months of security immersion warned Chekov that Sulu shouldn't have resisted an instant before the pilot shrugged off his escort. Red and black converged into a knot, one of them wrenching Sulu's arms behind his back while another pushed him facedown across the podium and a third clamped belt and restraining brace-lets into position around the pilot's waist. Chekov caught at the tether between the belt and bracelets, pulling them aside before the guards could lock them down. "You have to have some explanation—"

He felt the cold brush of the plainclothesman's phaser muzzle behind his ear and clenched his mouth shut without continuing.

"Please, don't interfere, sir. I'm working under strict orders." One of the guards looped an arm around the front of Chekov's shoulders to pull him with gentle firmness back away from the turmoil. "I really don't want to have to hurt anyone."

"Pavel, it's all right—I'm okay!" Sulu staggered upright when the guards flanking him dragged back on his collar. "I'm sure this is just some kind of formality. I'll be fine." But he looked a little too pale and uncomfortable for Chekov to believe him.

As if sensing his friend's worried thoughts, Sulu tossed him a crooked grin and suggested, "You can always see what your contacts in security can do about getting me a quick parole."

Chekov shrugged morosely. Even that made the plainclothesman's fist tighten on the front of his tunic, as though afraid the gesture heralded some sort of escape. "None of my contacts in security has graduated yet," Chekov said.

"I'll talk to Admiral Kirk," Uhura promised as the swarms of red and black made their way out the open doorways, taking Sulu with them. "There must be something he can do."

"I'd appreciate that." For the first time, honest concern flashed across the lieutenant commander's face, just before the classroom door swung shut between them. "And hurry, okay?"

Uhura didn't even wait for the second security team to make its exit. "Class dismissed." She spoke over her shoulder to the milling students, pushing the plainclothesman away from Chekov and motioning the intruder fiercely out the door at the same time. He departed with a last flip of his identification and a respectful nod. "We'll have to make up this lecture at another time. I'll post messages to your study accounts about possible changes in scheduling."

She turned to Chekov while the last students were still filing out the doors. "Are you all right?"

He nodded, nothing bruised except his ego. "Is Admiral Kirk even on campus?"

"I don't know. We'll have to call his office."

"Ma'am—" The wizened, white-haired old man pronounced the word more like a command than a greeting. Climbing down the steps against the flow of younger student bodies, he clacked his slim black cane against each riser, even though he didn't seem to truly need its support. He spared Chekov only a nanosecond's attention as he strode up to grip Uhura's arm. "You know I'm not without connections of my own. Is there anything I can do to help you out?"

Uhura squeezed his hand in appreciation before slipping it off her arm and back down to his side. "Thank you, Mr. Kahle, but I don't really know that you should get involved." A strange little smile twisted her lips. "I'm not even sure what it is we're getting involved *with!*"

"All the more reason to let me help you." Kahle waved off her dismissal with a diplomat's grace and ease. "I'm an old man with time and money to burn, Commander. Take advantage of my quixotic impulses."

"Unfortunately"—Chekov squirmed a little with embarrassment when they both turned as though expecting something useful from him—"I have neither time nor money," he explained reluctantly, "and I have to be back in Baltimore by five if I'm going to meet Dr. Piper on the testing range." He waved morosely toward the door Sulu had vanished through. "And my ride just left."

"Piper? Mark Piper?" Blue eyes sparkling with sudden keen interest, Kahle bent to peer intently into Chekov's face and thump a finger against his chest. "You the boy they got working on that Klingon disruptor project out at Hopkins, son?"

Chekov blinked, surprised by the question. "Yes, sir. Although I didn't think that project was common knowledge, sir."

"Son, none of my knowledge is common." Slapping a proprietary hand on Chekov's shoulder, the octogenarian aimed a triumphant grin at Uhura. "Ma'am," he declared, "you go see about getting that pilot friend of yours out of the hoosegow. I've got a private shuttle and the rest of the day with nothing to do." He turned the same fond smile down at Chekov. "I'll take care of this boy."

Sulu had always thought of himself as a patient man. His goals in life were long-term, and he was comfortable with the knowledge that he might have to wait years to achieve them. And, in times of conflict, his natural spirit of buccaneering recklessness had become tempered by his years of service with Mr. Spock. The Vulcan had taught him that it was generally better to tolerate situations about which you could do nothing than to tear yourself to pieces trying to alter them.

But after being arrested in front of his friends and led in handcuffs from the place where his parents had watched him graduate with special honors in piloting, Sulu found his reserve of patience and tolerance wearing dangerously thin.

It didn't help that he'd been thrust into a windowless security shuttle and flown for an hour without being told their destination, then politely blindfolded before being taken to what looked like a Starfleet briefing room but had the airless, locked feel of an interrogation cell. His two security guards had left him there, removing his blindfold and handcuffs but still not bothering to tell him where he was.

That had been three hours ago. In the meantime, Sulu had seen only one human being: a third silent security guard in an anonymous red uniform who'd brought him a meal and led him down a blank hall to a windowless bathroom. Neither the silence nor the unmarked uniform nor the lack of windows bothered Sulu, although all had obviously been designed to keep him from guessing his location. He'd known where he was the moment their shuttle had begun to land. Even the best Starfleet shielding technology couldn't keep out the skeletal sound of sand pattering over the hull from the gypsum-laden Tularosa Valley winds.

The knowledge that he was back at White Sands Experimental Flight Center had calmed Sulu's growing irritation. It told him his arrest hadn't been a mindless bureaucratic mistake, but had something to do with his assignment here. And, given the nature of the Wraith II project, it wasn't very difficult to guess what that something was.

So when the door finally opened on a tall dark figure with a commodore's gold braid glittering on his sleeve, Sulu demanded, "What happened to the cloaking device?"

Commodore Willis stopped short, his expression hidden by the glare of light from the hall behind him. Then he let out his breath in a short, sharp sigh and strode into the room, waving away the security guard at the door as he did so.

"The trouble with Starfleet officers," Willis said acidly, "is that they're just too damn smart." He swung a chair around to face Sulu across the briefing table, his strong, dark face looking grim but not hostile. "Has it occurred to you, Lieutenant Commander Sulu, that we've kept you in protective isolation all this time expressly to keep you from implicating yourself in what happened here today? Asking about the cloaking device before you've even been told that it's the focus of our investigation does not exactly clear you of suspicion."

"Oh." Sulu scrubbed a hand over his face, abashed. "Sorry, sir. But it was the only reason I could think of to arrest me."

The commodore frowned at him. "And, unfortunately, you were almost the only one we could think of to arrest. I'd advise you to be completely honest with me, Lieutenant Commander. Your future in Starfleet may very well depend on it."

Sulu straightened his shoulders, aware of the weight of

his new rank pins on the collar of his uniform. "I'd be completely honest with you whether my future in Starfleet depended on it or not," he said stiffly. "Sir."

"Good." Willis pulled a notepad from his breast pocket and tapped out its light pen. "Where were you at zero eight hundred hours this morning?"

"On day leave, flying a personal shuttle to Annapolis." For once, Sulu found himself grateful for the difference in time zones that forced him to leave at dawn in order to meet Chekov at the ensign's lunch break. "I logged in my completion of flight at the Security Academy shuttleport at eleven hundred hours EST."

Willis grunted and made a note of it. "And your activities while in Annapolis?"

"I waited for Security Ensign Pavel Chekov to meet me at the shuttleport, and we departed immediately for Starfleet Academy in San Francisco."

"You spoke to no one else in Annapolis during your ground time there?"

"Only to the port controller, sir."

"Good." Another scribbled note, followed by a few taps on the notepad's menu. "Flight control records show you logging in at Starfleet Academy two hours after leaving Annapolis. Why did the flight to San Francisco take half an hour longer than usual, Lieutenant Commander?"

Sulu cleared his throat, embarrassed now. "I—er—detoured slightly to show Ensign Chekov the base here, sir. I wanted to show him where I worked."

The commodore scowled across at him. "And had you received base permission for that overflight?"

"No, sir."

"Despite the fact that you planned to show a first-year security ensign some of the newest shuttles in Starfleet?" Cold suspicion leached some of the resonance from Willis's deep voice. "Were you aware that you were violating security restrictions?"

Sulu blinked at the base commander in surprise. "But I

wasn't, sir. Ensign Chekov has a Class A security clearance."

The furrows in the commodore's dark brow eased a little, but didn't completely disappear. "Isn't that unusual for a cadet?"

"Not if he's served most of a five-year mission aboard a starship."

For some reason, that unexceptional response made Willis's scowl deepen. He scrawled another note with his light pen, then glared up at Sulu. "For future reference, Lieutenant Commander, I'd prefer you request permission the next time you decide to do an overflight of my base."

"Yes, sir."

There was a long pause. If it was designed to goad Sulu into further admissions, it didn't work. His patience had returned, along with his ability to answer the charges leveled against him.

Whatever those might be.

Willis tapped his notepad a final time and grunted. "Well, Starfleet Flight Control confirms the overflight. I'm not sure that's a vote in your favor, but at least it shows you're telling the truth." He sighed and slid the pad away. "And the major point, of course, is that you're verified off the base at zero eight hundred hours."

Sulu kept silent, waiting. This time, he knew better than to betray himself with a guess as to what had happened, although his mind spun with speculation.

"Tell me, Lieutenant Commander." The commodore leaned back in his chair and regarded Sulu over steepled fingers, a new and more thoughtful note entering his deep voice. "Who else besides you and Dr. Nakai knew about the tests you were doing on the cloaked version of the Wraith?"

Sulu didn't have to stop and think about that. "No one, sir. We installed the device ourselves last Sunday, in a hangar we had security-sealed to our retinal scans only. No one but us has accessed the Wraith since then."

"And you don't think anyone could have detected the presence of the cloaking device during your test runs?"

"No."

"Even within Starfleet?" Willis gave him a skeptical look. "Your flight records show you've made two test runs this week. I assume you had the cloaking device enabled."

"Both times, sir, and it made us completely invisible. Dr. Nakai logged onto Starfleet's planetary surveillance net while I was up, and said there wasn't a whisper of response when the Wraith passed through."

"Dr. Nakai said that?" The commodore's dark eyes narrowed. "Now that's interesting."

"Sir?" Sulu decided it was time to risk a little cautious probing. "Has someone outside Starfleet found out that we're testing the cloaking device?"

Willis snorted. "You could say that. At zero eight hundred hours, Lieutenant Commander, someone broke into my office and stole the plans for the Romulan cloaking device."

Sulu's breath froze in his throat. The worst he'd expected to hear was that news about the Wraith test program had somehow leaked to the press, stirring up the usual public controversy about whether precontact civilizations should be monitored at all. To find out instead that the plans for the cloaking device had been *stolen*—his stomach twisted miserably at the thought. It had been his project, his responsibility, and it had become an utter disaster.

"But—" Sulu's mind darted after the first coherent thought it could find. "Why were there copies of the plans here at White Sands at all? We had the cloaking device itself, we didn't need plans—"

Willis scowled at him again. "And what if the Wraith had failed—failed disastrously—during one of your test runs? How were we supposed to figure out what had gone wrong if we didn't know what was aboard?"

Sulu ducked his head, reluctantly acknowledging the

truth of that. "But, sir, how could a thief get into your office?"

"He obtained a copy of my private locking code, then cut in an external circuit that convinced the computer it had gotten a valid copy of my retinal scan." Willis's voice held grudging respect. "That part of his plan was brilliant. Even though we found the bypass circuitry, there's no way we're going to trace it back to him. The whole thing looks home-built."

Sulu considered that for a moment. "Whoever it was still had to get past base security. How did they do that?"

"By being authorized to get past base security," the commodore said grimly. "There were no intruder alerts, no alarms. Once he was out of my office, the thief was safe. And that means he had to be one of us."

The sour taste of betrayal made Sulu wince. "You keep saying 'he,' sir. Does that mean you know who did it?"

Willis let out a long, unhappy sigh. "I'm afraid we do. That's part of why we've kept you here so long, Lieutenant Commander. I kept hoping our security alert would pick him up somewhere nearby, or at least discover an alibi for him. But as far as we can tell, he's been missing since dawn. We'll have to check with the Navajo Tribal Police just to make sure he hasn't gone back to—"

"Navajo Tribal Police?" Sulu's eyes widened. "Commodore, you can't mean—"

"Yes, Mr. Sulu." Willis's voice deepened in unwilling conviction and regret. "It looks like the cloaking device was stolen by Hernan Nakai."

Chapter Six

Johns Hopkins University
Baltimore, North America
Terrestrial Date: December 21, 2269
0848 hours EST

THE THERMOCOUPLE beneath the sidewalks at the Johns
Hopkins shot tower had broken down the night before.
Chekov exited the transit stop into a furry curtain of
white, his feet slipping when he came down on a sheet of
ice instead of the pavement he'd expected. A coarse ruff
of wind chased itself around the body of the brick shot
tower, and Chekov closed his eyes to breathe in the
stinging cold as it dashed over him on its way toward the
ocean. If this was truly the worst weather Baltimore had
seen in the last fifteen years, Chekov was just grateful
he'd been assigned to the East Coast at the right time of
year to enjoy it.

Giving himself a little running start in the snowy grass
beside the walkway, he leapt onto a promising patch of
ice and traveled a good seven meters before friction
worked its evil magic and slowed him to a sideways stop.
Sulu was insane if he thought New Mexico's winter
climate offered everything a man could want as far as
late-year weather. What could you possibly do for fun
someplace where it never snowed, or rained, or froze up
anything? With Sulu out of custody and free to amuse
himself with whatever local color existed, maybe the

pilot could investigate the subject of New Mexican winter sports for the holidays. They all had some free time coming up.

Aiming for a familiar figure another dozen meters closer to the facility, Chekov launched himself again in an attempt to cover the last distance in a single slide. Tim Anthony plucked another handful of tapes out of the snow, not even looking up when Chekov skated to a stop beside him. "Good morning, Mr. Anthony."

The grad student recoiled as though he'd been asked to lick a petri dish. His problem wasn't with Chekov, apparently, but with the concept of coupling "good" with anything surrounding himself right now. His knees and one hip were wet and stained with road dirt, the sleeve of his disheveled coat soaked all the way to the elbow. "What have you got to be so chipper about?" he demanded when the ensign squatted beside him to help excavate and wipe off his belongings. "Haven't you looked at the weather lately?"

"Well, yes, actually . . ." Chekov tried not to smile as he shook snow from another pile of disks. Anthony evidently wasn't as comfortable as Chekov with near-frictionless surfaces and blood-freezing winds.

"You're nuts." The lab tech snatched up his tape case and shook it with inefficient fury. "I *hate* this time of year."

Chekov held the bag open as Anthony jammed his clammy tapes inside. "Winter?"

"The holidays! Everything's supposed to be so happy —goodwill toward men, peace, mercy, all that stupid crap." He dragged himself upright on Chekov's proffered arm, then jerked his pack back into his arms as they started walking, more slowly, toward the Research Center. "But you know what you really get along with the weather and the finals and the god-awful snow? You get a bunch of greedy people too busy to look where they're going, rude waiters, thoughtless shoppers . . ." He swept them past the shivering guards with only a cursory wave of his ID. They were on the tiny elevator heading down for the research levels before Anthony finally grumbled, "It's the time of year that's supposed to make you glad to be a human being, and all it ever does is make me hate human beings even more."

Not sure how to respond to such an honest display of anger, Chekov satisfied himself with ducking out of the turbolift just ahead of Anthony to run his own datacard through the retinal scanner so he could hold the door open for Anthony to pass. If his simple attempt at politeness was recognized, Anthony gave no signal. Chekov was still holding the door in wistful chagrin when Piper hurried from the lab to shove him back out the door.

"If I could have a word with you, Ensign . . ."

He stumbled after Piper, hurrying to keep up with the arm the doctor had grabbed on his way past. "Uh, Dr. Piper . . ." The turbolift doors whisked shut on Chekov's coattails, rebounded lazily open again, then drifted closed just slowly enough for him to twitch his coat out of the way. "Sir, I didn't expect to see you this morning."

"It was a nuisance to get up so early," the doctor allowed, "but I wanted to make sure I caught you before you got into the lab." He reached out to hold the turbolift doors when they arrived at the surface. "Have you had breakfast?"

Chekov hurried out into the weather. "Yes, sir. At the Academy, sir."

Piper grunted. "In other words, garbage. Come on." He slapped at Chekov's shoulder as though redirecting a stubborn horse, and pointed at nowhere in particular across the windblown plaza. "Let's go someplace we can talk," he said as they wound their way between snowmen and students who scurried to and fro in their end-of-semester tizzy. Warm blossoms of illumination glowed from the Research Center's skylights beneath a patina of half-melted snow. "I'll buy you a bagel."

A somber carillon pealed the hour in slow, stately tolls, vibrating the air with its ringing. Flecks of color darted and swirled across the plaza, between the buildings, as students disregarded the weather and sprinted toward their various classes. Chekov followed Piper into a river of parkas and backpacks, wading upstream to the porch of some huge Victorian mansion, then down a winding stairway to a deserted mess hall that smelled deliciously of warm potatoes and toasting bread.

After almost a decade of Starfleet's small and convenient food replicators, Chekov had almost forgotten what it was like to pass through a line and choose from items displayed on a tray. "You like working at the lab?" Piper asked him, picking food out for both of them without slowing down. "Getting a good feel for the people there, and the equipment?"

"Yes, sir." He sniffed at the plate Piper handed him. Warm cream cheese and something with the sharp, inviting smell of smoke-cured salmon. His stomach growled in appreciation. "At least, good enough for the job you asked me to do there."

"Yes, well . . ." Two mugs of strong, black coffee joined the rest of the items on their tray. Chekov stopped Piper from dolloping either cream or sugar into his. Late nights and long hours at Annapolis had taught him how to drink the bitter liquid, but he didn't see much point in wasting other condiments on the beverage—it never tasted anything like what Chekov could consider good, no matter what sort of things were done to it.

"Your job at the lab's what I wanted to talk to you about," Piper admitted a little uneasily as he lightened his own cup to taste. "I'm afraid I misrepresented the situation somewhat when I asked you to join this project. I wasn't interested in you so much for your disruptor experience as for your security position." He fed his account card into the checkout with a sigh. "Ensign, I needed a mole."

Chekov shook his head, sure he couldn't have heard the doctor correctly. "Excuse me, sir?"

Piper retrieved his card, then motioned for Chekov to pick up their tray as he led the way to a vacant table in a far, quiet corner of the room. "I needed someone on the inside with the lab technicians," he explained, "Someone I was sure I could trust. I'd already made arrangements to get somebody in from the Security Academy, but the fact that you served under Jim Kirk made me sure you were the one I really needed. I couldn't go to just anyone about this." He seated himself while Chekov shrugged out of his peacoat, then lifted both mugs of coffee to offer one to the ensign as Chekov sank into his own chair. "Mr. Chekov, I think one of my lab technicians is a spy."

His first swallow of coffee suddenly diverted by a gasp of surprise, Chekov coughed and thumped his mug back down to the table. "What?" He could barely find enough breath for that startled squeak.

Piper made a face and pushed Chekov's coffee back into his hands. "Now, don't get your knickers in a knot," he grumbled. "I mean a corporate spy, from one of the civilian technical firms. They'll do damn near anything to get first crack at any kind of new design." He tore his cheese-smothered bagel in half, but didn't show any real interest in eating it. "Even something like an alien weapon might hold components they could use for what they consider more profitable undertakings. I'm just worried that dicking around on the corporate end will cause a security breach that endangers the rest of the project."

Chekov stripped a small piece of salmon away from the cream cheese. "Do you have any proof?"

The doctor sighed and shook his head. "Nothing concrete—nothing I could take to Starfleet. That's why I need you. I've made arrangements to meet Peter at lunch today—"

"Peter?" The fish turned as tasteless as ashes in his mouth. "Peter Broad?"

Piper drew back as though surprised Chekov hadn't known who they were talking about from the beginning. "I haven't been happy with his work since he got here. He's not familiar with procedures that ought to be second nature, and there have been too many times when

I think I've seen him running tests I didn't authorize. Turns out he worked for UniMed Technologies until about three weeks before he landed the assignment here. The rest of the information about his former employment is sealed."

"Then what do you expect to accomplish at lunch?"

"I just want to talk to him," Piper said, tracing an uneasy circle on the tabletop as though his mind and hands were on two different missions. "I want to see if I can get him to back down, or quit, or at least say something damaging. All I need for you to do is listen."

Chekov studied the doctor evenly across their dismantled breakfasts and coffee. "You mean monitor your conversation with him. From a distance."

Piper tipped his shoulder in something that was neither shrug nor nod. "He wouldn't agree to meet me anywhere Johns Hopkins security systems might see us, so I set up our meeting on the sixth-floor stair landing. He'll never even have to know you're involved."

"Dr. Piper, I'm not sure what you're asking me is legal."

"You're Starfleet Security," Piper reminded him. "This is a Starfleet research project. That makes it legal."

"But there are procedures, and special equipment—"

"I have the equipment." The doctor laughed at Chekov's gape of surprise. "Old friends in high places," he explained with a wink. Then, more seriously again, "I just need you a few flights up to see what we can get on tape. If I can't get Broad to quit, I want to be able to bounce his ass clear to Klinzai so he can never get a job like this again. Do you think we can at least accomplish that?"

Chekov sighed into the last of his coffee and ran a weary hand through his hair. "We can try."

"Ensign Chekov? Can you hear me?"

Chekov jumped, startled by the clarity of Piper's voice over the surveillance link, as well as by the booming, unaided echo that caromed up the open stairwell around him. Slapping a hand to the transceiver in his ear, he played with the gain on the control set until the dizzying overlap of voices resolved into a single one. Why on earth he needed surveillance equipment somewhere with acoustics like this was beyond him.

"Dr. Piper, please don't talk to me. You're supposed to be alone, remember?" He didn't even have to make an effort to speak loudly enough for the doctor to hear.

"I just wanted to make sure you're picking up well enough for the recording buffer—"

"I can hear you perfectly, sir." *Better than perfectly,* he thought. "The recording buffer is functioning properly. Now, please, be quiet until Mr. Broad gets here."

An indistinct rumble of complaint tumbled around the inside of the stairwell, but the surveillance equipment picked out the individual "condescending whelp" and "smart-ass" with phenomenal clarity. Chekov smiled and played with floating the omnidirectional transmitter into a more discriminate angle, just to see if he could refine reception to Piper's heartbeat, or the working sounds of his intestines. He was rewarded with a grotesquely loud *click-slosh* that he recognized belatedly as a magnified swallow; then a heavy, rhythmic pounding overwashed all other sound like peals of stunted thunder. A latch clunked and the stairwell whispered with displaced air as a door far below swung open. Then Piper's voice exploded in blurred magnificence, "Ah, Peter. Thank you for coming."

"Your note made it sound pretty serious," Broad's voice replied with a timid propriety that sounded particularly artificial at such a high volume. Chekov swept the transmitter back to its original position before all these casual comments could rupture his ears.

"Well," Piper said with a sigh. "This *is* serious, I'm afraid." Tense, unhappy shuffling filled the almost-silence. Then someone leaned against a stair railing with the cool sound of hands touching metal. "Peter . . . I have some questions about the circumstances of your employment here."

Nothing for a very long moment. "You aren't happy with my work?"

"No. As a matter of fact, I'm not." Someone started pacing again. Broad, from the irresolute sound of the footsteps. "You're not qualified for this position," Piper told him. "You don't know the techniques. You aren't familiar with the equipment." Piper made some small move in conjunction with the lab tech. "You didn't get this job based on your lab qualifications."

"Dr. Piper, if you brought me here just to insult—"

"Oh, cut the crap, Peter. I'm trying to talk to you like an adult, but we can make this childish if you want to. I know you were slipped in here by somebody associated with UniMed." One of them mounted the stairs leading upward with a thunderous bang. "I know you're after the disruptor," Piper went on with inexorable calm.

Chekov touched the transceiver again, frowning, as the pounding steps drew closer. No reverberation of the actual metal stairs, he realized suddenly. That's what was missing. Neither Piper nor Broad was going anywhere. "What I don't know is what could possibly be worth putting yourself in this kind of danger. Are you aware that what you're doing is treason? What did they offer you? Money? Some kind of management assignment? What?"

Then Broad's voice again, impossibly tiny. "Dr. Piper, who told you this?"

"Give me some credit, son. I *can* figure some things out for myself."

A crash like a shattering bulkhead smashed across the signal, and Chekov leapt to his feet with his shoulders pressed flat against the stairwell wall. When the door down below swung shut again, Chekov clenched his teeth against a shuddering sigh and touched a grateful hand to the door beside him. Even knowing that being found with elaborate equipment wouldn't earn him so much as a blink of surprise in a Starfleet research facility didn't make him any happier about the prospect of being stumbled across.

"Do you mind?" Piper's voice spiraled up from far below again, sharper this time but not quite angry. "This is a private conversation."

"No," Leong's voice answered him, coldly. "It's not."

Chekov nearly stumbled down to his knees in shock.

"Peter's been broadcasting since you first started talking with him, Doctor." No one moved in the lower stairwell now, all of their fidgeting and shuffling falling as still and silent as the snow outside. "So tell me," Leong asked with casual composure. "Who else have you talked to about this little problem?"

"About employee difficulties within my own lab?" Piper snorted. "Nobody!"

A howl of metallic sound blasted like a nova's pulse through the stairwell. Broad shrieked, covering Chekov's startled outcry as he jerked back into the wall behind him and cracked both elbows against the stone. His ears rang—one from the overloaded transceiver, one from the naked sound of the disruptor's wail—and he clenched the surveillance control panel against his stomach like a shield. Somewhere unseeable and impossibly distant, the surveillance equipment transmitter echoed with the splash of a body into a pool of fresh-spilled blood.

"Oh, my God!" Broad, his voice high and hysterical, clanged about on top of his own words. "My *God*, Leong! What did you do that for?"

Two calm, firm steps that had to be Leong. "You said we'd move at the right time." The sound of flesh on flesh as someone turned over an unyielding body. "It sounded like the right time."

"I thought nobody was supposed to get hurt. We were gonna be all clean and quiet—I'd take care of things at the lab, and you'd have the kid arrested out of his room at Annapolis!"

"Sounds good on paper, doesn't necessarily work that way in real life." Leong manipulated something on the disruptor with an eerie, sliding clack. "I hate loose ends."

Chekov bolted from the stairway without waiting to hear any more.

The hall beyond was dark and silent. Everyone gone to lunch, perhaps, or gone for the end of the semester. He hadn't considered what he would do if he ran across lab techs or students, yet now the thought of being trapped alone in this underground complex with no one but Leong and Broad brought his heart up into his throat. Switching off the control unit to preserve the words trapped in its memory, he ripped the transceiver from his ear and ran down the first side hallway he found. It might not lead anywhere immediately useful, but it didn't lead back to the stairwells, and that was the only criterion he cared about just now.

The doors to the glass-enclosed turbolift loomed, closed and silent, at the opposite end of the long central hall. Chekov sprinted the distance with the surveillance equipment bundled tightly in one hand, colliding with the lift almost without slowing and slapping at the controls as though the force of his request would speed up the turbocar service. A sound like broken footsteps started, then stopped, from somewhere unidentifiably nearby. He spun, hand clapped over his mouth to silence a cry, then backed quietly into the turbolift when he heard the gentle shush of its opening doors behind him.

The indicator above the door announced that they were going down.

"No . . ."

Leong was down. Broad and the lab were down. He punched every button above the lab, praying he was fast enough to stop the lift before it reached that level.

Folding the equipment, transceiver, and control panel back into their pocket-sized carrying case, Chekov found his fingers clumsy with adrenaline, his heart hammering too hard for him to breathe lightly. He'd left the transmitter somewhere back in the stairwell. If Leong located it, he might be able to trace the signal back to the unit in Chekov's possession, but if Chekov had already successfully delivered the damning memory chip to the authorities—

The doors whisked open, and Chekov jerked toward the back of the car with the surveillance gear clutched behind him.

Stern mimicked his startled gasp with a smile, then reached out to catch the doors before they could whisper shut between them. "There you are! Tim said he'd seen you come into work today."

"Yolande . . ." The indicator over the doors changed to UP, and it took every microbe of Chekov's control not to push Stern away from the entrance and let the lift slide closed. "I'm afraid I'm in a bit of a hurry."

"I'll bet you are." She smiled again and extended her hand. Chekov stared at it for nearly thirty seconds before he realized what she was asking.

"Please . . ." His stomach clenched around such a knot of confused despair that it almost stung tears in his eyes. "Please, don't be part of this."

Stern shrugged, but didn't withdraw her hand. "Everybody's part of this." She wiggled her fingers impatiently. "Give me the surveillance gear, Pavel."

He shook his head with halting courage. "I can't."

"Sure you can. Because if you don't, I'll just kill you and take it anyway."

Memories of the disruptor's scream ricocheted all through him and made him shiver. "If I give it to you," he said, very quietly, "you'll only kill me anyway."

This time she laughed gently, and cocked her head with all the fondness of a doting spinster aunt. "Leong warned me you were too smart for your own good."

"Hold the elevator!"

The squeak and slap of running footsteps rushed up on the open turbolift like a storm, and Anthony pushed his way underneath Stern's armpit with the oblivious rudeness of a prodigy. Wood, rolling her eyes at Chekov in mutual sympathy, waited until Stern had stepped clear of the doorway before slipping herself into the tiny space. "Thanks!" she breathed, flashing Stern a smile and squeezing Chekov's hand with a friendliness he thought he'd only imagined on his last visit to the lab. "You guys don't mind us barging in like this, do you? I hate having to wait for this thing."

Chekov shook his head, afraid to move his eyes from Stern's. "No, that's all right. We were only just leaving for lunch anyway."

"Great—I'm starved." Anthony grunted to reposition himself, an uncomfortable bundle of bony knees and elbows. "Yolande, if you're not coming, could you let this thing go?"

"Sure, Tim. I've still got things to take care of here." Laying a hand on Wood's shoulder, she winked at the girl as she leaned inside to pry the surveillance case from Chekov's numb fingers. He didn't even look down when she did it, afraid of what she'd do to Wood and Anthony if he resisted. "You guys go ahead without me. And *you*—" She tapped her finger on Chekov's nose just before the doors hushed shut between them. "I'll see you later."

Chapter Seven

IT HAD TAKEN UHURA several transcontinental calls to locate a suitable restaurant for her usual Friday night dinner with Sulu and Chekov. It had to be someplace close to a public shuttleport, so Sulu could return immediately to White Sands. For Chekov's sake, it couldn't be as expensive as a steakhouse or as unusual as a sushi bar, but Uhura drew the line at a greasy-spoon diner. In the end, she settled for a quiet Russian tearoom at the Chesapeake shuttleport and made reservations for four.

"I hope you like Russian food," she said to her companion.

Admiral Kirk made a noncommittal noise, scanning the menu that the dark-haired waitress handed him. "Well, I've never had anise-flavored vodka before." He sighed and set the menu down, shaking his head at the waitress. "And shouldn't have any now. The Romulan Territorial Conference is coming up next Tuesday, and I've got a lot of diplomatic briefings to catch up on before it."

"Next Tuesday?" Uhura looked across the table at him, concerned. "But doesn't Starfleet Command know that's Christmas Day?"

86

Kirk snorted. "Starfleet does, Commander, but the Romulans don't. They insisted on meeting Tuesday." He sat up, alerted by whatever sixth sense blessed starship commanders. "Ah, Mr. Sulu. I'm glad you could make it."

Sulu materialized beside Uhura, for once dressed in a nondescript civilian sweater and trousers instead of his distinctive silver flightsuit. "I'm glad *you* could make it, sir." He slid into the booth beside Uhura. "I know you're busy."

Kirk's mouth twisted in what was not quite a smile. "Not too busy to try and figure out what happened to our cloaking device." He cocked an inquiring eyebrow at the pilot. "Chekov didn't come with you?"

Sulu shook his head. "He's been doing some research up at Johns Hopkins University. He said he'd come straight from there to meet us."

"Ah." Kirk beckoned, catching the waitress's attention with his usual ease. "Three coffees for now."

The waitress tipped her head apologetically. "No coffee, sir, only tea. Sorry."

"Three teas, then." The admiral waited until she left, then speared Sulu with a flashing hazel glance. "All right, Mr. Sulu. Rep—" He caught himself with a wry shake of his head. "Old habits die hard. Update me on the situation down at White Sands, Lieutenant Commander, if you will." He cast a warning look at Uhura. "You've just been authorized for privileged communication. You know it goes no further than this table."

Uhura nodded while Sulu pushed back his sweater sleeves and propped his elbows on the table. He looked as calm as usual, but Uhura noticed that there were fine lines of strain around his eyes that hadn't been there last Friday.

"The plans for the Romulan cloaking device disappeared at eight hundred hours Wednesday morning." Sulu dove into the story without preliminaries, the way Kirk had taught them to relay information. "So did Hernan Nakai, the Wraith's project engineer. Security

87

hasn't found him since, although they've searched all of the area around Alamogordo and a lot of the Navajo tribal lands, too. Commodore Willis is convinced Nakai was the thief."

"But you don't think so," Kirk said, obviously reading the same unease that Uhura saw in Sulu's eyes.

The pilot shook his head. "No, I don't think so. For one thing, Dr. Nakai and I were the only ones who had physical access to the cloaking device in the Wraith. Why would he take the risk of breaking into the base commander's office for the plans, when he could just stroll into our hangar and walk out with the device itself?"

The tea arrived before anyone could answer, steaming in an ornate silver samovar. The waitress poured it into clear glass cups, then added a small pot of something that looked like plum preserves to each saucer before she handed the hot brew around. "Order now?" she suggested.

Kirk glanced at his watch and frowned. "I think we'd better. I have to catch the cross-country transporter back to Starfleet Headquarters in two hours." He handed his menu to Uhura with a quirk of his lips. "Admirals learn real fast how to delegate unnecessary work. You order for me."

"Me, too," Sulu added tiredly.

Uhura blinked and scanned the menu. "Three smoked salmon appetizers and three orders of braised beef with dumplings," she told the waitress, who nodded and took the menus away.

"All right." Kirk pushed his tea aside untasted, obviously more concerned with the matter at hand. "Forget the question of who stole the cloaking device for now, since we can't possibly answer that. Let's ask a more productive question: Why did the thief take the plans rather than the actual device?" He lifted an eyebrow at Sulu again. "Would you say your locked hangar was impossible to break into?"

The pilot frowned, drumming his fingers against the

table. "Not impossible, Admiral. A thief would only have needed the same things they used to break into the commodore's office: a copy of the entry code and a circuit to bypass the security computer's retinal scan."

"So we can assume the thief took the plans because they wanted the plans." Kirk sat back as the salmon arrived, glistening and garnished with caviar. He forked some up, then pointed across the table at them with it. "Now, tell me why."

Uhura felt the familiar sharp-edged joy of rising to a commander's challenge, tinged with sadness over the knowledge that she might never serve directly under this particular commander again. "Maybe the people who wanted the device wouldn't have been able to figure out for themselves how it worked," she suggested, stirring a spoonful of preserves into her tea to sweeten it. "Maybe what they really wanted was Starfleet's analysis of it."

"So they'd know how to manufacture more," Sulu finished the thought for her through a mouthful of salmon.

"Or maybe the thief—whoever he was—had no way to physically transport the device to the buyers," Kirk said slowly. "Plans are information, and information can be transmitted."

Startled, Uhura dropped her fork onto her empty plate. "Off-planet?"

"Why not?" Sudden understanding gleamed in Sulu's dark eyes. "After all, that's where the final buyers would be."

"Yes, and Earth is a free-communications planet," Uhura said soberly. "We can't cut off or control what's transmitted on privately owned subspace frequencies. Much less—"

"—jam the old radio bands." This time, it was Kirk's turn to finish her thought. "Even simple shortwave could transmit a code-stream of information to a ship sitting outside the system limits. It would only take a few hours."

"But who do you think is behind—" Uhura broke off when their dinners arrived, medallions of beef steaming on beds of tiny golden dumplings.

Kirk glanced at his plate, as if it surprised him to see it there. Then he eyed the ornate gilt clock on the restaurant wall and frowned. "Is Chekov usually this late for dinner?"

"No." Uhura threw an anxious look at the front door, but no hurrying young Russian came through it.

A faint line creased Sulu's brow. "Chekov would have called by now if he was delayed in transit. You know he's anal about things like that."

Uhura nodded. "Maybe something came up to keep him at Dr. Piper's lab."

"Piper's lab?" Kirk's first forkful of beef stopped halfway to his mouth, then clattered back onto his plate. "You didn't tell me Chekov was working with the Starfleet research sector at Johns Hopkins."

"He just started this week," Uhura admitted. "Is it important?"

"We'll see." The admiral fished a slim communicator from the inside pocket of his black civilian jacket. "One of the few privileges of rank," he said in answer to Uhura's questioning look. "I'm allowed to access Starfleet's main communications center in Iceland."

He flipped the communicator open, with only a tastefully muted chime of its usual activation whistle. Suitable for high-level Federation meetings, Uhura guessed. "Kirk here. Give me Reykjavik Central."

"Linking." There was a pause, then a startlingly familiar human voice. "Starfleet Intelligence, Rand here."

"Janice. This is Jim Kirk." A note of pleased surprise entered the admiral's voice as he recognized his former yeoman. "I'm glad I got you. I need to contact Mark Piper's lab in Baltimore. Can you link me there?"

"One moment, sir." Silence fell across the communications channel from Iceland. Uhura tried to eat some of her dumplings, but her growing anxiety turned them tasteless in her mouth. She pushed her plate aside, noticing that Sulu had done the same.

"Admiral Kirk." Janice Rand's voice came back, still professionally crisp but sounding far more grave than before. "I can't get through to Dr. Piper's lab. My records show all subspace receivers there locked down by Starfleet Security as of twelve hundred hours EST."

Kirk's frown jerked into a scowl. "Can you find out why that was done, Lieutenant?"

"I'll try, sir." Another long, nerve-grinding pause. "Admiral, right now the only explanation coded into my computer records is that Starfleet is investigating a Federation-level breach of security."

"Damn!" Without closing the communicator, Kirk gestured the waitress over, then pulled out his account card and tossed it to her. She ran a troubled look across their untouched plates, but took the card obediently. "Rand, see if you can get me through to someone in Security's East Coast headquarters who knows what's going on up there. Sulu, go flag us an autocab that can take us to Hopkins. Uhura, call my office and tell Riley I might be arriving late tonight."

"Aye, sir." Their responses chimed together as efficiently as if they were all still aboard the *Enterprise.* Sulu jumped to his feet at once, but Uhura lingered just long enough to ask Kirk worriedly, "Is it trouble?"

"More than trouble," the admiral said grimly. "Betrayal."

A drizzling mist met them when they exited the autocab at Johns Hopkins University, not quite solid enough to be rain, but still cold enough to send a shiver through Uhura. She wrapped her wool coat tighter, wishing the cloudy night wasn't quite so dark. The glare of red and blue security lights, flashing around some plaza close to the center of campus, seemed doubly ominous in the wet darkness.

"Something's happened," she said unnecessarily.

"Yes." Kirk glanced around, then chose a rain-slicked sidewalk that seemed to lead in the right direction. A murmur of crowd noise reached them when they emerged from the shadow of the ancient Victorian building that guarded this side of the campus. On the far side, Starfleet Security's light-emitting tapes ringed what looked at first like a flat, abstract sculpture. Closer up, Uhura could see that it was the transparent aluminum crest of a modern underground lab building.

"Let's walk up to the security tapes and see if we can catch any rumors," Kirk said quietly.

Uhura nodded and followed him, with Sulu a silent shadow behind her. As they approached, she could see that the crowd around the security tapes consisted of a constant flux of college students, each pausing to peer down inside the building and exchange interested comments with their neighbors before continuing on their way across campus.

Uhura took the initiative when they threaded into the crowd, partly because she knew her warm, quiet voice would be less intimidating, and partly because both men were intent on scanning what they could see of the activity inside the isolated lab below. She stepped up to the tape, beside a young woman whose book-laden backpack almost threatened to overbalance her, and said, in what she hoped sounded like surprise, "What happened here?"

The student gave her an amazed look. "You didn't hear? There was some kind of break-in at the Starfleet lab down there." She pointed with her chin, since both her hands were occupied in hefting her pack higher on her shoulder. "Some kind of secret alien weapon got stolen."

"Really?" The one word was all Uhura could manage to get past her tight throat. She was aware of Sulu's and Kirk's sudden switch of attention beside her, but both were smart enough to remain silent.

"Yeah. And one of my professors said someone got killed trying to stop it." Unaware of her fiercely intent audience, the student made a disapproving face. "I don't think they should do research on something that serious at a college campus, do you? How secure can a Starfleet lab be with twenty thousand college students noodling around it every day?" She shrugged her backpack up again and turned to go. "And hordes of them from off-planet, too!" she called over her shoulder, then strode off, shaking her head in teenage condemnation.

Uhura took a deep, shaking breath. "Someone got killed trying to stop it," she repeated numbly. "And Chekov never came to dinner . . ."

"Steady." Sulu gave her mittened hand a quick, reassuring squeeze. "Even if it was Piper's lab that got broken into, we don't know for sure that it was one of his team that got killed."

"If *anyone* got killed," Kirk added. "Rumors always tend to exaggerate things like that. They could just be holding everyone for questioning." He paused, staring down at the brightly lit open core of the underground lab. Far below, Uhura could see the vague shadows of figures moving around on one of the balconies. "However, given the level of Starfleet involvement in this, I think it's safe to assume that the 'secret alien weapon' really has been stolen."

Uhura turned to frown up at him. "The one our friend was working on," she said, mindful of the press of student bodies around them. There was no sense starting even more rumors flying around campus.

Kirk nodded grimly. "And that being so—" He turned to Sulu. "You shouldn't be found anywhere close to here. Not after what happened back in New Mexico. I don't want any guilt by association rubbing off on you."

The pilot's mouth tightened in frustration. "No," he agreed at last, reluctantly. He took one step away from them, then paused to look back at Uhura. "You'll call and tell me as soon as you find out what happened to Chekov, right?"

"Before I do anything else," she promised.

"All right." Armed with that reassurance, Sulu turned and vanished silently into the night. After a moment,

Uhura became aware that Kirk had swung away from her, too. She turned and followed him over to the shelter of an ancient ginkgo tree, out of earshot of the straggling crowd.

The admiral had pulled out his communicator, but he wasn't talking into it. Uhura puzzled over that for a moment, then remembered its nearly silent chime. "Rand called?"

Kirk nodded, tipping the communicator sideways so she could listen in. "—reported the disruptor missing at eleven-thirty EST," Janice Rand said crisply. "The lab tech called campus police first, but they knew enough to summon Starfleet Security. Once they started searching the building, they discovered Dr. Piper's body."

Kirk cursed and Uhura pressed both hands to her mouth to stifle her gasp of shock. "How did Piper die?" the admiral demanded, his voice steely with the effort it took to keep it low.

"The preliminary medical scan indicated death due to wounds inflicted by a Klingon disruptor." Rand's voice shook, then steadied again. It sounded as if she was reading from a screen. "There's apparently an eyewitness, one of the lab techs, who identified a suspect in the murder. Someone who was seen leaving the building with Dr. Piper this morning—" Unexpectedly, her voice broke off altogether.

"Rand?" Kirk scowled at the communicator. "You still there?"

"Yes, sir. But this can't be right." Rand's disembodied voice lifted in stark dismay. "It says here that the main suspect in Dr. Piper's murder is a security cadet named Pavel Chekov!"

Chapter Eight

Duke of Gloucester Street
Annapolis, North America
Terrestrial Date: December 22, 2269
0307 hours EST

A CONE OF LIGHT swept the yards along Duke of Gloucester Street, and Chekov ducked behind a lighted plastic
sleigh to crouch in the wet, frost-brittle grass. He waited
while the autocab's tires hissed across the wet pavement
and the sleigh's sharp-edged shadow swelled to monstrous proportions to crawl along the house's bare white
wall. When the autocab finished navigating the corner
and hummed serenely off toward the intersection of
Duke of Gloucester and Main, he pulled himself stiffly to
his feet and crept back onto the sidewalk. The pause had
done its damage, though—his knees felt packed and
swollen, and his skin had finally begun to chill. He
couldn't stop himself from limping as he hurried to get
out of the cold.

Sometime early yesterday evening, needle-fine rain
had replaced the blowing snow. It signaled a rise in
temperature, presumably, maybe even the beginning of a
warming trend and a chance to clear the growing mounds
of snow. Four hours outside Baltimore, Chekov had been
hard pressed to appreciate the improvement. He'd left
straight from Johns Hopkins, without telling Wood or
Anthony where he was headed, without waiting to see

how long it took Leong to mobilize Starfleet Security, without trying to circle back to the lab and retrieve his peacoat from the coat locker. He almost regretted that last omission now. The wool mantle would have been nice while half-walking, half-jogging along the overpopulated Maryland coastal plains. As it was, its absence just gave him one more reason to break into a blood-warming run every time the breeze licked across his exposed torso and wicked his heat away.

He hadn't set any cross-country records that night. Thirty-seven shamefully flat kilometers—not even a full marathon—and he hadn't run even half of it. Or maybe half, just barely. By the time he reached the Annapolis outskirts, he was weak-kneed and gut-sick, shaking as much from pure fatigue as from cold. He wished he'd eaten lunch before following Piper to his rendezvous. He wished he'd refused when Piper first raised the whole hateful, stupid idea of cornering Broad about his credentials. He wished he'd never taken this research job in the first place.

Oberste, Cmdr. G.J., 213 Duke of Gloucester Street. Chekov had found her in a combox on-line directory, the only Oberste in Annapolis. He had remembered some side comment during one of their nightly training stints, something about the benefits of qualifying for off-base housing. He didn't dare go back to the Academy. Not until he knew exactly what Leong had gotten him into, and what Chekov could do to protect himself from it.

He worked one hand out from under his armpit, unable to make himself untangle further from his shivering huddle, and poked twice at her door signal before finally making contact with the pad. The broad-spectrum light above the door blinked on, showering him in raw brilliance. He covered his eyes with one hand and ducked his head away from the light.

After what seemed a slow, arctic eternity, a woman's hoarse voice asked bluntly, "Do you have the faintest idea what time it is?"

He lowered his hand and looked up at the monitor.

"Commander Oberste . . ." The light still wouldn't let him open his eyes beyond painful slits, but he could see well enough to tell that she'd activated the door's monitor function so she could inspect him without revealing herself in turn. "Commander, it's me—Pavel Chekov. I'm sorry, I—I didn't know where else to go." He hugged himself against a sudden violent shiver. "I need help."

Silence from the other side of the door. He kept his attention riveted on the pickup, praying that she hadn't left him, that he hadn't run all the way from central Baltimore just to be abandoned by the only security officer he trusted. Then, just when he would have leaned into the buzzer again just to hear her answer, she grumbled, "All right. Wait there."

Three minutes later she appeared in the doorway, blond hair loose and tangled about her shoulders, a gray Annapolis Academy sweatshirt pulled hastily over loose bottoms of flower-print flannel. Grabbing him unceremoniously by the arm, she dragged him across the threshold and ordered the door to close while abandoning him to stumble toward an inner doorway. Chekov hovered, dripping, just off the edge of her close-cropped almond carpet. He wasn't sure what constituted appropriate etiquette in situations such as this, and the touch of warm inside air already had him feeling feverish and just a little heady.

Some other room woke up and filled itself with light, and Oberste reappeared through that doorway, face still sleep-dulled, feet still shuffling. "We've got to have a talk about the importance of keeping curfew," she muttered as she pushed him onto the carpet and away from the door. ,

"Commander, I . . ." Chekov let her guide him around the spartan furniture, finally breaking into the light to find a small, neatly laid out kitchen with both a replicator and a larger, more primitive cooking device. The smell of brewing coffee made his stomach spasm. "Commander Oberste, there's been—something horrible has happened." She shoved him into a waiting chair.

"Yes, so I've heard." She dialed something into the replicator while passing, then ducked into another room, only to reemerge with an armload of what looked like terry bathroom towels. "You're a very popular fellow," she remarked as she draped a couple of towels across his shoulders and legs, then dropped one over his head and began to scrub at his hair. "I can't turn on a news broadcast anymore without you being all over it."

Chekov lifted one edge of the towel to peer at her. "Me?"

She nodded and slapped his hand back down into his lap. "Johns Hopkins. The authorities are saying you killed a researcher there and took off with some alien artifact." Finished, she tossed aside the now-wet towel and unfolded another to stuff it into his hands. "Strip and dry off."

He stared at her, too horrified to even realize she'd made the suggestion. "No! That isn't what happened—I never killed anyone!"

"Calm down." Considerably more awake than before, Oberste turned to shovel a tray of food from the replicator and balance a full carafe of steaming coffee on the edge. "If I thought you were a murderer," she said as she crossed back to him, "I would have never let you in that door. Not conscious, anyway." She slid the food and coffee onto the table, then hooked the leg of his chair with her foot and scooted him around to face her so she could undo the collar of his singlet. "Tell me what happened."

He tried to pretend this was just another class assignment, that he was quoting from someone's written account of events too far away to damage anything he knew. When that didn't work, he thought of the worst of his missions on the *Enterprise,* the trust he'd put in Kirk and the courage that had given him to do what the captain needed, no matter how unsure the outcome. Neither strategy worked very well. In textbook readings, you didn't know the victims or smell the richly sweet odor of their blood; on the *Enterprise,* he had never been completely alone in a crisis. Not like this. He listened as his voice stumbled numbly into silence, then looked down at Oberste as she knelt to finish tugging off his singlet. "I don't know what to do," he admitted in a tiny, frightened voice.

Oberste didn't answer right away. Rolling his uniform into a dripping bundle, she pitched it without looking toward the other side of the room, then stood and uncorked the coffee carafe with a sigh. "This is serious stuff you're talking."

Chekov nodded, accepting the mug of steaming liquid she pushed at him. "I know that, sir." The warming ceramic made his fingers hurt as they thawed.

"If what you're saying is right, we've got to be careful who we take this to. Leong didn't get those two lab techs smuggled into Johns Hopkins, and he didn't get hold of a concealable listening device to put on his buddy, without the help of somebody a lot higher up than any of us." She paused to commandeer one of the towels and roughly wipe him down.

"So what does this mean?" Chekov finally asked when she tossed aside the towel to pronounce him dry and disappeared through the far doorway again.

"It means"—she returned with an armload of clothes, neatly folded and dry—"that you're in some pretty deep trouble. But I think I've got an idea." Refilling his coffee cup, she shook out a soft rose turtleneck and presented it to him with one hand. "If we get some food and coffee in you, how much longer do you think you can keep moving?"

Chekov accepted the shirt, then reached for the heavy blue sweater she offered behind it. "As long as I have to."

He only hoped that was true.

"We're there."

Blinking, Chekov straightened in his train seat, momentarily confused about what he was doing on a public transit line and where he was going. Then Oberste plucked silently at the shoulder of his gray down jacket, and all the horrible events of the last two days crashed over him. He slid into the aisle, awake now, and limped after Oberste's retreating figure as she left the train and wandered out into the station.

The slog of predawn passengers dispersed like rarefied atmosphere just beyond the mouth of the train. Few of them—professional commuters, or unconcerned transients—slowed to glance at the transit maps and train schedules projected on the station walls, and none of them so much as noticed each other. Chekov wondered if Oberste had expected such indifference during the early dark before rush hour, even given her efforts to dress herself and him as casual civilians. It had never occurred to him that success as a security professional might require an ongoing knowledge of current clothing styles.

Oberste waited for him a few meters farther up the station platform. "Don't walk out with me." She picked up his hand and pressed an account card into his palm. "Hold back a minute, then come streetside and wait in the news kiosk at the mouth of the station. Pretend you're reading the sports page or something. I'll be in the combox about two blocks to the south of here."

He nodded, tucking both hand and account card in his jacket pocket, and she clapped him manfully on the shoulder before turning away. The blunt honesty of her approval flushed him with warmth, but he gave no sign of it as he watched her mount the stairs for the surface.

He stood with the huge wall maps beside the schedules, trying to appear fascinated with the details of urban Annapolis as he traced transit routes just to watch the lanes light up with red, blue, and green. The station indicator surrounded by the bright yellow *YOU ARE HERE* was so far from the Academy as to almost be in Virginia. He let his finger glide from state to tiny state, and marveled at the frightening closeness of everything along the East Coast. He could be in the Carolinas and still not feel far enough away.

"We've got to get you out of Leong's reach," Oberste had told him as she'd hurried into her clothes and he'd wolfed down two breakfasts. "Not to mention out of the reach of whoever's directing him." She'd sat on the edge of the table and frowned at him very seriously while she tugged on her boots. "Tell me straight, Ensign—will your Admiral Kirk stand up for you in something like this? Even if that means going up against brass at least as heavy as he is?"

"Yes, sir," he'd assured her, with all the certainty four years under Kirk's tutelage had given him. "I'd stake my life on that, sir."

Which was exactly what he was having to do.

They didn't dare send him cross-continent on anything resembling public transportation. Assuming state authorities hadn't already been alerted that he was a flight risk, there were still Leong and his people to worry about. Oberste believed their best plan was to contact Kirk and arrange for some kind of private pickup. "He ought to have a personal shuttle," she'd explained to Chekov on their way to the Academy train station, "or at least access to the transcontinental transporters. If he can come pick you up personally, I think there's a good chance we can get you into protective custody somewhere safe on the West Coast." After all, it was one thing to persecute a single frightened young ensign, another thing entirely to try the same tactics on a top-of-the-line Starfleet admiral.

Three more trains quietly came and went, disgorging no one, taking no one away. Suddenly chilled by the ringing emptiness of the station, Chekov turned away from the maps and schedules to trot the steps up to street level a few minutes behind Oberste.

Crisp dryness nipped the last of his grogginess away as he mounted the open sidewalk. Roofs still sported glossy caps of melting snow, and water flowed like mercury from teeth of hanging ice on every doorpost, street lamp, and window in sight. Chekov slowed his stride as he approached the hooded news kiosk, trying not to seem obtrusive as he scanned the empty streets for Oberste. He found her easily, waiting outside an occupied combox several buildings away, hands jammed into her coat pockets, toe splashing an impatient tsunami in the puddles at her feet.

Except for Oberste, Chekov, and the young man gesticulating wildly from inside the soundproofed com, the city might well have been deserted, for all Chekov could tell. For some reason, he didn't find that thought particularly comforting.

He slipped into the news kiosk just to keep himself from staring at his commander while waiting for her to make the call. The kiosk welcomed him with a blast of warm air and a softly spoken "Pon'Tok" from the unseen voice-over speaker. He fed it Oberste's account card— "A'hde"—then chose a selection at random just to let the words scroll past his tired eyes.

Chekov couldn't read Vulcan, or understand it when it was spoken. He'd always liked the liquid, musical quality of the language, though, always appreciated the intricate, artistic lines of Vulcan written script. It seemed appropriate—in a way he couldn't quite identify and would never have tried to express to Mr. Spock—that a race so proud of its accuracy and logic would develop such a beautiful way of preserving and communicating information. If knowledge was beauty, and information was art, didn't that make written language the most perfect blending of the two? Or maybe that was just a silly human interpretation of it all. He watched the words drift past without division, a lovely, black-and-white abstract darned in colored spider's silk.

The sharp, blocky outlines of Cyrillic printing interrupted the soothing flow just as the calm Vulcan voice-over pronounced "Pavel Andreievich Chekov" in precise, flawless Russian. Chekov flicked off the kiosk in disgust, evaporating both text and language as if they'd never been there. Nothing instilled one with quite the sense of despair as discovering your infamy has made it to the Vulcan newslines.

A flash like the refracting of light against glass caught his attention from out on the street, and he leaned to one side in the kiosk to try and see out the transparent aluminum walls. Oberste, alone now in the distant combox, stumbled drunkenly backward and slipped to the floor of the booth as though suddenly robbed of her balance. Chekov tried to lunge through the side of the kiosk, slamming uselessly up against the hard transparent wall, while another flash of rifle fire splattered melted fragments of communications gear in a fan across the booth's already blood-sprayed inner walls.

"No!"

His cry was muffled by the kiosk's soundproofed hood.

He scrambled out into the open without letting himself consider the consequences. Oberste had managed to drag herself from sight—Chekov glimpsed the bottom of the combox through the kiosk's wall, took note of the box's empty, blood-slickened floor—but that wasn't the same as having found her way to true safety. He swung around the edge of the kiosk, scanning the rooftops up and down the narrow road for sound or sudden movement, and steam roared up in a ferocious column off the wet sidewalk ahead of him. Someone screamed in pain—or shouted a warning, he couldn't tell which. Then another shot answered, and a figure peeled away from a darkened doorway to point a phaser into Chekov's face.

"Don't do it, Pavel."

Chekov slammed to a stop, backing up involuntarily as Broad crept forward. The phaser between them shone glossy black in the wet streetlight; a twinkle of ruby picked out the pistol's "kill" setting beside the blinking charge indicator. "Get against the wall," Broad ordered in a hoarse, uneasy monotone. He held the phaser pushed so far out in front of him that he looked as if he might fall over unless he was very careful. "I'm sorry, but you've got to start moving."

"Peter . . ." Chekov tried to see beyond Broad's shoulder, but the other end of the street was silent, the play of fire against winter steam now ominously still. His heel caught on the curb as he edged backward, and he stumbled up onto the sidewalk with a curse. "If you're going to kill me, just go ahead and do it."

Broad shook his head stiffly, nodding him to keep retreating so they could preserve the distance between them. "That's all right," he said, incongruously eager. "I'm not supposed to kill you. All I'm supposed to do is hold on to you until Leong gets here. He's the one who knows what—" Broad's mouth started to form what might have been a proper name, but he stopped himself before giving voice to it. "—what our employer wants done with you. But they both know I'll kill you if I have to." His second hand gripped, white-knuckled, around the first. "I'm not afraid to use this."

That, at least, was a pitiful lie. Broad was very much afraid—Chekov could almost smell it on him.

As if recognizing the transparency of his threat, the lab tech tried to straighten his stance and pitch his voice more firmly. "Now turn around and stand against that wall," he commanded with brusque audacity. "Hands over your head."

Chekov lifted his hands first, as slowly as he thought he could get away with. A running figure, lean and panther-silent, emerged out of the surrounding dark and padded toward Oberste's body where it sprawled across the sidewalk on the other side of the street. He tucked a plasma rifle upright across his torso, the way the Academy trained guards to do when performing stealth maneuvers. Oberste was dead—clearly, horribly dead—but the sniper stopped to prod at her body anyway. Chekov spun away in revulsion when the gunman, ever cautious, dropped the muzzle to the hollow of her throat and reached for the rifle's trigger.

At the sound of the shot, Chekov finished his turn with the full force of everything Oberste had taught him during those long nights of hand-to-hand drill. He contacted hard with the hinge of Broad's jaw, hearing the meaty *click!* of dislocation and feeling the warm strength of his follow-through as he staggered to keep from whirling himself to the ground. The phaser clattered to the wet concrete between them, and someone who was neither Broad nor the sniper shouted a violent curse in combination with Chekov's name. Aiming another blow for the lab tech's face, he lifted his eyes for the barest instant to locate the assailants on the other side of the street and assess his options for combat.

"Be careful where you decide to hit someone—not all the bones in a human body were created equal." Oberste's basic lecture on the opening day of combat class. Having never met her before that autumn morning, Chekov had been impressed by the reasonableness of her advice and the straightforward manner in which she expressed it. "Anything you throw designed to break one of your opponent's bones is just as liable to break one of your own if you're not extremely careful."

The pain seemed to lift him straight out of his body. He and Broad crashed to the cold sidewalk in a tangle, and Chekov felt like no more than a distant observer as he crabbed back away from the lab tech with his arm cradled crookedly across his stomach. The wall behind him bumped into his back with the hardness of phaser strike. He couldn't feel his own breathing anymore, but he could see his palm when he knew it should have been pressed flat against his side, and he could feel a loose disconnection, as though his wrist was no longer on speaking terms with his elbow. He thought about moving, of trying to stand up to Leong despite the pain, if he could just find Broad's fallen phaser. Somewhere under the layers of wool and parka, bone grated on bone when he tried to curl his fingers into an experimental fist, and twisted muscles ripped his arm apart with pain. He couldn't stop himself from screaming.

An angry voice, the singing of a plasma weapon's

power coil, then running footsteps woke Chekov's conscious mind to the dangers still swarming around him. Rolling to his knees away from the wall, he lurched to his feet without using his hands, strangling his scream this time by biting into his lower lip. He struggled to hug his arm against himself as he ran back for the underground, waves of nausea and dizziness chasing him along with the sound of rifle fire. Brick exploded from the wall just behind him; a crash of ice and snow shattered on the pavement, warning him against slowing. He ducked around the news kiosk in some half-formed belief the little structure might shield him. By the time plasma heat cracked the transparent aluminum siding, he had already reached the station mouth and started his plunge down the stairs.

The train at the station stood empty, the overhead voice announcing smoothly, "This shuttle now departing," as the train's waiting doorway slowly constricted in on itself. The last of his hopes for survival would close behind that door. Sobbing an incoherent prayer, Chekov dodged clumsily between the two or three bodies milling on the station platform and lunged for the tightening doorway just as the overhead voice advised, "Please do not attempt to board the shuttle while it is departing." He toppled to the empty car's floor, then scrabbled away from the doors to give them space to finish closing behind him. He still wasn't sure he had actually made it until the train glided forward and settled into the smooth, frictionless race of its normal function.

He granted himself the luxury of lying where he was for a moment, swimming in pain and not trying very hard to fight off uprushing tears. He'd have to get off at the very next stop. Leong would already know by now which commuter line he'd leapt onto, and precisely where it was headed. He could abandon this train and take another without even leaving the station. Yes, train hopping would be his only chance. If he could ride and switch randomly as far as the lines would lead him, maybe he could confuse things enough to risk contacting Kirk again in another day, or two, or three.

He didn't know where he might be by then. He didn't know where he was going now. He tried to find some fragile hope in the thought that Leong couldn't very well outwit him if he didn't even know his next move himself.

Chapter Nine

White Sands Flight Center
Alamogordo, North America
Terrestrial Date: December 22, 2269
1700 hours MST

"COMMODORE WILLIS, are you sure about this?"

Winter storm winds roared outside the open hangar, cloaking Alamogordo's ink-blue twilight in a haze of snow and sand. Sulu throttled down the Wraith's impulse engines to compensate for the buffeting noise, and tried to read his commander's expression in the amber glow of the shuttle's heads-up display on the pilot's viewscreen. Willis's face remained enigmatic, but his resonant voice echoed with assurance in the tiny cockpit.

"The order came straight from Starfleet Headquarters today: Continue testing." Willis conscientiously checked the subspace radiation counter on Sulu's flight helmet, then handed it back to him. With Hernan Nakai gone, there was no one else on base who could be trusted to help with the Wraith testing program. "I told them exactly what I told you—that I don't like letting the cloaking device loose anywhere on Earth—but the admirals insisted."

"Even though they know there's a thief at White Sands?"

Willis flipped switches, changing the frequency of the subspace transmitter to another of the channels reserved

108

for high-security Starfleet projects. The commodore didn't seem annoyed by the additional evening duty of monitoring the Wraith, although Sulu had warned him that the run could last until dawn. "Starfleet Security says Nakai's long gone. And Headquarters seems to feel that if we don't keep the Wraith II program going, we'll have lost the cloaking device for nothing."

"But should we keep it going *here?*" Sulu couldn't keep the sharpness of unease out of his voice, not when he knew that Chekov was being hunted across North America for a crime he didn't commit. Uhura's assurance that Admiral Kirk wouldn't let their friend be framed for the theft of the Klingon disruptor hadn't stopped Sulu's instincts from clamoring in alarm. That two such traitorous acts could hit Starfleet within one week was mind-boggling; that both should involve former members of Kirk's acclaimed bridge crew was beyond any kind of probability.

A thin flash of teeth in the twilight was all Sulu could see of Willis's smile. "Not after the way my security team has already botched this project," he agreed ruefully. "In fact, I strongly recommended moving the Wraith II program to a more controlled site on the moon or Mars."

"So why didn't they do it?"

Willis stabbed a dark finger at Sulu's silver flightsuit, surprising a grunt out of him. "Because of *you,* Lieutenant Commander. You're the only pilot Starfleet Command wants running these tests—and until we've concluded our investigation and found Nakai, you're legally required to stay within Earth's security jurisdiction."

"I see." Sulu busied himself checking the status of his safety systems on the viewscreen display, but he couldn't keep his mind from spinning into a disturbing whirl of speculation.

Was he being paranoid, or was something odd going on? Sulu knew he was one of the best pilots in Starfleet, but he certainly wasn't the only one capable of flying the troublesome Wraith. That meant someone high up in

Starfleet Command must have other reasons for assigning him to this particular project. Was Admiral Kirk weaving one of his magnificently clever strategies for outwitting a Federation opponent, or flushing out a hidden spy? But then why had Chekov's involvement in the Klingon disruptor project taken the admiral so much by surprise? Surely the two assignments had to be related—

Willis tapped on the shuttle's chronometer, bringing Sulu's attention back to the here and now. "Coming up on departure time," the commodore reminded him. "Anything else you need me for here?"

Sulu shook his head. "I'll check in with you once I'm off the base's visual tracking screens. I usually engage the antigravs and the cloaking device somewhere over the Mojave Desert."

"Affirmative." Willis swung up out of the copilot's seat, swerving to avoid the sleek black device that took up most of the small cargo space behind the Wraith's cockpit. "I'll be listening for you."

Wind wailed into the shuttle as the commodore opened the hatch, then cut off with a thud and the dying hiss of scattered sand. Sulu watched the tall figure disappear off the edge of his viewscreen, then donned his flight helmet and carefully sealed it down against his radiation-blocking suit.

While he throttled the impulse engines up to their usual smooth, soaring song, Sulu deliberately emptied all other thoughts from his mind. Piloting demanded absolute concentration, and Sulu's ability to summon it had been tested under the worst of planetary conditions. Later, the Wraith's computer-controlled cruising program would give him time to think. Right now, it was time to fly.

He reached out, kicking in the silent antigrav generator for a second to lift the Wraith a meter above the floor of the hangar. The impulse engines cut in when the antigravity pulse faded, thrusting the stubby-winged craft into the driving snow outside. It might not be the recommended takeoff procedure, but it was the easiest way Sulu had found to get the stubborn Wraith airborne.

He toggled his communicator over to the normal channels used for traffic control at the base while he taxied out to the approach lane. Eventually, he would try engaging the cloaking device in the hangar to see if the Wraith II could escape the intense ground-level detection systems of a Starfleet test facility. For now, though, Sulu simply filed a flight plan for unspecified maneuvers over the Mojave, and tested the cloaking device against the broader detection systems of Starfleet's Earth Defense Array.

"Test shuttle WKI-2 requesting permission for takeoff, flight lane one," he told his chin-mike.

Traffic control came back with unusual promptness, and Sulu guessed that the bad weather had caused most other training exercises to be canceled for the night. "Request acknowledged, WKI-2. Be advised that winter storm conditions are causing strong downdrafts along the eastern slope of the San Andres." A glowing map of the experimental flight lanes appeared on his viewscreen, with unsafe departure paths highlighted in red. "Revise flight plan accordingly."

"Affirmative." Sulu tapped the code for an easterly departure into his computer and it blinked back a lane change. "WKI-2 now requesting permission for takeoff, lane four."

"Permission granted, WKI-2. Lane four now clear for takeoff."

Sulu skated the Wraith across the bumpy wind and steadied it above lane four, then cut in the antigravs again, this time for a full moment. With a gut-wrenching leap, the shuttle launched itself up into the snow-shrouded night, carefully aimed toward the dim, white-crowned peaks of the Sacramento Mountains. Sand drummed loudly against the hull as he broke through the Tularosa Valley winds, and then the Wraith was up inside the dark turbulence of the storm system. By the time the antigrav pulse finally faded, the impulse engines had caught the ship's momentum and smoothly transferred it into lateral cruising speed.

It was too bad you couldn't always use the impulse and antigrav systems together, Sulu thought while he called up the computer routine that would take him to the Mojave. The trouble was that even the smooth purr of well-tuned impulse engines could be detected by a high-level precontact civilization. Once inside a planet's atmosphere, the Wraith II was going to have to maneuver on its silent antigravs alone. But unlike its predecessor—which depended on darkness and its own ribbed reflective surface to remain undetected—this new Wraith class could also hide behind a fully functional cloaking device.

Provided Starfleet's testing program succeeded.

The Wraith broke through the western fringe of the towering storm system and emerged into a star-frosted winter night, with only a few gauzy wisps of cloud to obscure the broken Arizona landscape below. Sulu saw the jagged volcanic rise of the San Francisco Peaks cutting into the starry horizon, with the lights of Flagstaff clustered like fallen stars around its southern slope. The map on his viewscreen told him what he already knew: that another few minutes of flying would take him to southern California and its protected wilderness of empty desert.

He toggled the communicator back to the secret frequency Willis had selected for that night's run. "Shuttle WKI-2 to White Sands Base. Come in."

"White Sands here." The base commander's voice rang strong as a mission bell, even across the subspace channel. "How's it going?"

"So far, just as we planned." Sulu spotted the tiny splash of lights that was Barstow, with the vast unlit lands of the Mojave beyond. He reached for the impulse controls. "Switching to antigravs—now."

The thrum of the impulse engines died away, replaced by a quiet rush of wind along the shuttle's flanks. The Wraith slowed, then swooped into a headlong dive toward the desert floor. Sulu waited until he could see the coalescing shadows of dry rivers below, then cut in the antigravs again. There was the usual tense moment of lag time, as gravity cancellation fought with downward momentum. Then, a few hundred meters above the stony ground, the antigravs took over and the Wraith kicked itself up again. Even to Sulu's hardened stomach, the switch from downward to upward velocity seemed to come sickeningly fast, although his brain knew there had to have been an instant of standstill between them.

He kept his hand on the antigravs for a long moment, enjoying their powerful upward surge. "Antigravs functional. Engaging cloaking device." He reached for the control beside his seat, bracing himself for the unpleasant shiver that meant the cloaking field had materialized around him.

Nothing happened.

"What the hell—" Sulu toggled a systems check on his display to be sure his senses hadn't misled him. No fuzz of white appeared around the image of the Wraith on his viewscreen. "Cloaking device not operational, White Sands."

"Not operational?" Willis sounded very startled. "That can't be right! Try it again, WKI-2."

"Running a glitch-tracking program first, sir." It had always been one of Hernan Nakai's rules to locate any break in operations before overriding with more commands. Sulu looked down to tap the correct code into the computer, and heard the series of clicks that meant it had begun debugging the shuttle's systems. When he looked back up at his viewscreen, though, the heads-up display had vanished.

Instead, silhouetted like a faint tattoo against the outside darkness, the face of Hernan Nakai scowled out at him.

Strings of colored lights coiled up the trunks of naked trees, blinking and glowing, and casting dainty holographic images into the nighttime air. Starbursts, miming angelic choirs, tiny dancing creatures with wings. Chekov stood, swaying slightly, and watched a fine dusting of snow blur the double line of footprints leading from someone's front door to a tree-hanging bird feeder and back again. He had no idea how long he'd been standing there. The footprints were half-filled with snow.

No transit station was immediately in sight. He must have walked here, through the still streets and pretty yards of this quiet suburb, past God only knew how many other people and things. No one had seen fit to arrest him, so perhaps he didn't look as fiercely criminal as he'd been afraid he did all this long, awful day. Or perhaps the people who lived in this dark and pleasant place didn't care enough to worry about Annapolis news.

He didn't even know for sure what country he was in.

Probably still America. He couldn't believe he had traveled all that far. Even ten or eleven hours on what seemed like a hundred different trains could only have taken him a few hundred kilometers. From dark until dark, premorning to early night. Two hundred kilometers, maximum. He hadn't seen the sunlight all day.

He should probably keep moving, before he got too cold to go on.

A horrible, grinding twist of pain wrenched at his arm on the very first step, and he sagged to his knees with a whimper. Some small, almost-unconscious part of him remembered that something like this had stopped him in the first place, but that was too long ago to corroborate any details. He crawled a hand across the front of his coat to finger the opposite sleeve. He didn't dare try to interact with the broken arm any further than that—he was dimly afraid he wouldn't live to regret it once the pain spasmed over his system.

Sometime on the third of fourth train he'd boarded that morning, he'd gritted his teeth against the pain and slipped his injured hand into a coat pocket to try and hide any obvious impairment. He'd been unconscious for almost an hour afterward. Now, he couldn't bring himself to repeat the maneuver, no matter how badly he wanted to inspect the damage. He was just too afraid of what would happen, and what he'd find.

I can't keep going like this.

And yet a hospital was out of the question. Even if he could find a tiny private practice, the authorities would be all over him the instant his ID hit the medical net. Without help, though, he was going to go facedown on someone's manicured lawn and no doubt be in custody —or, more likely, dead—by morning. He pinned his elbow to him with the flat of his good hand, then climbed to his feet one slow, painful step at a time.

He found a combox some hundred-odd meters past the last residential dwelling. A park of some sort, with a thick overgrowth of trees and almost no snow brightening the muddy swath of ground. At least if he curled up to hide here, no one was likely to find him until spring. He squeezed into the soundproofed booth, letting the door hum shut behind him. The cool touch of the combox's glass panels felt good to lean his head against as he waited for the call unit to speak to him.

"Thank you for using TranSpace Link Lines." It had a throaty, woman's voice that sounded like warm caramel when compared with the bleak snow outside. "Would you like to tell me the party you wish to contact?"

That meant he had to open his eyes. Turning awkwardly in the little booth, he picked out the letters one by one on the unit's keyboard. Assuming he could even talk clearly enough for the unit to understand, he didn't want to leave a record of his voice in the planetary communications systems. He didn't think there could be that many Russians avoiding Starfleet authorities in America.

"I'm sorry, but a residential code or direct number are required in order to place that call."

Squeezing his eyes shut against a moment of dizziness, he steadied one shoulder against the wall of the booth and toggled *HELP* with his thumb.

He only had to type four letters before the unit recognized "Baltimore" and obligingly offered all public numbers. When he called up everything beneath the

115

name "McCoy," he groaned to see that there were hundreds of them. But only one "Leonard, M.D.," listed at a temporary address in a hotel not far from Johns Hopkins hospital. Unable to focus on the keyboard any longer, he asked the unit to place the connection for him.

"That call requires a long-distance connection. Would you like me to proceed?"

Long-distance? Where could he possibly be that would require a long-distance connection to Baltimore? "Yes," he whispered hoarsely. "Place the call."

"Thank you."

Wind rattled past the edges of the com booth, shuddering it and the overhanging trees with the kiss of winter's chill. Chekov watched the silver glitter of snow-turned-rain-turned-snow-again ripple like silk curtains underneath the bare lamplight. It felt good to be away from the cold, he realized. Good not to be moving, good not to be standing, good to close his eyes and listen to the combox signal long-distance Baltimore over and over and over . . .

Chekov didn't mean to sink down to the floor and curl up on himself next to the com booth's heating vent. It just happened that way while he was waiting, oh, so cold, for someone—anyone—to acknowledge from the other end of the line. He didn't mean to lie in useless silence when the unit finally completed its connection, or to be, by the time a crusty, older voice finally rasped "Hello? Hello?" in irritation, too deep in fever dreams to answer.

Chapter Ten

Somewhere over the Mojave Desert, North America
Terrestrial Date: December 22, 2269
1740 hours MST

"DON'T SAY ANYTHING!"

The silent command flashed across the Wraith's viewscreen in fire-white letters, emblazoned with Navajo thunderbolts and Starfleet danger symbols. The warning was unnecessary—Sulu had already leaped from wordless surprise to the realization that he was seeing a pretaped message left for him by his project engineer. By the time Nakai's weathered face reappeared on the viewscreen, Sulu had already retracted the subspace antenna that guided his communications through the Romulan cloaking field. A little burst of static wouldn't alarm the commodore, especially on a stormy night.

Beneath Dr. Nakai's face, a question scrolled in smaller letters: *"White Sands listening in? If so, retract antenna."*

Sulu nodded, then realized there was no way the computer could note that. He reached out and typed "Antenna retracted" on his console.

"Good." Nakai's gruff voice replaced the letters, and his face faded to give Sulu a view of the desert floor rushing up toward him. The pilot cursed in Orion and slammed on the antigravs, then endured the agony of lag time watching night shadows coalesce into the distinct shapes of rocks and cacti and mesquite trees. A hundred meters above the ground, the antigravs bounced him back into the sky, and he misted his helmet's faceplate with a sigh of relief.

"—blamed for it," Nakai was saying when Sulu finally turned his attention back to the voice in his ear. He hoped he hadn't missed much of the old engineer's recorded message. "I know it, because I found the damned things under a loose floorboard in our hangar."

What things?" Sulu demanded, forgetting once again that this was just the computer talking to him.

But Nakai must have been prudent enough to program some interactive loops into his message. There was a pause, then the gruff voice said again, "Good. You probably know by now that the cloaking device plans have been stolen, and we're getting blamed for it. I know it, because I found the damn things under a loose floorboard in our hangar. Got up early on Wednesday to work on one of the Wraith's transtator chips and caught the transporter pulse on one of my subspace monitors. I got curious and tracked it down."

The Wraith's momentum switched from up to down, and Sulu hit the antigravs again. This time, the shuttle's huge bounce took it west, toward the looming darkness of the San Gabriels. Beyond that dark mountain wall, Sulu could see the massive, cloud-lit glow of Los Angeles. He guided the shuttle toward the dark mountains north of it that was the Tehachapi Federation Wilderness Sanctuary.

"As soon as I saw there were scanner marks on the plans, I knew they'd already been transmitted somewhere, probably off-planet," Nakai's voice continued. "But that still didn't clear us—after all, we both had access to high-security subspace channels in the Wraith. I didn't have any record of that damn transporter pulse I'd caught, and I couldn't think how to destroy the plans undetectably." The engineer snorted. "No matter what, we were going to look guilty. Only thing I could think to do was make just *one* of us look guilty.

"So I decided to take the plans and run."

California's jagged coastline solidified beneath the Wraith as it descended. Sulu hit the antigravs again and sent the little shuttle soaring toward the shining darkness of the Pacific Ocean.

"Not that I'm any too worried about getting caught." Nakai snorted again. "After all, if a hundred generations of raiding Apaches couldn't find the canyon where I'm going, there's no way Starfleet can. And I'll be underground, where satellite infrared can't find me. I'll be safe.

"But I won't be able to smoke out the real thief."

Sulu's eyes narrowed. "That's what you want me to do," he said in dawning awareness.

"That's why I rigged the Wraith to play you this message when you tried to turn on the cloaking device," Nakai confirmed, almost as if he'd heard him. The engineer's voice lost its southwestern accent, and took on the almost-Vulcan precision that meant he was thinking hard. "Here's what I know: It's got to be someone high up, maybe even someone from off base. Someone who could have smuggled a portable transporter unit into White Sands. And someone who could have authorized private use of a high-security channel with no one listening in."

Sulu silently added a fourth criterion: It had to be someone who wanted the acts of treason to be connected to the *Enterprise's* bridge crew.

"You'll have to be careful, Sulu." Gruffness crept back into Nakai's voice. "*Very* careful. Whoever these people are, they're well-organized and they're ruthless. They might still decide they want you framed along with me. Don't trust anyone."

"Don't worry," Sulu muttered. "I don't."

A chronometer beeped on the prerecorded tape and Nakai grunted. "Been five minutes. Better stick your antenna out before White Sands gets suspicious. Oh, yeah—once you figure out who's behind all this, you just stop by the old mission church in Alamogordo and buy some raw turquoise. You don't have to say nothing to nobody. I'll get the message. Nakai out."

Silence fell in the shuttle's cabin, a tense and lonely silence that made Sulu wish he could fly out over the shining Pacific and never come back. He sighed, then reached out to return the Wraith's subspace antenna to its normal position.

"White Sands calling WKI-2, come in." The raspy note in Willis's deep voice surprised Sulu. Surely, the commodore couldn't have been calling for him all that time. "White Sands calling WKI-2, come in."

"White Sands, this is WKI-2." Almost without thinking, Sulu kicked the Wraith into another soaring leap. It was easier to estimate lag times when your baseline was sea-level instead of mountains. "Sorry about that static, sir. I hit some t-storms over the San Gabriels." Which was a lie, but Sulu doubted Willis had a weather map in front of him.

The commodore let out an audible breath. "Thought I'd lost you for a minute. Everything all right?"

"All systems normal."

"Including the cloaking device?"

Sulu mentally kicked himself. He'd been so distracted by Nakai's taped message, he had forgotten all about the cloaking device he was supposed to be testing. "The glitch-tracking program just finished running, sir," he lied. "Looks like just a temporary malfunction."

"Can you engage the cloaking device?"

Sulu reached down for the control beside his feet, and this time felt the Wraith shudder as the cloaking field materialized around it. "Cloaking device engaged, sir."

"Acknowledged." Willis's deep voice regained its resonant timbre. "Good work, Mr. Sulu."

"Thank you, sir." Sulu watched waves come into focus as the shuttle swooped downward, each one outlined by a delicate froth of phosphorescent plankton. Six hundred meters above them, he hit the antigravs and waited for the bounce.

It was his instinct for gravity that warned him, long seconds before the shuttle's alarms began to wail. Instead of the gravitational braking he should have felt, Sulu's senses told him that his downward velocity was still increasing, at the familiar and inevitable rate of 9.816 meters per second per second. He smacked at the antigravs again, to no avail, then tried to cut in the impulse engines. Nothing happened.

Sulu cursed and slapped the communicator over to normal channels while he tried to wrestle the stubby shuttle into some semblance of a glide. "Shuttle WKI-2 in distress. All systems failing. Repeat, all systems failing—"

Heaving with phosphorescent fire, the Pacific rose to meet him.

"Don't say anything!"

Chekov stirred groggily against the press of a body above him, and clutched at the hand clamped over his mouth with a swell of rising panic. Thin fingers tightened threateningly along his jawline. He closed his eyes and fell back against the floor of the combox, shivering.

". . . ambulance has already been dispatched to your location. I cannot cancel the emergency order without the direct instructions of a licensed physician."

"I *am* a licensed physician, you glorified answering machine! Commander Leonard McCoy, Starfleet, retired, Earth medical license number 4138884. Now I'm telling you, cancel the damned ambulance request! There's nobody here but me, and I was fine until you started harassing me!"

Chekov reached up again to grip the doctor's arm, and this time McCoy returned the frantic pressure with a reassuring one-handed squeeze of his own. Relief washed over Chekov in a wave.

Somewhere in the middle distance, ambulance sirens stretched to encompass every corner of the sky.

"Computer?" McCoy's words had taken on a sharp, southern twang of concern. "Are you listening to me?"

"Voiceprint verified for Dr. Leonard McCoy, license number 4138884."

Abruptly, the sirens stopped.

"Ambulance order remanded, ambulance recalled." Some invisible transition took place out of sight or sound of the remote combox, and a different, happier voice wished them, "Have a nice day."

McCoy grunted and slapped off the com unit's listening device. "The only thing we could have possibly done to make medical science more inefficient was to automate it." He bent over Chekov again to scowl in doctorly warning. That craggy southern face had never looked so welcome. "Don't you even *blink* till I decide whether or not it's all right to move you. If you're gonna drag me out here in the middle of the night, you're gonna have to put up with my temper." But the hand he lifted from Chekov's mouth was gentle as it began its swift probe of his bones and muscles.

"Doctor . . ." The thin dryness of his voice horrified Chekov. "How did you get here? How did you *find* me?"

McCoy surprised him with a crooked half smile. "Well, I don't get that many anonymous com calls." He pressed his hands along the length of Chekov's collarbones, across his shoulders, down. "When the computer told me the booth was still occupied but nobody was talking to me, I took a wild guess that something was wrong and had it play back the only thing you'd said while you were here."

"Yes," Chekov remembered whispering into the combox pickup. *"Place the call."* He couldn't believe he'd been stupid enough to say anything.

"You sounded like hell."

McCoy's hand slipped below his right elbow, and pain slammed Chekov back against the wall of the booth, causing a howl he didn't even have the breath to sustain. The doctor clenched a fist in the front of his parka to hold him when he would have stumbled to his knees. "Don't move, dammit!"

"I'm sorry . . ." Chekov tried to relax, but the reawakened agony burned him up like brittle paper until even his breath could only come in short, useless hitches. ". . . It's broken . . ." he gritted between clenched teeth. "I'm sorry . . ."

McCoy nodded grimly, waving him back into silence. "All right, I hear you." But he touched Chekov's shoulder in quick apology before moving on to continue his inspection elsewhere. "I got the com unit to tell me what booth you'd called from, then called an autocab to haul me out here." He picked up his explanation as though the interruption had never happened. "It's a good thing for you the lecture circuit pays me so well. Otherwise I never would have been able to afford the fare."

"Why?" Chekov frowned out the clear-plate sides of the booth, only to find the world obscured by driving snow and endless, primal black. "Where are we?"

"All the way out on the Delmarva Peninsula in some little town called Pocomoke City. You're not even on the map." Shifting clumsily, the doctor ducked to pull Chekov's good arm across his shoulders and work his own arm behind the ensign's back. Their first step up and forward was pure agony.

"I know it hurts," McCoy grunted, staggering as Chekov slewed against him. "But it looks like all we've got to deal with is that arm. I want to try and get it set before the swelling gets any worse."

"No . . ." Chekov pulled weakly at McCoy's grip, but only stumbled back into the doctor when McCoy tightened his hold on him. "I can't go to a hospital."

"I know that, son." McCoy kicked open the door of the autocab and turned slowly sideways to lower Chekov inside. "Don't worry—I've already made other arrangements."

McCoy's "other arrangements" turned out to be an hourly motel along the coast of the Delmarva Penninsula. None of the other rooms appeared occupied when the autocab eased to a stop outside their lodgings, and once they'd made their way inside, Chekov could understand why. A low, mirrored ceiling reflected carpet and bedspread, both patterned in Andorian erotic cuneiform, and a clashing wall display of Klingon pillow art took up most of the opposite wall. It occurred to Chekov that this was the only place he could come to where the pain of a broken arm would seem not so bad in comparison.

Pushing Chekov with gentle firmness onto the edge of the bed, McCoy growled, "Lie down," before ducking back outside into the windy dark and snow. Chekov looked after him a moment, sweaty from the combox's heater vent and the close confines of the autocab, then slowly started the numb task of unfastening the front of his parka. McCoy slipped back in the door when he was only halfway down the coat's long front.

"Oh, hell, Chekov . . ." The doctor tossed both black bags onto a nearby table, then hurried over to gently move Chekov's hand aside so he could quickly finish the job. "I was just going to cut that off you."

"I need it," Chekov protested weakly. He let McCoy reach behind him to slide his left arm out of its sleeve. "I've already lost one coat to this mess."

McCoy grunted, but didn't contradict him as he started to carefully work the right side of the coat off Chekov's body. "So," he said with deceptive lightness. "You want to tell me what the hell is going on?"

"I can't." Chekov clutched a rumpled handful of blanket and squeezed his eyes tight against an insane urge to jerk away from the pain. "I don't want you to have to lie to Starfleet Security."

McCoy pressed both hands to Chekov's chest until he finally relented and lay back across the top of the bed. The mattress was hard and oddly lumpy. "Then let's start with what I already know." Chekov heard McCoy rise and go to pop the latches on one of the little black cases. "I know you didn't kill Mark Piper, son," he said above the rattle of whatever equipment he was sorting. "And Jim Kirk knows it, too."

Chekov raised his head, startled by the mention of Kirk's name. "You've talked to the admiral?"

"I didn't need to." Chekov's heart fell, but he said nothing as McCoy came to kneel by the side of the bed again. "Jim Kirk knows his crew. He trusts you." Picking up the edge of one cuff, McCoy tucked a cutting tool inside the sweater's soggy sleeve and sliced it clear to the shoulder. "Rose and aqua," he commented dryly as he did the same thing to the turtleneck. "Not the colors I would have picked for you, Chekov."

Chekov visualized Oberste shoving the unfamiliar clothes at him in her kitchen, and a rueful smile twisted his mouth. "My selection was somewhat limited."

A hypo hissed against the bare skin of his shoulder, washing him with cool relief and dispersing the worst of the pain. When he opened his eyes to meet his own haggard reflection in the overhead mirror, he looked only long enough to see the bruised, distorted ruin of his arm atop the bedspread, then quickly turned his face aside. For all his horrific imaginings on the train and in the autocab, he still hadn't been prepared for the brutal reality.

"Computer. World broadcast news." It was something else to look at, at least, something to take his mind off what he'd done to himself, and what McCoy was about to do.

"You want my learned medical opinion?" McCoy asked. He didn't wait for Chekov's answer. "Don't watch. It'll just depress you."

"I need to know what they're saying." He flinched again as McCoy slipped one half of a molded splint beneath his arm. "I need to know what they know." On the display screen, a sincere weatherman made circles with his hands above a storm off the coast of Florida.

"You're gonna hate me for doing this . . ," McCoy's cool grip closed resolutely around Chekov's thumb. "But, I promise, you'll thank me when it's over."

He told himself he didn't know what was about to happen, that he'd do better if he relaxed, that nothing, absolutely nothing, could hurt more than what he'd already suffered through most of this horrible day. Then the hand around his tightened, the bones twisted and snapped back into place with a crack, and he would have ripped out of his own skin to escape that instant of soul-splitting pain. But by the time his body registered it and took in a breath to scream, he'd exploded out the other side, into a foggy, floating limbo of relief.

"That's it—all done." McCoy's voice sounded farther away than before, soft-edged and blurry. "The hard part's over." His arm responded with only the most viscous throb of protest as the doctor fitted the rest of the splint and began to expertly tighten it.

Alertness crept back over him as the pain at last receded into a distant, sickly ache. Chekov opened his eyes to the muted colors of the display monitor, McCoy's soothing voice blending into a seamless nonsense with the monotone announcer's dialogue. When Sulu's slim, smiling face first dominated the oversized viewscreen, Chekov thought his mind had woven some reassuring phantom from the threads of his longings, the screen's presence, and McCoy's words. Then the movement of the announcer's lips somehow fell into place with his speaking, and Chekov bolted upright in sudden horror.

"Chekov!" McCoy grabbed at him with both hands. "Hold still!"

"Quiet!" *Oh, please, let it be a lie, please, don't let it be true!*

"—destruction of a military aircraft from the White Sands Experimental Flight Center. Starfleet officials aren't discussing details about the missing aircraft, except to say that the night flight over the South Pacific was part of a series of classified tests conducted by Lieutenant Commander Hikaru Sulu, who was declared dead upon the loss of the aircraft."

McCoy broke the silence between them with a rasping whisper. "Oh, my God . . ."

Chekov stared at the viewscreen until McCoy ordered

it off. Even then, the afterimage of Sulu's laughter hung on the darkened screen, as though reluctant to fade.

McCoy stood, hovering by the side of the bed as though unsure where he meant to go. "There has to be some mistake."

No mistake. Piper. Oberste. Sulu. However this all fit together, it was connected by a chain of corpses.

"I'm going to see if I can get in touch with Jim—"

"Not from here." It was something Chekov felt very strongly about, but it came out as a numb suggestion, devoid of either emotion or strength.

"No, not from here," McCoy agreed. He'd already retrieved his coat from somewhere, and shrugged it over his shoulders as he talked. "I can try to get through to him from the combox where I found you. I want you to stay here and wait for me. Whatever's going on, we'll be better off if we face it together." He caught Chekov's jaw in one hand and forcibly turned the young ensign's head to face him. "You hear me? Stay here."

Lies came too hard for him to construct any sort of proper answer, but McCoy didn't wait long enough to force him into one. "I'll make that an order if I have to, Ensign." He tossed a pale gold account card onto the bedspread beside Chekov. "See if the replicator will give you anything but coffee and get yourself something hot to eat. I'll be back in under an hour." A swirl of snow chased McCoy out the door, then settled into a fading ribbon across the patterned carpet. The room felt very cold and empty once he was gone.

"What is the first vow of a Starfleet security officer?" Oberste's voice echoed grimly from somewhere on the other side of death.

What difference does it make now? Chekov rubbed at his arm, overwhelmed with his helplessness to promise anything. *A guard's first vow is to protect and serve.*

"And what one duty must you uphold above all others?"

I must preserve the lives placed under my protec-

tion . . . He looked out across the night-dark water and the smear of barrier island holding back the ocean waves. The narrow stretch of land reached into the darkness like a bridge between realities, and the first flickers of a plan began to form at the back of Chekov's brain. ". . . even at the expense of my own."

Chapter Eleven

Starfleet Academy
San Francisco, North America
Terrestrial Date: December 24, 2269
1030 hours PST

"Sir?"

Uhura looked up from her desk, startled out of her round of unhappy thoughts. If there was one thing a semester of teaching had taught her, it was that students never came in during Monday morning office hours unless they were studying for an exam. And finals week had ended last Friday, just before Starfleet Academy had emptied for the holiday break. Only the professors and senior officers remained on campus, along with a scattering of off-planet students who hadn't been able to afford the starship fare home.

The snub-nosed face peeking shyly around her door belonged to the second category. Ensign Dana Cercone had the dark eyes and easily tanned skin of her Italian ancestors, but her lilting accent marked her as a resident of Sherman's Planet, an Earth colony whose native tongue was New Esperanto. Uhura forced herself to smile and greeted the student in that language.

Cercone switched to it herself, looking anxious. "I don't want to disturb you, sir, if you're busy. Do you have time to talk to me now?"

"I'm only grading papers. I don't mind being disturbed when I do that." Uhura swept a stack of exams from the chair beside her desk and gestured Cercone to sit. "Did you have a question about your test? I haven't gotten to it yet."

"Oh, no, sir." The ensign looked down, fingering the winter-issue cadet cap she'd folded in her lap. "I think I did okay on it. I really enjoyed your class."

"So did I. You were all good students." Uhura set her grading notepad down. "What can I help you with, then?"

Cercone looked up, eyes dark and serious now. "It's my senior honors thesis in communications, ma'am. I thought I'd work on it over winter break, since I'm stuck here—uh, I mean, since I decided to stay—"

Despite herself, Uhura smiled again. "'Stuck here' will do fine, Ensign. What's your thesis on?"

"Data compression in planetary subspace relays. I'm trying to eliminate linear lag time by using a transporterlike system to send data in simultaneous intact bundles."

Uhura nodded. "That's a good idea. Does it work?"

"Well, not yet," Cercone admitted. "I still have to find a way around the quantum-gate problem, but I've been running some promising tests down at Starfleet's main transporter facility. The problem is—" Her smooth brow creased in puzzlement. "I've been getting a lot of strange interference in my subspace test messages, just lately."

"And you'd like me to look at it," Uhura guessed.

"Yes, sir. I don't think it has anything to do with my thesis problem," the ensign added hurriedly. "If it did, I wouldn't ask you to explain it to me, of course. But if it's just an extraneous planetary effect—well, I know you've had a lot of experience untangling that kind of thing."

"And enjoy it a whole lot more than grading papers." Uhura frowned at the stack of exams on her desk, estimating the work she still had to do. "Tell you what, Ensign. I should have the rest of these done in about an hour. If you bring your data back here then, I'll take a look at it."

"Great!" Cercone sprang out of her chair with the infectious energy of the young. "I'll go put everything in order, just the way it came in. Thanks, Commander."

"No problem." Uhura watched her out, then turned her attention reluctantly back to the stack of tests. She sighed. At least grading exams was better than thinking about—

"Excuse me, ma'am."

Uhura recognized the polite voice even before she glanced up at the tall, stoop-shouldered man in her doorway. "Good morning, Mr. Kahle." She forced another smile. "Have you come to check your grade?"

The multibillionaire snorted. "Never was much of a grade-chaser, ma'am. Just took the test to see if I could still handle the pressure." He cocked one iron-gray eyebrow at her. "Did I pass?"

"With flying colors," Uhura assured him. "Would you like to come in and see it?"

Kahle waved his cane regretfully. "Don't have time today. I only stopped in to see if you'll be going to the Academy Christmas party tonight."

"I was planning to." The thought of that party—and the men who had been supposed to attend it as her guests—brought Uhura face-to-face again with the looming uncertainty of what had happened over the weekend to Chekov and Sulu. She bit her lip and said less steadily, "If I can make it. Something might—might interfere."

"Understood, ma'am." Kahle gave her a somber nod of sympathy. It occurred to Uhura that there weren't many secrets in Starfleet that this former starship captain wasn't privy to. "Hope the news will be good, and that we'll see you there. Your old colleague Mr. Scott has promised to come down for it." He snorted again. "Had to promise him Saurian brandy to get him away from the *Enterprise,* though."

"That sounds like Mr. Scott, sir." Uhura managed a shaky laugh. "Tell him I'll try to stop in and see him, even if I can only stay a little while."

"Good." Kahle tipped his cap to her, then departed with a stride not much slower than the young ensign's had been.

Uhura sighed again and forced her attention back to the exams she had to grade. She knew that if she let herself think about her lost friends, she would wind up repeating the same useless cycle of worry, heartbreak, and outrage that she'd spent most of yesterday trapped in. And none of it would help Sulu and Chekov. If only she could think of something that *would* help . . .

"Uhura."

She recognized the new voice and jerked her head up, staring at the slim, wiry figure in her doorway with mingled hope and fear. "Admiral Kirk! Have you found out—"

Kirk shook his head and came into her office, letting the door swing shut behind him. "Still no word on Chekov's whereabouts. And still no luck locating the Wraith's crash site."

"Oh."

The admiral must have seen the dismay in her eyes. "Uhura, that's *good* news. If Sulu really had gone down near the coordinates of his last transmission, we'd have found evidence of it by now. The search team has scoured the ocean top to bottom for fifty kilometers around the site. They haven't found so much as an oil smear, much less any trace of wreckage."

Uhura nodded. It was what she kept telling herself, in between fits of being sure that the Wraith had completely annihilated itself in some freak explosion. "And is it good news for Chekov that they haven't found him?"

Kirk sighed and pulled a chair around to straddle in front of her desk. His face had the usual sharp edge it took on in a crisis, and the hazel eyes were smudged with uneasy shadows. "That," he admitted, "I'm not so sure of. I wish that boy would turn himself in so we could stash him away and find out who's out to get him." Half-exasperated and half-chagrined, he looked a question at Uhura. "Dammit, doesn't he trust us?"

"I think it's Starfleet Security he doesn't trust," said a new voice from the door.

Uhura gasped, and Kirk swung around with a curse, his hand dropping to a phaser he didn't have. The familiar willowy figure in the hallway looked back with calm blue eyes that defused their tension, the same way they used to quell Dr. McCoy's most irate tirades. Christine Chapel's air of quiet composure had always seemed serene enough to rival Mr. Spock's. Now that the nurse had graduated from medical school and was finishing her doctorate in research, her poise had been strengthened by a great deal of self-confidence.

"Christine!" Uhura sprang up and pulled her friend into the office, closing the door more securely behind her. "How on earth do you know about Chekov?"

"Leonard told me, of course." Chapel perched on the edge of Uhura's tape-littered desk, waving Kirk back to the chair he'd offered her. "That's why I'm here. I came to give you his news."

Kirk paused in the act of sitting down, looking surprised. *"Bones* has news about Chekov?" Then his face lit in swift comprehension. "That's right, McCoy's been giving lectures at the Johns Hopkins Medical School this month, hasn't he? Don't tell me Chekov's hiding out with him?"

Chapel shook her head. "No, not anymore. Dr. McCoy told me—"

"In person?" Kirk interrupted grimly. "Or through Starfleet channels?"

"Neither." She smiled faintly. "He said he couldn't trust the official mail net, and you know how he hates flying. So he sent a message on the medical net from Johns Hopkins to Stanford, coding it as a confidential patient file for my consultation."

Kirk whistled approval. "Good work, Bones! What did the message say?"

"That Chekov had called him from a public com somewhere along Maryland's Eastern Shore on Saturday night." Chapel's voice took on the carefully measured tones of a doctor reciting a case history. "He was injured—" She heard Uhura's gasp of dismay and added reassuringly, "Just a simple ulnar-radial fracture to his right arm. Leonard took an autocab down to meet him, but Chekov refused to go to the hospital. They managed to splint his arm at a hotel, but when Leonard left to call for help, he walked right into a swarm of Starfleet Security. He managed to talk his way out of getting arrested, but by the time he got back to the hotel room, Chekov was gone." Her eyes crinkled with faint humor. "Along with Leonard's account card, apparently."

Kirk scowled. "Did Chekov tell Bones where he was going? Or how he got hurt?"

The doctor shook her head. "No. He said he didn't want to force anyone to lie to Starfleet Security. That's what makes Leonard think Chekov doesn't trust them. Why else would they need to be lied to?"

Kirk cursed and sprang out of his chair again, pacing the narrow length of the office like a caged cheetah. Uhura and Chapel exchanged glances, both recognizing the signs of impending action in their former commander. If they had still been aboard the *Enterprise,* the next words out of Kirk's mouth would have been an order to fire photon torpedoes.

But this wasn't a fight that could be won with a starship's weapons. Uhura could tell from his scowl of concentration that Admiral Kirk knew that. He paused in his pacing and cursed.

"That's why Chekov can't turn himself in to anyone." Kirk smacked one fist into the other, so hard that Uhura nearly jumped from her chair. "Security must be in on this, at the highest level! Even if the field patrol that arrested him was loyal, somewhere along the line he

knows he'd get turned over to the people who are trying to frame us—"

"Frame *us?*" It was the one thing Uhura hadn't permitted herself to think, although her mind kept circling back to it like a moth beating on a windowpane. It was the thought that scared her the most. "You mean, the crew of the *Enterprise?*"

"All my main bridge crew, at least." Kirk's seething strides vibrated Uhura's desk when he passed, sending her exams cascading unnoticed to the floor. "Dammit, it can't be a coincidence that Sulu and Chekov are getting blamed for the two most serious acts of treason to be committed against Starfleet in a century! Someone— someone very high up—is arranging it to look like my crew is behind all of this." Kirk paused again, his mouth twisting as if he'd swallowed something very bitter. "And I think I know why they're doing it."

"To discredit *you,*" Chapel said quietly.

Kirk nodded grimly. "There are a hell of a lot of factions in the Federation Council that don't like me— or any of the other admirals, for that matter. But since I'm Starfleet's diplomatic troubleshooter right now, I'm the best one to attack." With a wordless growl of frustration, he started pacing again. "I just wish I knew who they were—and who they found to do their work for them inside Starfleet!"

Chapel frowned. "If we could find that out, we'd know who the real traitors are."

"Yes. Which is exactly why they've hidden their tracks so well." Kirk scrubbed a frustrated hand across his face. "I've had Riley run every computer check he can think of to pin down other suspects in those thefts, but the damn traces keep coming up blank. I don't know if it's because they're getting interfered with, or if the thieves were so damn clever that they left no trace at all."

Uhura pressed her interlaced hands against her mouth, thinking hard. "But there's one place they can't cover their tracks," she said into the taut silence at last. "They have to sell their stolen technology somewhere, don't they?"

Kirk came to a dead stop, an arrested look on his face. "And the buyers will want to know who they're dealing with, to be sure they're getting the real goods. All we need to do is find them and convince them to testify . . ." He crossed the office in three long strides and swept Uhura up into a brief bear hug. "Bless you, Uhura."

"Thank you, sir." She stepped back, breathless but happy. "Will you need help tracking the buyers down, Admiral?"

Kirk drummed his fingers thoughtfully against the edge of her desk. "I will, Commander, but I don't think it's the kind of help anyone on Earth can give me. The buyers are off-planet, and that's where I'll have to go to find them. What I need is a neutral being, someone all of our allies and our enemies will talk to. Someone everyone knows and trusts, and someone I can persuade to help us. . . ."

"We saved Ambassador Sarek's life a little while ago," Uhura reminded him. "He owes us a favor."

"So he does." Kirk's smile regained its gleam of laughter. "And isn't it convenient that he's stationed right here at the Vulcan consulate in San Francisco? I think I'll go have a chat with him right now."

"What should we do?" Chapel asked.

Kirk handed Uhura the rank pins he'd stripped off his uniform. "Keep these for me until I can convince Starfleet I deserve to get them back. And call in all the communications contacts you have. See if you can locate Sulu and Chekov without anyone in Security finding out. Get them into safe hiding, or at least put them in touch with Kevin Riley. He'll know what to do." Kirk peeled his wrist communicator off next and tossed it to Chapel. "Doctor, I want you to take this with you back to Stanford. If anyone calls for me, tell them I'm undergoing my annual physical and can't be disturbed."

Chapel lifted a dubious eyebrow at him. "If I remember correctly, Admiral, you always come up with an excuse to avoid your annual physical."

"Which is exactly why it's going to take me at least a day to undergo all those delayed tests," Kirk retorted. "Right?"

A smile flickered across Chapel's face. "Right, sir. Good luck," she added as he swung toward the door.

Kirk glanced over his shoulder, suddenly somber again. "I'm not the one who's going to need luck, Doctor. Whoever the people are behind this plot, for the next twenty-four hours I'll be completely out of their reach." He pointed at Uhura. "But you won't—and with Spock off on Vulcan, you're the only remaining member of the bridge crew. Be careful they don't make you their next target."

"Don't worry, Admiral." Uhura squared her shoulders so he wouldn't see the shiver that ran through her. "I'll be safe enough here at the Academy. After all, there's nothing that the traitors can want from me."

A big, blunt fist pushed at Chekov through the walls of the thermal sleeping tube, nearly rolling him onto his side. He told himself he should probably ignore it, but when another insistent nudge jostled at his arm, the pain forced him to pull aside the head flap and scowl at the long, bewhiskered face hanging over him. "Do you mind?"

The pony blasted a loud snort of surprise and danced off, shaking its head as it minced a few meters away to regard him. The four others milling with it made a token dash toward the underbrush, then all five seemed to forget their resolve and wandered back to foraging. *How depressing to know you aren't even capable of routing a band of wild ponies,* Chekov thought.

Thunder pealed across the curdled black sky, and a lash of wind whipped from no discernible direction to scatter bits of frozen brush all over the clearing. It could have been midnight or midday; Chekov guessed from the ponies' lazy wanderings that it was still fairly early in the evening, and maybe not even that late. Either way, he still had plenty of work to do.

He wormed his way out of the thermal tube, no longer even bothering trying to keep the sand out of it. The stuff was insidious. When he'd first been struck with the "inspiration" to come here, he hadn't realized the "island" was nothing more than a long bar of sand, with just enough stunted bushes and sparse grass to keep the whole thing from washing away. He hadn't yet found a water reservoir that wasn't stagnant and briny, as bitter as the sea. Yet the ponies must be drinking something. Or maybe not. He couldn't say for certain how long a horse could go between hydrations; he only knew you had to water reindeer copiously and often.

Marina Franz had made Assateague sound so charming and quaint when she'd talked about it. "I spent a summer there with the World Conservation Corps," she'd told him as they'd walked between classes in the early part of the year. "Except for park management and emergency care of the ponies, no one's allowed to interact with the island—no visitors, no tourists, not even full-time rangers. It's wonderful!"

Now, with his mouth dry for lack of water and every inch of his skin itching from the blowing white sand, Chekov couldn't begin to imagine why visitors, tourists, or even ponies, for that matter, would ever want to come to Assateague Island in the first place.

All the more reason to stay here as long as possible. No one who wasn't completely insane would even think about camping on Assateague in the middle of a stormy December. *Which sums up nicely what I've fallen to.* He smiled ruefully as he rolled up the sleeping tube and stuffed it into its carry sack.

Franz had talked about the ranger stations dotting the length of the island. "Along the main road," she'd said. "These cute little houses where the Conservation Corps would sometimes store measuring equipment and com-

138

munications gear." He'd been hoping to escape the weather inside one of these "little houses" when he'd first crossed the Assateague land bridge two miserable nights ago. But, so far, a day of walking along the island's only road hadn't turned up so much as a hint of the promised stations. Maybe, he figured wryly, they seemed closer together when you didn't have to cross the island on foot. Chekov was just glad he'd thought to abscond with McCoy's account card so he could buy camping gear. He promised himself he would pay back the doctor's unwilling donation just as soon as all of this was over.

He'd taken to walking the island at night simply because that's when he'd first arrived there. After walking as far as he could possibly push himself, he'd sealed himself into the sleeping tube and struggled to bite open the end of a packet of winter camping rations. He fell asleep with the packet unopened, the stubborn pull-tab still held between his teeth.

It made for a convenient breakfast when he finally roused again. The weather had deteriorated into a perpetual angry glower, blanketing the sky with blackness and pelting the already desolate landscape with snow and rain in equal measure. By the time he'd rolled himself into his sleeping gear after that night's hike, he'd lost all track of the hour or the day. All that mattered was that he keep surviving long enough to locate someplace better to hide.

Hefting the lightweight carry sack, he tugged his mitten back on with his teeth and wished, not for the first time, that the fingers of his right hand were more useful than painful. At least the discomfort hadn't crescendoed past the point of a few warning stabs since McCoy had pulled the bones back into alignment. He ought to be thankful for even that simple improvement—fugitives couldn't be too picky about the details of their exile. Squeezing between two nervous, ice-slicked horses, he pushed into the underbrush and headed resolutely for the road.

The flat, straight access lane made for the easiest walking he'd known so far on this long ordeal; his weary legs and aching back were grateful. He didn't bother forcing himself to jog anymore. What was the hurry? Once he reached the end of the island, he had nowhere else to go, no other brilliant plan to fall back on. He might as well delay confirmation of his fate as long as possible, since he wasn't sure he'd be able to keep himself going when he no longer had a goal to aim for.

The arrhythmic *clop-clop* of pony steps echoed through the dark on either side of him. As light-footed and quiet as they were among the dunes, the horses clattered up a racket on the roadway, covering any sound his own booted footsteps might have made. He'd been shadowed since his first night by the same five docile males. The rangers must have offered handouts when they came to stay among the horses. Or maybe the lack of bothersome tourists kept the ponies from learning just how dangerous human presence could be. Whatever the cause, they'd proven reasonably pleasant travel companions, and their unflagging hoofbeats had served as sensor pings to sound out the width and distance of the road ahead of him. As storm winds thickened the darkness around them, he found himself relying more and more on that ringing report.

So he noticed immediately when the hoofbeats stopped.

Slowing to a careful tiptoe, Chekov felt his way forward with his limited human senses. The wind shredded all subtle sound, but he thought he heard the smack and lick of open water, just before his foot stepped over the precipice and plunged him to the knee in frigid, foaming soup.

He caught himself against a pony's rump, managing to stumble back out of the shallow lake without soaking anything higher than his parka hem. One trouser leg and hip, though, sloshed a great splash of water across the road in his retreat. A slice of wind cut through the wet fabric, and he cursed himself aloud for being too stupid to look where he was going. Snorting in reply, the pony swerved out from under his hand and flicked its heels in equine protest.

Waves and rain had washed out the road for a good five meters or more. Chekov stood on the edge of the drop-off and let water lap over his toes. If he could hold on to one of the horses, he might make an effort to slog through the dark, frothy mess. But from the way they'd already drifted out beyond his easy reach, he judged that option to be just about as likely as his leaping the expanse in a single bound. That left returning to the underbrush and trying to pick his way around the washout, with no guarantee he'd find a clear passage back to the road.

"Oh, how much worse could it possibly make things?" It wasn't like he'd find Leong or Broad in ambush there, so it was already better than anywhere else along the seaboard. Stooping to squeeze as much water as he could from his pants leg, he followed the last retreating pony into a wall of bushes, on the theory that the horses at least had some idea where they were going.

Sand slipped and moved beneath his feet; branches snapped off in handfuls when he grabbed them for balance. The ponies navigated a narrow, winding path through the scrub growth, traveling each with a nose to another's tail as though linked together like big paper dolls. When they snaked leftward as a group, Chekov marked it down to whatever random whims guided ponies. Then the final horse in the line exerted his independence by stepping just as calmly right, and Chekov realized with a start that they were making their way *around* something that the brush and their bodies hadn't at first let him see. He stopped to let them trail away, then climbed into the weeds and started digging.

The long metal hamper had managed to catch every torn limb and kelp knot tossed up by the encroaching storm. Chekov dragged the debris away from the lid, then groaned in disappointment when he saw the bold, sand-scoured lettering there: RANGER STATION 13, ASSATEAGUE ISLAND WILDERNESS SANCTUARY.

"Ah, Marina . . ." For some reason, when she'd said "little houses," he'd thought she meant structures a human being could actually fit inside.

He bypassed the station's simple lock by popping two circuits with his thumb. At least he'd come away from security school with some useful practical knowledge. Inside he found scientific notepads, emergency medical kits (one for humans, one for horses), a collection of various sampling vials and data disks, and an inset communications hookup. He kissed the little transmitter before pulling off his glove and punching in the connect code.

He hoped it wasn't too late Pacific Standard Time. Without access to a Starfleet communications node, he had to try and reach Kirk at his office. Security was bound to have that line monitored—he'd prepared himself for that. But if Kirk was there—and if Chekov could talk to him—he was sure Kirk wouldn't let anything happen to him. All he had to do was succeed in making contact.

The communications circuit closed with a ping. "Starfleet Headquarters, Admiral Kirk's office."

Chekov took a moment to wrestle his voice under control, worried with a sudden spurt of panic how the wind and thunder would sound across the transcontinental channel. "Could I speak with Admiral Kirk, please?" He would have given anything to speak unaccented English these last few days.

The voice at the other end of the line was silent for a moment, as though distracted by too many memos, or searching for the note that would clarify when Kirk was allowed to be bothered. When he spoke again, the secretary sounded stiffly wary, his voice laced with concern. "I'm sorry, but Admiral Kirk is in the hospital until further notice and can't be contacted." Then, with careful interest, "Ensign Chekov? Is that—?"

Chekov severed the communications with a twist of his hand.

Admiral Kirk . . . hospitalized. He sank to the ground beside the ranger station, propping one elbow on the casing to bury his face in his arm.

Chapter Twelve

Starfleet Academy
San Francisco, North America
Terrestrial Date: December 24, 2269
1130 hours PST

THE ORIGINAL MESSAGE transmitted to Starfleet's main transporter facility had been simple: the word "peace" in New Esperanto, repeated fifty times. It had come back transformed into a nightmare gibberish of letters, all meaning lost and no pattern discernible in it. Uhura scanned the flimsy printout twice, then shook her head.

"I can see why this confused you, Ensign." She drew a dark finger across one line of text, noting the total lack of gaps between the letters. "Did you check this output against the Communications Library's records of planetary interference?"

Ensign Cercone nodded. "The library computer couldn't figure it out at all. That's why I came to you, sir."

"Hmm." Uhura glanced across her desk at her student's expectantly alight face, and couldn't bring herself to say that she couldn't figure it out, either. In any case, she reminded herself tartly, puzzling over a communications problem was far more productive than sitting here wondering how Admiral Kirk could possibly find proof of his crew's innocence in time to save them. Which was how she'd spent most of her time since she'd finished grading the exams.

"Do you think it could be neutrino interference, Commander?" Cercone asked. "From solar flares?"

Uhura found herself shaking her head before she'd even thought about the question. She had to stop and search her mind to find out what made her so sure.

"I don't think it can be any kind of natural interference, Ensign," she said slowly. She traced a finger down the flimsy again. Every garbled line was completely filled with English letters, just as the original message had been. "You used Federation standard transmission code to send this, didn't you?"

"Yes, sir."

"Do you know how many bits of information are needed to correctly identify a single letter in Federation standard?"

"Sixty-four," Cercone said promptly. "The minimum number needed to transmit the seven major alphabets and pictographs of Earth, plus the five Vulcan alphabets, the six branches of Andorian letters, and the entire Tellarite trading symbology."

"Very good." Uhura hid a smile, remembering when she had been just as quick to spill out everything she knew in response to a simple question. Admiral Kirk had cured everyone in his crew of that habit—except, perhaps, for Mr. Spock. "Now, if natural interference was randomly altering some of the individual bits of code you sent, do you think all the altered packets would still code out as English letters?"

The ensign's mouth opened to reply, but what actually came out was a yelp of surprise and dawning comprehension. "No, of course not!" She skated her fingers accusingly over the all-English letters on her printout. "Some of these should be Russian *shcha*'s, or Arabic *qaf*'s, or Vulcan *iluzal*'s . . ."

"Precisely." Uhura tapped at the flimsy. "What we have here, Ensign, is a deliberately miscoded message."

Cercone looked stunned. "You mean someone's trying to sabotage my senior honors thesis, sir?"

Uhura paused in surprise. She was so used to encountering coded messages in distant and unfriendly parts of the galaxy that it hadn't occurred to her how odd it was to find one here on Earth. "I'm not sure. The only way to find out is to analyze and see if the miscoding's random, or if there's a message embedded inside it."

"Can we do that?"

"Very easily." Uhura swung around and retrieved her optic pen, then ran it across the flimsy printout and transferred it into her desk console. The computer beeped an error code and verbally repeated the first line of the message.

"Eunhtuerrapirmiasleievne?" The console's artificial monotone clicked and stumbled over the awkward combination of letters. "Language reference?"

"It's a coded message, of unknown cipher," Uhura replied soothingly. She couldn't break the habit of being polite, even when talking to a machine. "Run standard pattern analysis, spacing two to begin."

"Analyzing." The console's pause was only an eyeblink long. "Analysis complete. Ten-letter pattern discovered at spacing two, repetition frequency nine."

Uhura sighed, wishing computers could be programmed to foresee obvious questions. "And do the ten letters make a word?"

"Affirmative. The word is 'Enterprise.'"

Uhura's breath froze in her chest, so numbly that for a moment she felt almost phaser-stunned. *Enterprise?*

"Enterprise?" Ensign Cercone's eyes rounded with astonishment. "But, sir, that's the name of the ship you—oh!" Understanding flitted into her dark, intelligent gaze. "Commander, that hidden message is for you!"

"I think so." Uhura reached out to freeze the console's analysis, afraid of what it might spit out next. "But who could have known . . ."

"Someone who found out I was in your class, and

hoped I'd consult you about this," Cercone guessed. "Or hoped I'd bring it to you, if I managed to decode it myself."

Uhura took a deep, steadying breath. "Do you *want* to decode it yourself?" she asked the ensign, then added, "Before you answer, let me tell you that someone in the Federation is trying to make Admiral Kirk look like a traitor. I don't want you to get caught up in that fight, Ensign, but this message is part of your research. I can't take it away from you."

Cercone's brows drew together thoughtfully. "Sir, I don't think I—"

The beep of Uhura's communicator band interrupted her. Uhura reached down to activate it. "Uhura here."

"Uhura, this is Janice Rand in Iceland. Are you alone?"

Uhura opened her mouth to say no, but the click of her door's electronic latch stopped her. She glanced up at her empty office, then down again to see that Cercone had pushed her flimsy all the way across the desk before she left, clearly consigning it to Uhura's care.

"I am now," she told Rand. "What have you found out?"

"A lot of things." The other communications officer sounded bleak. "And most of them are bad. Is it true Admiral Kirk's been hospitalized for a day or two?"

"That's what I've been told." All good communications officers knew the trick of conveying official information that might not necessarily be true. Rand's quiet indrawn breath told Uhura that she understood. "He'll definitely be out of touch with us for that long."

"Well, he couldn't have timed it worse," Rand informed her. "I pulled a message this morning off Security's communications net. Computers reported an unauthorized transmission from the Assateague Island Wilderness Sanctuary. I didn't think much of it at the time, but just a few minutes ago, Security's recon satellite reported that there was one stray infrared signal on Assateague."

"So?" Uhura tapped at her console while she listened, programming it to remove "Enterprise" wherever it occurred and to decode what was left of Ensign Cercone's garbled message. Preoccupied as she was, she didn't see why Rand's news had made her sound so glum. "That infrared could be from anyone out there—a ranger, maybe, or a visiting scientist. For heaven's sake, it could even be one of the wild ponies!"

Rand snorted. "Uhura, have you looked at a global newscast lately?"

"No. Why?"

"Because there's a Class Four hurricane about an hour away from landfall on Assateague Island!" Exasperation sizzled beneath the other woman's competent voice. "All personnel were evacuated early this morning."

Uhura bit her lip in gathering dismay. "But the ponies must still be out there!"

"Yes, but believe it or not, the rangers know exactly how many ponies they have. And what they know, Starfleet Security knows." Rand paused meaningfully. "There is one *stray* infrared signal on Assateague Island."

"And that's Chekov." Uhura tugged helplessly at her earrings, her ultimate gesture of frustration. "And Admiral Kirk left just an *hour* ago—"

"You can't call him back?"

"I doubt it." She stared unseeingly at the output scrolling down her console's screen, her mind sorting out possibilities. "I could call Riley. He might be able to—" Uhura broke off abruptly as the console screen stopped scrolling and came into focus.

"To do what?" Rand inquired, after a brief silence. "Uhura, are you still there?"

"Oh, yes." Uhura stared at the console screen, seeing the reflection of her incredulous smile over the words printed there. "Don't worry, Janice. I know exactly what to do now. Uhura out."

The com-band beeped itself off and Uhura hurriedly reactivated the console's audio output, just to make sure she wasn't dreaming. "Uhura," the computer's toneless voice said. "I'm alive in Tasmania with Kyle. Tell Kirk Wraith sabotaged to blame us, but now repaired. Chekov found yet? Reply through transporter."

It was Sulu.

"Oh, *Christ!*"

Chekov jerked to his knees at the sharp, distinctly human shout. Blind instinct warned him to be frightened before his brain even identified the source of the sounds. Ducking down behind the ranger station, he listened to the crash and rattle of pony feet through the dead brush around him and tried to calculate how long he'd been sitting since trying to contact Admiral Kirk.

"What?" The second voice sounded more irritable than angry, almost drowned into a blur by the thunder. "What is it?"

"Oh, just another one of those damned horses." Delays between their speech were filled with waves of rain and lightning. "What have they got us out here for? If they've got some fugitive loose on the island, leave him one night in this storm and he'll be dead by morning."

"Come on, Adam, that would be inhumane."

"Sending us out in this weather is inhumane. Aw, dammit! The road's gone!"

Chekov crept away without listening to more.

Could they have traced his call to the admiral so quickly? Even if they'd been expecting him to contact Kirk, he hadn't kept the line open long enough for a trace to reach farther than the East Coast multiplexer. Could there be some system that registered unauthorized calls from the wilderness ranger stations? That option seemed more likely. Upon their recognizing a linkup with a long-distance node, it wouldn't have taken a tactical genius to figure out Chekov must have initialized the call. That meant they knew for certain who they were looking for, and that his options for evasion were drastically limited. He rose up from his crouch and started to run.

The ponies led the way, as usual. Trotting and grumbling, they criticized Security's presence on the island with their stamps and snorts and lashing tails as they wended through the maze of brush. Chekov didn't try to impose himself on their pathways, keeping instead to the scrub on either side. The tangled roots and weeds made for treacherous footing, but he didn't dare push in between the jostling horses—there were dozens of them now, all intent on their own destination and indifferent to his frailties. He wasn't sure how easily a man could be trampled to death, and didn't want to find out.

As searchlights carved white tunnels out of the sky, the scream of a passing flier dashed the horses apart like startled fish. They melded almost thoughtlessly together again, but Chekov had to force himself to move from the thick cover when the pack flowed up over the dunes and into the open.

Cruel sheets of blinding ice rain crashed in from over the ocean, chasing great, foaming waves up onto the beach and eating at the sand there with each hungry lick. The horses topped the rise and scattered, directionless as autumn leaves as they trotted onto the open beach. They had no point in coming this way after all, no place of pony safety where they could all hide and wait for the search parties to pass. Chekov wanted to fall on his knees and cry.

A roar like the rending of heaven exploded across the storm front. Chekov recoiled to fall full-length in the sand, startled out of his despair by the violence of the sound, and the ponies screamed into a chaos of flight. A long patch of beach erupted into rooster tails of sand and sleet, throwing tide debris everywhere. Kelp and grass blasted upward to carve a deep, irregular pit in the dunes, and the next wall of water to crash up onto the beach caved in on itself to leave a huge, misshapen hollow behind. Chekov had only climbed as far as his knees when the spectacle of ocean violence in front of him rippled and shred to reveal the glossy black surface of an interatmospheric shuttle.

"No criticisms!" a familiar voice declared as the side

of the ship cracked open and slid inward. *"You* try and land one of these things in the worst weather since Noah built the Ark." Sulu had to hold on to the doorway to keep from slipping backward into the shuttle, thrown off-balance by the uneven beach and the distinctly uphill cant of the Wraith's blunt nose. "Well? What are you waiting for?" He waved impatiently when Chekov returned his shout with only a disbelieving stare, and nearly slid out of sight beyond the doorway for his efforts. "Don't just sit there like you've seen a ghost—get in!"

Chapter Thirteen

Assateague Island
Delmarva Peninsula, North America
Terrestrial Date: December 24, 2269
1600 hours EST

ANOTHER CRASH OF THUNDER shattered lightning across the sky, and Chekov dug his fist into the sand to duck away from the explosion. Four days of running had scrubbed his nerves raw, sensitizing him to both his vulnerable position here and the ever-looming danger of security searchlights.

"Chekov? Are you deaf?"

He jerked his attention back to the eroding shoreline. As if bolting awake out of a nightmare, he was suddenly aware again of Sulu's silver outline and the very real presence of the off-kilter Wraith.

"Come on!" the pilot shouted, bending his knees to weather the impact of another wave against the Wraith's exposed side. "We've got about a ten-minute window before either the storm or your Security buddies kill us! Get *in* here!"

If this be madness, he thought as he clambered forward, *then let us make the most of it.* He let the wet sand drag him down the crumbling dune, clawing back to his feet at the bottom and running into the maelstrom as hard as his aching legs would carry him. What difference did it make how wet and cold and filthy he got now? He was on the verge of rescue or death, and either way the ordeal was over.

When he tumbled against the too-high lip of the Wraith's threshold, the pain of flesh striking polished metal had never felt so good.

"What are you doing here?" He reached up to clasp the hand Sulu stretched to him, pulling against the helmsman's grip and scrabbling up the wet bulkhead at the same time. "They said your shuttle was destroyed! Why aren't you dead?"

"Because I've been ordained by the gods to be the protector of wild ponies and dumb Russians. Here"—Sulu tossed him a scrap of silver flightsuit and signaled the outside hatch to close—"put this on." He darted back toward the front of the shuttle without waiting to see if Chekov obeyed.

"Wait a minute!" Gathering up the reflective fabric, Chekov scrambled after him, wet boots sliding on the awkwardly tilted floor. "Sulu, don't do this to me—I'm too tired to deal with sarcasm." He threw himself into the copilot's seat and shook out the flightsuit one-handed. "Why aren't you dead?"

Sulu smiled and flashed his hands across the Wraith's controls. "The persistence of antigravity."

Chekov bent to work his foot down one leg of the flimsy suit. "What?" he prompted wearily.

As if in reply, the little shuttle bounced upward and her forward thrusters roared into life. "See, you can temporarily knock out an antigrav with a negative phase generator, but you can't disable it permanently. As soon as I figured out that the source of the negative phase shift had to be my cloaking device, I just turned it off and the antigravs came right back on." Sulu shrugged as though this were the most trivial of piloting feats. "Of course, with both my thrusters and the cloaking device out of commission, I had to spend the entire trip to Tasmania bouncing from one wave-top to another to avoid detection. I've never been so seasick in my life." He made a face and swept the shuttle keenly eastward. "Have you got that flightsuit on yet?"

"No." Chekov squirmed into a more manageable position, then growled when he still couldn't find sufficient grip to drag the suit up any higher than his hips. "I don't think these things were designed to fit well over wet parkas."

"Well, make it fit," Sulu suggested. "I didn't fly all the way through Hurricane Kevin just to toast you when I turned on the cloaking device."

Chekov flashed his head up in surprise. "You flew through a hurricane?"

"And we're going to do it again." Rain crashed across the viewscreen with the fury of a demon. "Now quit arguing with me and put that flightsuit on!"

Snapping the seals down the front of the parka proved only the first of Chekov's problems. Twisting sideways in his seat and using the console as leverage, he managed to scrape his left arm out of the sleeve; then he yanked his right arm free, without worrying about what would happen if he disturbed the splint. As it was, pain kicked him twice as he struggled the parka off his shoulders and out from behind him, but his arm lodged no protest at all when he shoved it down the flightsuit sleeve and tabbed shut the throat closure.

"All right." It was still too tight—not designed to fit over double layers of wool and heat-weave, either—but the front stayed firmly closed, even when he bent to dig the helmet out from under the panel between his knees. "I'm ready."

Sulu snapped down his own helmet's locking rings. "Then here we go."

A crackle of coruscating lightning seemed to arc through the enclosed cabin. Chekov felt the invisible wave pulse skitter along his nerve pathways; then the viewscreen flashed white and a single darkened readout on Sulu's console silently sprang into life. They were cloaked.

"Sulu, if we're invisible, can't we please avoid flying through Hurricane Kevin?" It felt weird to be considering flight plans based on Starfleet's inability to detect them. He suddenly knew how the Romulans must feel.

"Sorry," Sulu told him. "With this much precipitation —especially the snow—those searchers will notice the turbulence in the air when we fly past." His faceplate reflected a grim Asian smile. "That's something Dr. Nakai never thought of." He flicked bright eyes across a string of readouts. "Our only chance of getting out of here unnoticed is by cutting through the worst of the storm where our pursuers can't follow."

Chekov felt around the edges of his seat for the copilot's shoulder strap. "Does it count if we don't actually make it through your escape route in one piece?"

"What are you worried about? A Class Four hurricane's no worse than your average ion storm."

Chekov decided this wasn't a good time to mention how many starships perished in ion storms every year.

They smashed the face of the onrushing storm, and sweeping curtains of sheeting rain hissed and tore at the Wraith's outer hull. Chaotic waves echoed the roiling sky, buffets of wind blasting the ship like hammer blows. Chekov clutched the panel in front of him, desperately wishing for something constructive to do. A shot of anguish up the bones of his right arm disabused him of any thoughts of helping to pilot, and he made himself let go of the console and settle both arms back into his lap.

When the Wraith first burst into sunlight, Chekov thought for certain they'd intercepted a phaser blast and the light was just a trick of the resultant explosion. He remembered they were cloaked right about the time his eyes caught on the debris-riddled ocean chop below, and Sulu kicked the Wraith nose-upward to begin their final climb. Chekov let the acceleration push him back into his padded seat, closing his eyes against a ringing surge of vertigo and counting the seconds until the phantom pressure lifted.

He cracked one eye to steal a look at Sulu as the Wraith

settled into a silent, lateral track. "Anything?" he asked at last.

Sulu shook his head, but didn't look up from scanning the Wraith's sensor arsenal. "Nope." Just watching the rapid, rhythmic movement of Sulu's hands made Chekov's head loop in circles. "Looks like we made it clear." Sulu pushed away from his console with a sigh, dragging a hand across the front of his helmet as though unconsciously reaching to wipe sweat from his eyes. "You know, being dead's a whole lot easier than having half of Starfleet on your tail."

"But not as much fun." Chekov closed his eyes again. The warmth inside the well-sealed Wraith bordered on narcotic. "What do we do now?" he asked when it occurred to him he should say something.

Sulu sighed. "I've been thinking about that. We can't hope to hide out on Earth for any length of time— somebody's bound to zero in on the Wraith eventually, if only by tracking our ion trail. But they didn't build this thing with enough range to fly out-of-atmosphere to anyplace farther than Luna."

"So we need to find somewhere within Earth orbit that's big enough to hide both us and the shuttle, but where no one will stumble across us until we're ready to be found." Even as he said it, Chekov saw the answer to their riddle like an angel spread across a tapestry of silk and stars.

"Well," Sulu said slowly, "there's one place I can think that just might fit the bill."

Chekov turned and flashed his friend a tired smile. "The *Enterprise*."

"Uhura, are you sure this is a good idea?"

Hot and burdened with the weight of a coat she wouldn't need until she reached Annapolis, Uhura cast a harried glance back over her shoulder. Christine Chapel stood somewhere behind her in the crush of holiday travelers at Stanford Station, the main West Coast terminal of North America's cross-continental maglev train. The doctor's plaintive voice could barely be heard over the multilingual chatter of reunited families and the background jangle of harpsichord music. Uhura didn't even try to reply. She was too busy politely excusing herself into the line that led to the ticket counter.

An austere congregation of Vulcan monks parted as silently as a school of fish and let Chapel emerge beside the waiting line. The doctor lifted an eyebrow at the distance separating Uhura from the nearest automated check-in position. "You're never going to get a ticket before the next train gets in," she said, not bothering to lower her voice in the sound-swallowing din. "Why don't you wait for Sulu to call before you go running off to Assateague?"

"Because that might be too late." Uhura refrained from looking at the chronometer on her wrist, knowing it would only depress her. Janice Rand had called with the news about Chekov just before lunch, and it was already midafternoon. For all she knew, the Russian could be in custody at this moment. "If I can't get on this train, I'll just wait for the next one. They're only three hours apart."

Chapel's smooth brow creased with worry. "But what if Sulu manages to rescue Chekov in the meantime? How will they get in touch with you?"

"I told my office computer to route all my calls to Admiral Kirk's office. Sulu will know he can talk to Riley there, even if Chekov doesn't." Uhura edged her way a step closer to the distant ticketing machine, swallowing despair at how long that tiny advance had taken. "Right now, it's more important for me to go to Assateague and find out if Chekov's been captured than to sit here waiting to hear that he's safe. If he *is* safe, I've only wasted a train trip. If he's in custody and I get to him before Starfleet Security does—"

"—they can conveniently kill you both." Chapel's refined voice held a more acid note than Uhura had ever heard in it before. "Uhura, listen to me! Just because nothing's happened to you yet doesn't mean you're somehow immune from this plot."

Uhura opened her mouth to reassure her friend, but a sudden flux of red-and-black-clad security cadets jostled past them and silenced her. She exchanged dismayed glances with Chapel. "The train from Annapolis must have just arrived," Uhura said, trying to keep her voice steady. "Would you go see if the return train is leaving on time?"

"Uhura—" The expression on her face must have told Chapel further argument was useless. The doctor sighed. "Oh, all right. Stay here."

Uhura managed a half-choked laugh, gesturing at the sluggish line in front of her. "Don't worry. I'm not going anywhere."

Chapel nodded and ducked back into the milling crowd. Left alone for the first time since she'd run into Christine on the commuter train down to Stanford, Uhura felt her doubts and hopes rise in a paralyzing swirl of anxiety. If only she could be sure that Hurricane Kevin wouldn't stop Sulu . . . if only she could convince herself that the forces sent to capture Chekov couldn't *all* be involved in this spiderweb of treachery . . . if only she knew where Kirk had gone and how much time he would need to prove them all innocent . . .

"Madam, I'm a doctor, not an information booth!"

"Dr. McCoy!" Uhura spun around, searching the passing crowd of westbound travelers in mingled disbelief and delight. That caustic Georgian drawl couldn't possibly belong to anyone else. She raised her voice to a singer's practiced level of projection. "Dr. McCoy, are you here?"

"Uhura?" A wiry figure draped in a coat a size too large emerged from the passing stream of security cadets. Uhura beckoned at the doctor, unwilling to leave her place in line even for this most welcome of chance encounters. McCoy scowled and cut rudely across the queue toward her.

"What the dickens are you doing here?" he hissed when he'd gotten close enough for normal sound to carry through the din.

"I'm going to Assateague, to see if Chekov's been captured."

"The hell you are!" With unusual force, the doctor grabbed Uhura's wrist and yanked her out of line. Ignoring the complaints that rose around him, he towed her back across the queue and out toward the station's main concourse. The swarming mob of travelers parted around them, as if they could somehow sense the urgency radiating from McCoy.

Uhura started to protest, then noticed the lines of strain etched into the physician's craggy face. His blue eyes, creased sharp at the edges with apprehension, scanned the crowd. "What's wrong? Has something happened to—"

McCoy turned and clapped a hand across her mouth, shaking his head down at her in exaggerated warning. "Not here," he mouthed silently.

Uhura's eyes widened in sudden realization. This much caution couldn't arise just from McCoy's one encounter with Chekov, she knew. Something else must have happened to the doctor since then, something much more threatening.

She bent her attention toward finding someplace they could talk safely, protected from the surging hordes of maglev passengers. They passed a game arcade along the concourse, noisy and crowded with children, and then an even more crowded cappuccino stand. Finally, just when Uhura had resigned herself to the risk of going outside the station to talk, she spotted a nearly empty electronic newsstand.

She pointed it out to McCoy and he grunted, then led them across the concourse toward it. Antiphase sound mufflers dropped a soothing curtain of silence across them when they entered, broken only by the quiet whisper of someone printing out a flimsy at one of the newsboards. McCoy glanced around, then pulled Uhura into the shelter of a Tellarite-language newsboard, with its projected waterfall of glowing three-dimensional symbols.

"Aha. Alone at last." Tension crackled under McCoy's usual whimsical humor, turning it awry. "Sorry if I scared you back there, Uhura."

She shook her head, ignoring the apology. "What's the matter? Is someone following you?"

"Damned if I know." McCoy grimaced. "I've never been much good at spotting that kind of thing. All I know is . . ." The doctor paused, wiping a hand over his damply furrowed brow. "Well, if I was one of the people behind this damned conspiracy, *I'd* have followed me."

"Then they probably did." Uhura turned and took a step out from behind the cascade of luminous Tellarite symbology, to where she could keep an eye on the passing crowd. "What happened?"

"I got a package this morning," McCoy said bluntly, "Containing a recorded message from Mark Piper."

Uhura threw him a startled glance. "Sent before he died?"

"No. After." McCoy cleared the gruffness from his throat. "The package came from his sister in Boston. She said he'd left instructions to give it to me in the event of his death."

"He knew something was wrong in his lab," Uhura guessed. She scanned the concourse, hoping to spot Christine Chapel before she returned to find Uhura gone from the ticketing line. God only knew what Chris would think of that. "And he didn't trust Starfleet Security with the information."

McCoy nodded grimly. "That's why he asked Chekov to come work with him at Johns Hopkins, to help him catch the person he suspected of treachery. He said he knew he could trust a member of Jim Kirk's bridge crew."

Uhura felt her throat clench with regret. "But that played right into the spies' plans, didn't it? They killed

Dr. Piper, and threw the blame for the disruptor theft on Chekov."

"Yeah." McCoy blew out a snort of vast disgust. "Makes me wish I'd just stayed down in Georgia and drowned myself in mint juleps. If it hadn't been for me taking Piper out to dinner that night in Baltimore—" The doctor caught himself with an exasperated snap of his teeth. "Never mind that now. The important thing, Uhura, is that Mark Piper didn't underestimate how ruthless these damned traitors could be. He guessed they might kill him, and he took precautions."

A flash of pale blond hair in a distinctive coronet caught Uhura's attention, far across the train station's concourse. She stood on tiptoe to peer out, trying to make sure it was Chapel before she waved at her. "What kind of precautions?"

"He put all the evidence he had of the traitors' identities into a package . . ."

It *was* Chapel. Uhura ducked around the corner of the Tellarite newsboard and lifted a hand to wave. From behind her, McCoy's worried voice continued.

". . . and somehow managed to send it up to the *Enterprise.*"

Without warning, the artificial silence of the newsroom exploded into a roaring blast of fire. Agony seared across Uhura's raised hand, turning her reflexive outward dive into a screaming curl of pain. She had just enough wits left to jam her fire-glazed sleeve into the dense folds of her coat and hug it suffocatingly tight, but somehow that didn't seem to stop the burning. Gasping, Uhura wrenched herself to her feet and turned to look for water.

Strong hands caught her and yanked her hand out from the smoldering folds of her coat. In the blur of smoke that surrounded her, Uhura couldn't see who it was, but she heard something hiss and then felt cold foam spatter across her hand. It smelled like ammonia and stung like wasp's venom against her seared skin. Uhura shrieked in anguish and tried to pull away.

"It's all right, it's all right." That was Christine Chapel's voice in the smoke, cool reassurance against the blaze of pain. Uhura closed her eyes and leaned into the hands that held her, gathering her strength to face the pain. Sirens wailed in the concourse, overwhelming the gathering shouts of alarm that surrounded them. She clenched her teeth on a long breath that threatened to become a whimper, and opened her eyes again.

Most of the smoke was gone, letting Uhura see the scorched circle of black that had engulfed the little newsroom. Long fingers of fire still smoldered in gouts across the floor, a strange green-gold fire that smelled more like sulfur than smoke. Halon mists drizzled out from darkened newsboards, slowly drenching what was left of the flames. Ignoring her pain, Uhura turned with dread to follow the scorched pattern back into the newsroom, past the Tellarite display that had shielded her from the worst of the blast, and then on to the blackened, crumpled form—

"Don't look." Christine Chapel's voice shook beneath its professional calm, but the hand that turned Uhura's face away never wavered. "It's Leonard."

Chapter Fourteen

Stanford Medical Center
Stanford, North America
Terrestrial Date: December 24, 2269
1500 hours PST

THE FAMILIAR HUM of antigrav generators sounded eerily out of place to Uhura, caged as it was inside the antiseptic white walls of Stanford's intensive-care burn unit. She edged her way inside, careful not to jostle the intricate web of tubing that shuttled oxygen, synthetic blood, and bioplasma to the transparent aluminum sarcophagus in the center of the room. Inside that massive skin-regenerating unit, McCoy's gaunt figure hung suspended by antigravs to protect his burns from contact trauma. The stillness of the doctor's blistered face made Uhura wince.

"Christine, are you *sure* he's going to be all right?"

Dr. Chapel turned away from her intent scan of McCoy's life-support computer and lifted a quizzical eyebrow at Uhura. "Of course I'm sure. I wouldn't have told you his condition had been upgraded to good if I didn't know that for a fact."

"Sorry." Uhura rubbed at the plas-skin bandage around her right hand and wrist. Despite having spent an hour with her arm immersed in a miniature version of McCoy's bioplasma unit, the scorched nerves beneath her brand•new skin still insisted they hurt. She suspected

163

that was why McCoy was so heavily sedated. "It's just that I can barely believe he survived, with the explosive device planted right on the back of his coat."

"He was lucky," Chapel said soberly. "There's only so much eruptive resin you can hide in a button-sized bomb, and his coat absorbed most of it." She tapped at the reassuring blue of the human schematic on her medical scanner, freckled in only a few places with urgent pinks and reds. "The worst damage is to the back of his head and neck where the resin hit bare skin. His clothes got an instant dose of flame-retardant from the Tellarite newsboard."

Uhura frowned, remembering the glittering mist triggered by the heat of the explosion. "Whoever set off the bomb must not have realized that the newsboard would have fire extinguishers built into it."

"Or they didn't even know you were standing next to a newsboard." Chapel led her out of the burn unit and into the quiet hospital corridor outside. "I found some metal fragments buried in McCoy's coat and gave them to the nano-technician at the hospital this morning. She's not a hundred percent sure, but she thinks there might have been an audio pickup attached to the explosive device. It couldn't have had much transmission range, but the person who planted it could easily have been out of sight when they triggered the bomb."

"Eavesdropping on us." A shiver crawled up Uhura's spine when she realized what information that unseen listener had been given by McCoy. "Then they know—Christine, I've got to get out of here!"

She began to turn away, her mind already charting out the safest and quickest route from Stanford to San Francisco. Chapel caught at her shoulder before she could take a second step. "Uhura, don't be stupid!" the doctor pleaded. "Do you want to give whoever planted that bomb a second shot at you? Stay here, where you're safe."

"I don't know that I *am* safe here," Uhura told her

friend bluntly. "Or that you are, if I stay here with you."
She saw an obstinate look appear on Chapel's face and
added unfairly, "Or Dr. McCoy, for that matter. If the
person who planted that bomb followed the ambulance
shuttle back here, then they know where we are. Once
they find out we're still alive, they might try to kill us
again."

That made Chapel pause and tap her fingers worriedly
against compressed lips. "They might," she admitted at
last, then glanced at the chronometer on her wrist. "Of
course, it's only three P.M. The hospital hasn't issued any
official statements to the evening news nets yet. If we
don't say anything about Dr. McCoy—"

"The traitors will know he's alive." Uhura rubbed at
her aching wrist again, trying to think what Admiral Kirk
would do in a situation like this. Her eyes narrowed with
a sudden shrewd thought. "But if you issue a statement
saying he's *dead,* and that I've been taken into custody by
Starfleet Security . . ."

Chapel frowned down at her. "Why would they do
that?"

"To question me about McCoy's death, or to keep me
in protective custody. Whatever sounds good to you."
Uhura set off down the corridor again, and this time the
doctor merely followed her out to the main bank of
elevators. "By the time the traitors find out it isn't true, I
should be safely back at Starfleet Headquarters." She saw
the unspoken question in the other woman's eyes and
answered it. "I have to go, Chris. Our reputations—and
our lives—may depend on it."

"But how are you going to get there?" Chapel demanded sharply. "These traitors, whoever they are, are
going to be watching all the hospital exits!"

"I hope they are, because we're going to give them
exactly what they expect to see." Uhura tugged Chapel
into the open elevator, then pointed at the row of
medical abbreviations on its control panel. "Which of
these is the morgue?"

* * *

Body bags, Uhura decided one uncomfortable half hour later, were simply not meant for live people to inhabit. The heavy plastic that surrounded her was not only skintight and sweat-sticky, but also bristled with bumpy handles and information tags that stabbed at her ribs no matter what position she squirmed into. At least it was no longer airtight—Christine Chapel and a sharp pair of surgical scissors had made sure of that before Uhura had left the morgue—but it did smell depressingly of formaldehyde.

Uhura squirmed again, trying to rub at the persistent ache in her right wrist. The trip to San Francisco had taken longer than she'd expected, probably because the morgue's shuttle pilot had elected to follow the coastline rather than use the fast traffic lanes over the peninsula. As far as he was concerned, this was merely a routine run up to Starfleet's service mortuary. Only the two morgue attendants who'd carried Uhura aboard knew that the body inside their bag wasn't dead yet.

The morgue shuttle banked and began to descend at last. An anonymous outside hand steadied Uhura against the inertial drag, and a muffled voice said, "Almost there, ma'am."

A mixed blessing, Uhura thought wryly. As eager as she was to get out of this body bag, she wasn't necessarily looking forward to meeting the Starfleet pathologist who opened it. Assuming he or she survived the shock, there was always the distinct possibility that Uhura might have to take violent measures to prevent her unorthodox arrival from being reported to Starfleet Security.

The morgue shuttle settled on the ground, creaking like a rusty old chair. Uhura felt a familiar San Francisco breeze buffet her when the side door opened, but the brief exchange of words outside was drowned under the whir of the impulse engines. She felt herself being lifted and carried, but only knew she was inside the mortuary building when she was dropped on a surface so instantly cold that it could only have been a stone morgue slab.

There was a long, nervous silence. Then, somewhere far away, a door gonged shut. Uhura held her breath, wondering if she was imagining the rapid thudding of footsteps back toward her.

The hiss of the body bag's electrostatic seal answered that question, dazzling her with a sudden blaze of halogen light. Uhura shielded her eyes with one hand and levered herself up with the other, trying to see who had opened the bag. The worried face that met her gaze was as dark as her own, and startlingly familiar.

"Dr. M'Benga!"

A brief smile chased the anxiety from the former *Enterprise* physician's eyes. "Lieutenant Commander Uhura." M'Benga helped her shed the rest of the clinging body bag and sit upright on the morgue table. "I hoped it might be you."

Uhura's eyebrows shot upward incredulously. *"Hoped?"* she demanded, pointing at the body bag she'd arrived in.

M'Benga grinned down at her. "Well, I knew *you* were alive." He twisted the body bag's identification tag around to show her McCoy's name. "But I wasn't so sure about Leonard. I saw Christine announce his death on the news net just a few moments ago, and I thought she didn't seem upset enough for it to be true. He *is* alive, isn't he?"

Uhura nodded, distractedly. "But what on earth are you doing here, Ben? I thought you would have transferred to another starship by now."

"And missed my chance to get back aboard the *Enterprise?* Oh, no!" The doctor rubbed a hand across the pathologist's badge on his uniform, smiling. "Anyway, I've always thought I might like pathology. This was a good chance to get a year's experience without committing myself."

"But why didn't you tell me you were stationed here?" Uhura demanded, feeling hurt. "I've been working around the corner from you for three months!"

M'Benga shrugged, his chiseled mouth tightening a little with embarrassment. "Ah, well. I kept meaning to call, but I didn't want you to think I was—um—pursuing you. Making a pest of myself."

"But I wouldn't have—" Uhura broke off, shaking her head in disgust. *"Men!* I don't suppose it occurred to you to let me decide whether or not I wanted to see you?"

"No," M'Benga admitted, humbly. *"Do* you?"

"Yes." Uhura jumped down from the table with sudden decision. "In fact, you can take me to the Starfleet Christmas party right now, if you want."

M'Benga's thin face turned somber. "Why do I get the feeling this isn't a social invitation? Uhura"—he gestured at the body bag behind her—"if someone's trying to kill you, shouldn't you call Starfleet Security and let them handle it?"

"No. *Especially* not Security." Uhura met his frown. "I don't know exactly who, Ben, but someone in Starfleet is trying to frame Admiral Kirk and his old bridge crew. And Security is involved."

"Ah." The doctor's mobile eyebrows rose with enlightenment. "That's why Sulu is missing, and Chekov is on the run?"

Uhura nodded. "And why I have to get to the Starfleet Christmas party tonight. Mr. Scott will be there, and right now, he might be the only man on Earth who can help us."

"Then we'll get you safely to him," M'Benga said with firm decision. He cast a discreet glance down at her clothes and cleared his throat. "You weren't planning to wear what you have on, were you? If someone in Security *is* looking for you, those burns will be a dead giveaway."

Uhura glanced down at her uniform and winced at the noticeable scorch marks across it. "And after an hour in that body bag, I probably smell like a pickled frog, too. I could try to sneak back into my quarters and change—"

M'Benga shook his head. "Too dangerous, and unnecessary in any case. I have a whole stock of dress uniforms right here." He led her out of the morgue and down the mortuary's long main hall. It was deserted in the Christmas Eve hush. "Try to find one in medical colors. I have an idea that I think will get us past Security."

"Yes, but . . ." Uhura peered through the door he had politely paused outside of, and saw racks of uniforms filed like spare parts on tall, utilitarian shelves. It clearly wasn't a quartermaster's shop. "Ben, why do you have all of these?"

The doctor smiled at her wryly. "For funerals, of course," he said, and left her there.

The main rotunda of Starfleet Headquarters glittered like a miniature nebula, its soaring dome filled with a thousand floating luminarias whose candle glows warmed the dying afternoon with light. The whispers of all those tiny antigravs were lost under the sound of Andorian winter solstice music being played by an interplanetary chamber orchestra at the far end of the room. Nearer to the doors, a receiving line of dignitaries greeted the arriving officers and their spouses, shaking each hand with a practiced blend of charm and swift efficiency. Each name was announced by the security guard at the top of the portico stairs.

Uhura took a deep breath when M'Benga handed over their identification card, feeling her borrowed blue medical uniform tighten around her tensed shoulders. The security guard scanned the card, then glanced up at them. His face tightened a little.

"Dr. M'Benga?" he inquired.

"Yes," Uhura answered, trying to sound matter-of-fact about it. The rigid line of the guard's mouth was making her extremely nervous.

"And spouse?" The security guard looked more carefully at the tall man in civilian clothes standing behind her.

"Yes." M'Benga's hand dropped onto Uhura's shoulder with an air of casual affection. "My first visit here," he confided to the security guard in an undertone. "A little intimidating, isn't it. Good thing I have my wife around to protect me."

"Yes, sir." The guard's mouth quivered into a betraying smile, then was ruthlessly jerked flat again. Uhura realized that it was suppressed amusement at their contrast in heights, not suspicion, that had made the man eye them so oddly. She let her breath out in a silent sigh of relief and gave the first elderly admiral in line a dazzling smile. He blinked and smiled back at her.

"Dr. M'Benga, eh? Pathology, I think?"

"Yes, Admiral." Fortified by their initial success, Uhura managed to make her voice sound confidently merry now. She moved down the receiving line, smiling back at all the warm faces, answering all the cordial greetings, introducing her polite civilian "husband" to one senior officer after another. The only thing she was really aware of was that the one face she would have liked to see—Admiral Kirk's—was disappointingly absent.

They got to the end at last, only to be handed a glass of champagne and efficiently swept into the buffet room by an Academy student doubling as a waiter for the evening. The ensign gave Uhura's blue medical tunic a slightly startled look, and she tensed. It would be ironic if she had managed to deceive all of Starfleet's high command, only to be exposed as an impostor by an ensign. But after showing her where the buffet line started, the young man nodded respectfully and left without a backward glance.

"One of your students?" M'Benga murmured to her, handing her a buffet plate. He'd obviously noticed the sidelong look too.

"No." Uhura absently transferred salmon in puff pastry onto her plate while she searched her memory. "Probably just someone who's seen me on campus regularly. Not many medical officers serve as regular lecturers at the Academy, but some do."

"That must have been why he looked surprised." The doctor heaped his own plate with a salad made of smoked artichokes, marinated asparagus, and water buffalo cheese, then reached for the croissants. "Uhura, have you thought about how we're going to find Mr. Scott in this mob?"

"Oh, that will be the easy part." Uhura filled her plate with steamed shrimp, baked Brie, and crabmeat-stuffed mushrooms, suddenly aware of how long it had been since her last real meal.

"It will?" M'Benga paused in the doorway that led from the buffet room back out into the main rotunda, looking harried and overwhelmed. The huge room was already jammed with officers in Starfleet colors and their spouses, not to mention flocks of extraterrestrial dignitaries holding court in various corners. The chamber orchestra was now playing an ancient and energetic Earth waltz, and the noise level in the room had risen accordingly.

"Of course." Uhura joined him, scanning the room with a practiced eye while she forked up salmon and Brie. "All we have to do is look for the bar." She spotted it after several more quick mouthfuls of food, discreetly screened by a row of luminous Orion fern trees. Even from here, she could see the familiar burly figure leaning against one end. "There it is. And there he is."

"Oh. Of course." M'Benga followed her through the crowd. "So, if that was the easy part, what's the hard part?"

Uhura smiled and handed him her plate. "The hard part," she said, "is getting him away from it."

"Uhura, lass!" Montgomery Scott's brown eyes lit with undisguised delight. "I was hoping I'd see ye here!"

"Oh, Mr. Scott." Uhura had to restrain an urge to hug as much of the stocky engineer as she could encircle. She knew that would embarrass him, though, so she smiled up at him instead. "You have no idea how much I was hoping I'd see *you.*"

"Missed the old crew, eh?" Scott sighed and shook his head. "Aye, lass, so have I. I was just telling my friend"— he motioned at the silent bartender—"how hard it is to walk around the ship and not see the people who ought to be on it."

"Yes, I know." Uhura glanced over her shoulder, to where M'Benga stood guard outside the ferns. The doctor interrupted his scan of the crowd to give her a reassuring nod. "Mr. Scott, I need to talk to you. Can you give me a minute?"

"For you, lass, all the hours in the world." Scott drained his glass and handed it back. "Another of the same, if you will, laddie. That's a fine, rare vintage of the Saurian."

Uhura stifled a sigh, but she knew enough to wait for the glass to be refilled and handed back before she tried again. "The thing is, Mr. Scott, I need to talk to you more . . . more privately. It's very important."

Something in her voice must have broken through the cheerful air of sociability she was trying to project. Scott paused with his glass halfway to his mouth, peering down at her with real concern. "Lass, what's wrong?" His gaze traveled to M'Benga's tall silhouette and narrowed. "The doctor's behaving like a good gentleman with you, isn't he?"

"No, it's not that." Uhura glanced around and saw no interested faces close to them at the bar. She stood on tiptoe and whispered to Scott, "It's about what happened to Chekov and Sulu."

"Is it, then?" The engineer's intelligent face remained totally unenlightened. "And what happened to Chekov and Sulu?"

This time, Uhura's sigh was audible and exasperated. "Mr. Scott, don't you ever read anything but technical journals?"

"Not when I'm rebuilding a starship, lass." Scott followed her with reluctant obedience when she tugged on his sleeve, leaving the bar for a sheltered niche between the luminous white ferns. On the other side, the orchestra had segued into a solemn Vulcan year-end chant. "Why?"

"Because if you'd listened to the news nets at all this

week, you'd know that Chekov's been accused of murder and Sulu's missing and presumed dead!" Uhura saw the warning glance M'Benga shot her through the ghostly fronds and forced her voice back to a whisper. "Captain Kirk's gone off-planet to try and prove they're not traitors, but I just found out from Dr. McCoy that the evidence we need is hidden on board the *Enterprise.*"

"The *Enterprise?*" Scott lowered his voice when Uhura winced and laid a shushing finger across her lips. "But how can anything be hidden aboard her, lass? She's barely half-reconstructed, and there's not a speck of cargo in her."

"There's not?" Uhura stared up at him, appalled. "But Dr. McCoy said that—"

The lift of Scott's gaze warned her to fall silent, long before she felt the tiny shift of air that signaled another person's arrival. Expecting M'Benga with a warning, Uhura swung around and gasped.

"Evening, ma'am," said Jackson Kahle. The former starship captain nodded sociably to Mr. Scott, but his keen gaze never left Uhura's face. She tried to arrange it into suitably welcoming lines. "Have to forgive my barging in like this, I'm afraid. After what I heard happened down in Stanford, I wanted to be sure you made it back here safe and sound."

Uhura's smile looked only a little forced. "Thank you, Mr. Kahle. I appreciate your concern."

Kahle grimaced and waved his cane self-deprecatingly. "I'm just a nosy old man, that's all. Had some of my young classmates looking out for you tonight, and I got a little worried when they said you'd come out of uniform."

Uhura brushed her hand self-consciously over her borrowed medical tunic. "I—um—didn't have time to make it back to my apartment, so I borrowed some things from my friend Christine Chapel in Stanford."

"The young lady who spoke on the news nets? Ah, yes." The billionaire frowned. "Sorry to hear about Dr. McCoy, you know. He was a good man."

"Yes." Uhura reached out for Mr. Scott's elbow as if to steady herself against grief, but her fingers tightened in warning on the engineer's forearm. He scowled but remained silent. "Yes, he was."

Despite her best efforts, something in her voice must not have sounded right. Kahle's steel-blue eyes caught and held Uhura's gaze with sudden, relentless focus. "Is something wrong, ma'am? Something I can help with?"

Uhura swallowed past tense throat muscles, then decided that partial truth would serve to deflect this well-meaning threat better than total falsehood. "Yes, Mr. Kahle. I'm afraid a lot of things are wrong. But I can't ask you or anyone else for help with them."

"Sure about that?" Kahle cocked a grizzled eyebrow at her. "I have lots of resources, you know."

Uhura managed a slight smile. "I know, sir. But the only resource I need right now is Admiral Kirk, and he's not available."

The octogenarian snorted. "Easy enough to fix that problem, ma'am. Just come to the Security Academy in Annapolis tomorrow. Kirk promised me he'd be there for the Romulan Territorial Conference."

"He did?" This time, Uhura didn't have to fake her smile. "Mr. Kahle, that's wonderful news! Thank you."

"Glad to be of service, ma'am." Kahle nodded politely at M'Benga, who had just slid breathlessly through the ferns to check him out. "Evening to you, Doctor. Enjoy the rest of the party."

M'Benga's eyes widened as he watched the billionaire stride away. "Does that guy know who I am?" he asked Uhura.

"I guess so." She shook her head in renewed amazement. "Sometimes, I think Jackson Kahle knows everything in Starfleet."

"Well, that explains why he knew to send me over." M'Benga saw the question in her eyes and shrugged. "He came by and told me one of the Vulcan ambassadors had choked on something and was having trouble breathing."

Uhura frowned. "And was the ambassador really choking?"

"Oh, yes." M'Benga rubbed at his fist, wincing. "You have no idea how hard it is to punch exactly the right place on a Vulcan's diaphragm."

Mr. Scott coughed abruptly and drained the last of his drink. He shot Uhura a wistful look. "I don't suppose I've got time for one more brandy, do I?"

"No." Uhura threw a longing look of her own at the mostly full dinner plate M'Benga had brought with him, then took a deep breath and turned away. "You heard Mr. Kahle: Admiral Kirk will be in Annapolis tomorrow. That means we have to do it tonight."

Scott scowled down at her. "Do what, lass?"

"Find out who the traitors are." Uhura tugged at his sleeve again. "Come on. You and I are going to transport up to the *Enterprise*."

INTERLOGUE

U.S.S. DeGama
Donatu Sector, Coordinates Unknown
Terrestrial Date: December 24, 2269
2330 hours shiptime

"DeGama bridge calling Admiral Kirk."

The tense edge in the communications officer's voice jerked Kirk out of his seat and over to the wall communicator in two long strides. He hit the reply pad with more force than it required, then winced at its howl of feedback. "Kirk here," he growled over the noise, trying to ignore Sarek's lifted eyebrow. "What's happening?"

"Sir, we've docked with the *Kozain,* but her commander refuses to grant us entry to his ship."

This time it was Kirk's turn to cock an eyebrow at Sarek. The Vulcan ambassador gave him back an impassive stare, which Kirk assumed meant he was thinking hard. They had discussed many possible receptions on the way to this rendezvous, but this had not been one of them.

"Have you asked the commander why he bothered to dock with us, if he doesn't intend to give us any kind of hearing?" Kirk demanded.

This time it was *DeGama*'s captain who answered, her crisp voice sounding more annoyed than distressed. "Admiral, the *Kozain*'s commander says that he just

179

wanted to see if he could really get this far inside Federation space without getting shot at."

Kirk snorted and took his hand off the transmission pad. "That's a lie."

"Is it?" The Vulcan regarded him over steepled fingers. "Given the tribal mentality of our friends on the *Kozain*, Admiral, I believe their commander's statement may well be true."

"Then why bother to dock with us at all? Why not just leave us a message buoy and run for the nearest neutral zone?" Kirk scowled and shook his head. "No, they're here to talk to us. This is just a test to see how desperate we are."

Sarek absorbed that reasoning and meditated over it. "We can accord that hypothesis a high degree of confidence and proceed accordingly," he agreed at last, with a scrupulous Vulcan precision that made Kirk long for Spock's quicker, half-human judgment. "How desperate are we, Admiral?"

Kirk suppressed a sigh, knowing Sarek meant the question literally. "Not desperate enough to be stupid, I hope." He pressed his palm against the communicator's reply pad, trying for some Vulcan patience this time. The comlink opened with only a tiny hiss of protest. "Kirk to *DeGama* bridge. Is the *Kozain* keeping a communications channel open to us?"

"Yes, Admiral."

"Then give her commander this message." Kirk paused, gathering his words with care. "His next war will not be waged against the Federation, but humans will have started it for him. End of message."

"Aye-aye, sir." The stifled note of complete bafflement in the communications officer's voice made Kirk grin. He turned away from the communications panel and saw a milder echo of that emotion in the dark gaze Sarek slanted him.

"An illogical prediction, Admiral."

Kirk nodded, his grin fading. "But an accurate one. And I'm betting that the *Kozain's* commander knows it."

Sarek spread the fingers of both hands, a highly eloquent gesture for a Vulcan. "But what purpose do you expect it to serve?"

The last of Kirk's coffee had congealed to bitter syrup in the bottom of his cup, but he drank it anyway. It gave his tense stomach something real to protest about. "I expect it to make them mad," he told Sarek. "Preferably mad enough to demand that we come over and explain."

ENTERPRISE

Chapter Fifteen

Starfleet Shuttle WKl-2
Somewhere over Earth
Terrestrial Date: December 24, 2269
1730 hours shiptime

"HEY—*Hey!* It's all right! It's just me, okay? Pavel? It's just me. . . ."

Chekov pushed away from the hands that reached to pinion him, and the side of his helmet cracked sharply against the unyielding bulkhead beside him. He flashed his eyes open, not realizing until then that they'd been closed, and pulled both feet up under him in preparation to bolt.

In the Wraith's pilot seat, Sulu stared at him with his hands poised over his shoulders in the age-old expression of surrender. "Hey, Pavel, are you all right? It's me."

Chekov uncurled his fingers one joint at a time from the edge of his seat's padded back. "Did I hit you?" he asked, horrified.

Sulu nodded, lifting one shoulder in a quick, dismissive shrug. "I shouldn't have startled you." He deflected any further comment by aiming Chekov's attention beyond the forward screen. "We're there."

Scooting into a more conventional position, he leaned across the console to follow Sulu's gaze. More magnificent and stately than she had ever seemed to Chekov from inside, the *Enterprise* filled the space around her

185

with a splendor heightened by the lacework of scaffolding surrounding her frame. Her missing main hull and dismantled warp drive made her look even more like some infinite angel, stretching on in all directions until she disappeared into eternity.

Across the curve of the world, a blinding glare of sunlight backlit the ship's fragile structure and kissed a watery gloss across every brand-new strut and plate. In only another few months, this ship would shake off her restraints and race into space's eternal darkness. Until then, Chekov thought, it seemed only fitting that she be cradled, and pampered, and worshiped for the mythic creature she was. How could anyone content himself with a land-bound existence, he wondered, when something like this waited just beyond the bell jar of his atmosphere?

"I've never seen her look so lovely."

"Yeah." Sulu sounded significantly less enamored with the sight. "Now if only we could get inside her."

Chekov turned to frown a question at him, and Sulu waved dispiritedly toward the stern of the ship's secondary hull. The shuttle bay's shell doors stood shut tight and solid. There wasn't even a rain of customary floodlighting from the surrounding dry-dock orbital platform; everyone gone home for the holidays, and everything closed up behind them. "I hadn't thought about that."

"Neither had I." Puffing gently on the maneuvering thrusters, Sulu eased them away from the tail of the big starship, starting a leisurely circuit of the dry dock. "It looks like there are plenty of workbee ports along the orbital platform." He nodded to the closest bay as they drifted past. "Maybe we can park in the scaffolding and get across on the maintenance catwalks."

"And do what?" Chekov wanted to know. "Leave the cloaking device constantly engaged and hope no one tries to park a workbee on top of it? No, we have to put the Wraith in the docking bay if we're going to stay here."

Sulu shrugged and ducked the ship neatly under one of

the many long, transparent catwalk tubes. "Well, all I know is, we're not going to go in through the hangar doors."

Chekov twisted in his seat to watch the catwalks and hangar bay disappear behind them. "Maybe we are." He turned to Sulu again as they glided around the primary sensor shell. "Is there anything like an environmental suit on board this shuttle?"

Sulu glanced at him, frowning, then looked back up at the forward screen. "You're wearing it. The flightsuits won't withstand a vacuum forever, but they're designed to make do in case of an atmosphere breach. Why? What are you thinking?"

"I'm thinking," Chekov said, starting to feel out whatever atmosphere seals he could find on the second-hand flightsuit, "that Mr. Scott has been too busy to change the manual access procedures for the external bay doors. If we can key the bay to open from outside, it should be much easier to close it once we're inside."

Sulu busied himself with the pilot's controls for a moment, nudging the Wraith gently starboard, adjusting their attitude. "Look," he said at last, "I don't want to talk down to you, Pavel. But there's no way you'll be able to fly this thing, much less make a controlled landing with it in a confined docking space."

"I know." The thought of flying the Wraith had not even occurred to him. "That's why I'm going to be the one outside."

"Chekov, you're crazy! You can't even talk straight, much less handle a spacewalk."

"All the more reason why I shouldn't try to fly." He unlatched the copilot's shoulder strap, then slipped carefully out of his station so that Sulu wouldn't notice how hard it was for him to move. His friend didn't look particularly mollified.

"Hikaru, listen: If there's one thing I've learned from all this, it's that we survive or fail on our own. I'm not going to sit here until our atmosphere runs out, arguing about what we should or shouldn't do. Are you going to tell me how to open your airlock, or do I have to prove they teach us something in Security and override your command code?"

Sulu studied him for a long, quiet moment, then asked with no sign of rancor, "Can I give you just one piece of constructive advice?"

Chekov scowled at him. "What?"

"Hook up your air module before going outside." He yanked the package loose from under the console and offered it to Chekov with a smile. "Your suit will work better that way."

Silence.

Deep, eerie, bone-cold silence, the likes of which Chekov had never experienced before. Even a high-risk environmental suit journey involved a helmet communicator and sometimes the sounds of an on-board computer—he'd never been prisoner within a flimsy suit that didn't at least provide contact back to some relay. Now, he had only the deafening sound of his breathing against the face mask and the heavy *thud, thud, thud* of his heartbeat in his own ears. Neither sound struck him as particularly soothing, especially in conjunction with the other. He slipped along the welds that formed the tip of the Wraith's dorsal surface, then drifted slowly supine to walk hand over hand toward the wing.

He would never have tried this with anyone but Sulu at the controls. The slightest twitch, the slightest quiver, and Chekov would have found himself divested of any contact with the shuttle and imparted with just enough momentum to describe a pleasing arc before impacting with the outer atmosphere. Inertia was an evil thing when working in microgravity.

"I'm there." He said it uselessly, into the vacuum, as he rose up onto his knees at the angle of the wide, ribbed wing. It made him feel better to go through the motions of reporting to someone, to make believe someone could save him if he took a wrong step and headed Earthward. "I'm going to try and land on the shell door lip. That should give me some margin for error." How much margin wasn't really at issue. He would either make the leap or miss it—statistics beyond a certain point meant nothing.

Committing to the step only required the slightest tip of heel and toe. No drag against his flightsuit warned him. No sense of acceleration substituted for seeing the bay doors approach. He kept his eyes locked grimly on that tall, white expanse and counted down the seconds aloud until the instant before the doors passed inside his point of focus and he made contact.

The full-body impact blasted pain off his splayed fingertips and knocked him breathless in a short, explosive grunt. A banshee of panic screamed at him to flail. He smothered it, letting his body gently rebound until the contour of the hull in front of him drifted into reference, and he could reach down slowly, easily, calmly to grasp the external handhold to the left of the doors. After he'd pulled himself into position and slipped an arm through the grapple to anchor himself with one elbow, he relaxed and let the tremors take him.

The external controls sat not an arm's length from him, open, blinking, the edge of their inset housing crumpled as though someone had backed a workbee into it. Crooking his elbow more tightly through the grapple, he leaned to his left to punch the activation pad, and heaved a monstrous sigh of relief when it answered him with a bright green glow. Contacts and circuits closed with blessed smoothness, and he shoved the control rod forward as far as his fingers could push it. The ship beneath him seemed to rumble as the doors glided majestically open.

Shivering, the inside of his flightsuit now chilly with sweat, Chekov clung to the outside grapple with both hands and watched Sulu swing the Wraith into position. He threaded the bay doors like silk through a needle;

Chekov could have touched the black surface when it passed, and felt the solid *boom* of the Wraith's clean landing. Feeling for a grip around the edge of the half-open doors, Chekov abandoned his perch with but the tiniest push, drifting inside to let the artificial gravity take him.

He landed with a silent thump on the inside lip of the hangar bay. The ship felt good, and real, and solid—the Wraith looked proper stashed away inside this alcove, and the reapplication of gravity reminded him shrewishly that he hadn't had painkillers since leaving McCoy in Delmarva. If he didn't need to walk the whole long length of the bay to operate the inside door controls, he could have stayed here forever, enjoying the relative merits of simply sitting down.

Chekov didn't notice the doors trundle closed behind him, but he noticed the growing pressure of atmosphere on the outside of his suit, the gradual blossom of sound in the hangar bay around him. Looking up, he registered Sulu, poised in the Wraith's open doorway with his face a mask of horrified surprise, just before a booming Scottish voice rang out, "Well, speak o' the devil, and he shall appear."

Montgomery Scott ducked into sight around the nose of the uncloaked spacecraft, hands on his hips and a paternal scowl on his Gaelic features. "It seems you lads got here just in time. If half of what Uhura tells me is true, you've both got a lot of explaining to do."

The Wraith II shuttle chattered to itself as it cooled, steam rising off its ribbed black hull inside the chill, humid air of the docking bay. Sulu vaulted out through the open hatch, looking for the source of the voices that had hailed them. He saw Commander Scott's burly figure first; then the slighter shadow of Uhura slipped around the engineer and came to greet them. She was wearing a blue medical tunic instead of her usual uniform, but her smile was as bright as a fire on a winter night.

"How on earth did you two know to come here?" she demanded, catching Chekov's gloved hands between hers and squeezing hard.

The Russian didn't reply, looking as if the task of undoing his silver flightsuit, latch by careful latch, was all his mind and muscles could manage for the moment. Now that his hood and faceplate were off, Sulu could see that Chekov's face was haggard with exhaustion, frost-pale except for where a blasting wind had chapped it red across his cheeks and nose.

"We didn't know." Sulu shed his protective flightsuit with the ease of long practice, then went to help Chekov wrestle the rest of his suit off. Beneath the metallic fabric, the Russian was soaked to the skin and shuddering. "The *Enterprise* was just the only place we could think to go that wouldn't be swarming with security guards. Mr. Scott, are there any emergency medical kits in here?"

"Aye, lad." The engineer ran a knowing eye over the skeletal girders that constituted the *Enterprise's* new docking bay. "We have to keep a wee kit in each sector for the workers. Ah, here it is." He hauled up one of the heavy steel plates on the floor with ease, and extracted a medical kit from below.

Sulu took the case and rummaged in it, finding one hypospray for shock and another that contained a metabolic stimulant. Chekov sat and watched with vague detachment while Uhura rolled up the sweater sleeve over his left arm and Sulu pressed both hypos to his skin. The unwelcoming chill of the *Enterprise* seemed to be making the Russian's shivering worse instead of better.

"That lad needs to be somewhere a whole lot warmer than here," Commander Scott said, sizing up the situation with his usual blunt practicality, then putting his analysis into action by the simple expedient of stooping and lifting Chekov into his arms. "Get a thermal blanket or two outside of him and some piping-hot food inside, and he'll do."

"Yeah." Sulu followed Uhura and the burly engineer

out of the docking bay and down one rough hall. Welded plates of steel and aluminum stuck out at odd angles along the way, draped with tangles of fiber-optic cables and insulated bundles of superconducting power lines. Sulu felt his stomach clench, a feeling almost akin to pain. He'd seen other ships in this half-completed phase, of course, but somehow it felt different seeing it happen to the *Enterprise*. It was hard to believe that anything could be built in this seeming chaos, much less a top-of-the-line starship.

Mr. Scott ducked under a low beam and turned down another half-finished corridor. Sulu frowned as he took his bearings. "Is this the way back to the orbital platform?"

"No. We don't dare take you lads over there." Scott turned down another, more smoothly finished hallway. "There's naught a soul officially up on the platform now but me and Uhura, and the computer will be sure to notice that there's two more life-forms aboard than should be. We'll be safer staying here."

"But there's no place warm enough here," Uhura said worriedly.

"There's one place." Scott paused before a sealed door and palmed its lock. Lights automatically brightened inside when the door slid open, and a reassuring warmth floated out to meet them. "Auxiliary sickbay. We had to finish it first and gave it full life-support, in case of a construction accident."

"Thank God for safety regulations." Sulu helped maneuver Chekov over to one of the examination tables. The Russian sank down on it with a groan, while Uhura bent to tap the diagnostic panel and bring it humming to life.

"We need to find out what's wrong with you," she told Chekov when he rolled a suspicious eye toward her. The antishock medication must be kicking in, Sulu thought in amusement. Chekov now looked more grumpy than vague. "Hold still."

The overhead medical computer probed at the figure beneath it with ultrasonic whispers and a shimmer of laser light. "Patient has ulnar-radial fracture of the right arm, sustained approximately seventy hours ago," it reported at once. "Patient has also suffered severe exposure to cold, and is both undernourished and slightly dehydrated. Recommended primary treatment: acoustic stimulation to reduce posttrauma swelling followed by carbon-resin casting of right arm. Recommended secondary treatment: oral intake of hot fluids and nutrients, external application of insulating materials, prolonged bed rest."

"There, didn't I tell you?" Scott had already dug silvery thermal blankets out of a storage compartment. He handed them to Sulu, while Uhura went to pull out one medical equipment drawer after another. "I'll just jog over to the orbital platform and bring back a portable food synthesizer, and we'll have Chekov shipshape in no time."

The engineer ducked back out into the hallway, letting in a clammy shiver of air while the door opened and shut. Sulu shook out one of the insulating blankets and laid it over Chekov's legs, then wrapped another across his chest and torso, carefully sliding it under the broken arm to leave it accessible for treatment. By the time Sulu began shaking out a third blanket, Chekov had recovered enough strength to scowl at him.

"What's that for?" the Russian demanded.

"Your head." Sulu arranged the last blanket to cover Chekov's damp hair and shoulders. "Don't you know you lose most of your body heat through your head?"

Chekov's eyes narrowed in an increasingly irritated frown. "That doesn't mean you need to wrap me in a turban." He jerked his head away when Sulu tried to tuck the tail of blanket under his chin. "That's enough!"

"You must be feeling better—you're getting grumpy." Sulu anchored all the blankets along the sides and bottom of the bed, turning it into a silver cocoon. "I probably ought to bounce a coin off you to be sure I tucked these in tight enough. . . ."

"Try it, and I'll bounce *you!*"

"What are you two fighting about now?" Uhura scurried back to the examination table with a pen-sized medical device. A smile crinkled her dark eyes as she took in Chekov's blanket-wrapped figure. "You look just like an egg roll."

"Thanks. Does that mean you're going to cut me up with chopsticks?" The Russian was definitely feeling better. He sounded hoarse but alert, and Sulu noticed that a pale tinge of color had begun to warm his waxy face.

"No, I'm going to use this acoustic stimulator on your arm and get the swelling down." Uhura paused beside the bed. "We'll have to take the splint off to get at the swelling," she said uncertainly. "Sulu, do you think you could? . . ."

Sulu winced, but bent over the plastic splint, running careful fingers across its binding straps. "Did Dr. McCoy melt these things shut?"

Chekov shook his head. "I think there's a release tab at the top."

Sulu grunted and slid his hand up along the splint. "I can't find—oh, there it is." Something popped and the plastic straps that held the sides of the splint together sprang free. Chekov gritted out a Russian curse, but managed to hold his arm rigidly still while Sulu and Uhura unwrapped the rest of the splint. Uhura flicked on the acoustic stimulation pen and began to move it slowly across the multicolor bruises that splattered Chekov's arm.

Sulu reached out and swung a desk chair across the aisle, then sprawled in it tiredly to watch. "Exactly how did you do this to yourself?" he asked Chekov.

The Russian let out a grunt that at another time might have been laughter. "I hit someone—too hard," he said between stiffly held breaths. "And not in the right place.

It's easy to break a bone—in unarmed combat. Especially when you don't know what you're doing."

It sounded like a passage recited from a class at the Security Academy, colored faintly bitter by experience. Sulu frowned, noticing that some of the marks on Chekov's arm were more faded than others, and that they extended far past the actual area of the break.

"And what about the rest of these bruises?" he inquired. "How did you get those?"

Chekov tried to shrug one-armed, then winced. "One of my classmates gave me those. The same one who killed Dr. Piper."

"One of your classmates killed Piper?" Sulu groaned and fell backward in his chair. "Don't tell me a security cadet is behind this whole plot!"

"No, he was just the hired gun. There were two others involved up at Hopkins. Peter Broad and Yolande Stern. Lab technicians."

"Huh." Sulu swung himself back to a sitting position, thinking about that. "Lab technicians and security guards at your end—and I have no idea who at my end, except that it *wasn't* Hernan Nakai." He reached out and tapped at the plas-skin bandage visible under the sleeve of Uhura's borrowed medical tunic. She jumped a little, as if the skin underneath were still tender. "And what happened to you? That bandage didn't come from wrapping too many Christmas presents."

"Dr. McCoy got attacked by a remote firebomb at the Stanford maglev terminal," she said briefly. "I was standing next to him." She saw their worried looks and added, "He's all right, and safe in intensive care. Christine Chapel promised not to let anyone in his room unless she knew them personally, and I sent Dr. M'Benga down to Stanford to help her guard him. But Starfleet Security hasn't arrested anyone for the firebombing yet."

Chekov snorted. "Of course not. Whoever these people are, they have someone in Starfleet Security in their pocket."

"And someone at White Sands, too." Sulu's frown had become a scowl. "Dammit, I hate to think that career Starfleet officers can be bought that easily!"

"I know. I wish Admiral Kirk was back. Right now, he's the only superior officer I trust." Uhura finished running the acoustic stimulation device over Chekov's arm.

Sulu cocked an eyebrow at her. "Chekov said the admiral was in the hospital, too. Can't we just go talk to him?"

Uhura sighed as she went to search sickbay for the equipment they needed to cast Chekov's arm. "He's not in the hospital—that's just the story he told his secretary to tell everyone. He took off this morning in a high-speed courier with Ambassador Sarek, saying he knew how to get some proof against the traitors. I don't even know where he was going." She stopped in front of some clear shelving, her face a frustrated reflection in the transparent aluminum. "And not three hours after he left, Dr. McCoy got the evidence we needed from Dr. Piper!"

"Evidence?" Sulu demanded.

"Dr. Piper?" Chekov demanded simultaneously.

Uhura glanced back over her shoulder at them, looking startled. "Didn't I tell you—no, of course not, we haven't had time. The reason Dr. McCoy came out to California was to tell me that Dr. Piper had shipped some sort of evidence about the disruptor theft up to the *Enterprise.*"

"Where is it?" This time, Chekov's and Sulu's voices chimed together urgently.

"I don't know!" Uhura turned to face them, her voice rising, as if the stress of the last few days had finally broken through her rigid control. "Dr. McCoy said it was in a package, but Mr. Scott says there isn't any cargo aboard. I can't even guess where to look for it. How am I supposed to find anything in this mess?" She threw her hands wide, helplessly. "I can't even find Chekov a resin-casting machine!"

Sulu made a wordless, reassuring sound and came to help her. "There's the resin-caster," he said, drawing her attention up to the top shelf of the equipment case and the familiar curving silhouette of the medical device. "Go get a cart, and we'll bring it over to Chekov, okay?"

"Okay." Uhura dabbed at her eyes surreptitiously before going to pull a cart from across the room.

Sulu loaded the resin-caster onto it, then patted at Uhura's hand. "See, don't worry. If we can find this, we can find McCoy's package too. It only seems impossible now because we're tired and sick and hungry. When was the last time you ate?"

Uhura managed a quivering smile. "Actually, about an hour ago." Sulu gave her an aggrieved look, and her smile grew more real. "At the Starfleet Christmas party. I had salmon in puff pastry, baked Brie, and steamed shrimp."

Sulu groaned, pretending to collapse against the cart while he rolled it across to Chekov. "You rat! While poor Chekov was starving and I was eating emergency rations out of the Wraith!"

"I hadn't eaten much the day before that, when I thought you guys were dead!" Uhura defended herself. She watched Sulu position the resin-caster as low as it could go over Chekov's torso, then carefully helped the Russian slide his arm into it. The machine hummed to life immediately. Chekov yelped out another curse when it began processing his injury, but Sulu noticed his face didn't whiten with pain this time. The analgesics in the antishock hypospray must have finally made it into his system.

"Maybe the food synthesizer will be able to make some steamed shrimp and salmon for us." Sulu looked up as the door slid open on a puff of cold air and let in Commander Scott, a miniature food synthesizer riding easily on his broad shoulder. "Do you think your synthesizer can make seafood, Mr. Scott?"

Uhura regarded the little box dubiously. "I'm not sure something that small can make *any* real food. Can it, Mr. Scott?"

"Well, I know it can make haggis." The engineer straightened up, grinning at them crookedly. "I just don't know if that qualifies as food."

Chapter Sixteen

U.S.S. Enterprise
Earth Sector, Standard Earth Orbit
Terrestrial Date: December 24, 2269
2000 hours shiptime

THE VIEW FROM the *Enterprise* was beautiful. As always.

Chekov stood as close as he dared to the transparent aluminum airlock, carefully avoiding all the moorings and temporary seals as he watched the last wink of Sol's corona disappear into the black of the southern Pacific Rim. Nighttime closed across North America like a sigh.

A fairy dusting of cities rimed the edges of the continent, twinkling from the bottom of the atmosphere like chips of Spican flame gem. Roads and maglev paths intersected top to bottom, shore to shore, until the landmass seemed to pulse and breathe with the lifeblood of a thousand sparkling arteries. A million kilometers away from that beauty, Chekov could almost imagine that every fleck of twinkle and color represented the strings of lights so popular in the yards and houses of North America at this time of year. So different from the quiet ice sculpture and window paintings of Russia. Still, it made for a better holiday experience than hiding in the secondary hull of a gutted starship, waiting for his career—and maybe even his life—to come to an end.

"There you are."

Chekov glanced briefly over his shoulder, incapable of

feeling startled by the helmsman's arrival. On a ship so empty and distant from everything, it was hard to believe anyone unexpected would appear.

"Uhura and Mr. Scott are trying to get something foodlike out of the synthesizer," Sulu volunteered as he padded up to stand beside him. "You have any requests?"

Chekov shrugged and turned back to the planet. "At this point, anything warm would be fine."

"Okay." Sulu rose up on curious tiptoe, pressing one hand carefully to the transparent portal. "So what're you doing out here?"

"Looking for Moscow."

"Uh, Chekov . . ." Something very like amusement fluttered in Sulu's voice. "We're in geosync over North America."

Chekov spread his hand beside Sulu's on the cold, transparent barrier. "I know."

"Oh." Sulu shifted to lean his back against the last finished segment of hallway, stealing a look down the skeletal framework that stretched out ahead of the airlock, then looking resolutely spaceward again, as though the sight of the unfinished ship made him uneasy. "This isn't what I intended to do with my holiday, either," he admitted after a long, companionable silence. "I was kind of looking forward to a nice, rainy weekend in California with nothing better to do than wander around Sausalito looking for expensive restaurants."

Chekov shrugged one shoulder, then abandoned his view and turned to Sulu. "At least you were going to get to go home."

"That's true." Sulu reached across to clap Chekov's shoulder with a sigh. It made a pitifully wet slapping sound, and the helmsman recoiled fussily. "I'll tell you what," he said around a theatrical grimace. "We've got a little while before the food's ready. Why don't you let me see what I can do about curing those holiday blues?" He fingered the front of Chekov's sweater and wrinkled his nose clear up to his forehead. "I think I've just figured out the perfect Christmas present for you this year."

"Somehow, this isn't what I thought you had in mind."

Sulu glanced up from rummaging through Scott's open bureau, his face alight with that blend of mirth and mischief that marked the helmsman at his most vexatious. "Then consider it your Christmas gift to me and Uhura. I feel I can speak for both of us when I tell you we have no intention of sleeping in any sickbay with *anyone* who smells the way you do right now. *Don't sit on that!*"

Chekov leapt to his feet before even making contact with the chair, and ended up halfway across the small dry-dock quarters before stopping to fix Sulu with a punishing glare. "You made me walk through every corridor and catwalk between here and the ship," he complained. "You flew me through a hurricane! The least you can do is give me a chance to sit down."

"And you're stealing Mr. Scott's clothes," Sulu reminded him. "The least you can do is not get ocean smell all over his furniture." He stood with a tunic and trousers draped across either shoulder and crossed the room to throw them both onto the bed. "Strip down, Ensign—that's an order. I am going to throw out your current apparel. You are going to take a shower."

"Mr. Scott and I are not even slightly the same size." But he dragged the heavy sweater over his head before Sulu could yell at him again.

Sulu took the sweater from him and dropped it primly behind him. "Are Mr. Scott's clothes dry?"

"I assume so." Chekov tossed the turtleneck on top of the sweater.

"Do they smell bad?"

"No."

Sulu kicked the whole filthy pile toward the open cabin door. "Then the size is close enough. Go get in the shower."

Whether or not stealing Mr. Scott's clothes was the best idea Sulu ever had, Chekov thought, the shower more than made up for it. He stood under the pounding spray, almost tumbling into sleep as the heat and steam and vibration scoured the salt scum from his body and worked their magic on his beleaguered sinuses. If he could have spent the night in the shower, he would have. As it was, he settled for a scaldingly decadent twenty minutes, then stumbled out into the humid lavatory and toweled himself dry for as long as was reasonably possible.

The clothes, as he'd expected, didn't fit.

"I'm going to be arrested for impersonating an officer." He tried rolling up the tunic cuffs, but the gold commander's stripes kept getting in the way.

"Hell, they already want to arrest you for treason." Sulu slipped off his belt and held it out for Chekov's taking when it became apparent the trousers would never stay up on their own. "You might as well be dressed as snappily as possible when they get you."

The Russian told himself wryly that at least the engineer's tunic was red.

The hike back to the sickbay only seemed to take half as long as the journey out had. Chekov wondered if he was simply better disposed toward walking without twenty kilos of waterlogged sweater weighing him down or if Sulu had looked up some better route while he was fighting off sleep in the shower. Whatever the answer, they made it back to the better-insulated starship corridors while Chekov was still trying to finger-comb order into his wet hair, and the warm, simple odor of replicated rations wafted out to greet them. His stomach twisted around itself as a reminder of how long he'd gone without food.

Uhura looked up from one of the workstations as they entered, her hands stretched out in front of her so she could balance a motley assortment of cups, bowls, and platters on her arms. "Where's Mr. Scott?" Sulu asked as he hurried forward to take over half her burden.

"Down in the shuttle bay. He said he wanted to make

sure Kyle serviced all the Wraith's systems correctly before letting you leave Tasmania." She smiled and rearranged the dishes into three equal assemblies. "Personally, I think he just wanted to get a closer look at how the Wraith goes together."

"Who can blame him? It's not like you get to see a lot of Wraith shuttles on a starship."

"Very true." Uhura settled into one of the chairs around the workstation, raising a playful smile to Chekov as he came to steal a glance at what foodstuffs she'd collected. "So, Sulu, who's this handsome, sweet-smelling young fellow you've brought back with you?"

Chekov scowled sidelong at her, blushing, and Sulu laughed as he dropped into a chair of his own. "I picked him up over on the orbital platform. He claims he used to work here."

"Does he?"

Chekov tipped one of the bowls of food, aware from long experience that the best way to avoid their bouts of teasing was to ignore them. "Did you replicate this food for us to look at, or can we start to eat now?"

"You can start to eat if you want to." Uhura sat forward in her chair and tapped with weary skepticism at his bowl. "Just don't hold me accountable for what you might find."

Chekov lifted the bowl, sniffed at it, and shrugged. "It looks like food. It smells like food. It's better than anything else I've had lately." At least he was fairly certain nothing out of a replicator could kill him.

"What's this?" Sulu thrust out the steaming mug in his hand accusingly.

Uhura didn't even glance at it. "I think it's supposed to be gazpacho."

"It's warm!"

"I said, 'I think.'"

"And this?" Chekov asked. Whatever it was, it smelled deliciously like cabbage.

"Salad." But she didn't sound completely certain.

Sulu, on the other hand, was scandalized. "It's cole-slaw!"

"I *like* coleslaw," Chekov protested. Sulu shoved the bowl across to him without further comment.

"And then we have tortellini with"—Uhura angled an anxious frown into another of the dishes—"some kind of red sauce."

Chekov had to take only one bite to solve the mystery. "Ketchup."

That earned him both their bowls, and a strangled sound of disgust from Sulu. "But what are you two going to eat now?" Chekov asked, feeling a little guilty. "Don't tell me you both like haggis."

"We," Uhura said with a sly lift of her eyebrows, "get to eat dessert." She cradled a clear glass goblet in the palm of her hand and offered it grandly across the workstation to Sulu. It looked as though it were filled with wet breadsticks and milk. "Tiramisù."

"*Tiramisù?* Out of *this* piece of junk?" Sweeping up the tiny goblet, Sulu clutched it to his chest and raised eyes skyward. "There *is* a God."

It still looked like soggy bread to Chekov. "What's tiramisù?"

"A disgustingly rich dessert made with ladyfingers, espresso, mascarpone cheese, and rum."

He grimaced and pushed the dessert over to Sulu, then nodded his permission to Uhura when she stole his warm gazpacho. The coleslaw and tortellini didn't complement each other as well as Chekov might have expected, but after nearly seventy-two hours of nothing really solid to eat, he didn't feel much like complaining. When Sulu finally lowered himself to steal a few tortellini from the one remaining bowl between them, Chekov climbed away from the table to refill the empty water pitcher.

"Is it just me," Sulu asked after a moment, "or is this really pitiful?"

Chekov clunked the refilled pitcher back into the center of the workstation. "It's not just you."

Uhura sighed at the bottom of her tiramisù glass, but didn't offer a contradictory opinion.

"I had a lot of time to think on the way to Tasmania," Sulu said. He dropped his fork into the bowl with a clatter. "I couldn't imagine why anyone would want to do this to us, what they could possibly hope to accomplish by getting us blamed for such horrible acts of treason. Then somewhere around Fiji I realized that this wasn't about us at all—it was about the one thing Chekov and I had in common."

Chekov picked up Sulu's fork to scrape the last of the food out of the bowl. "Admiral Kirk."

"We were both part of the admiral's command crew." Sulu leaned back in his chair to prop his feet tiredly on the edge of the table. "I don't know why, but I think the traitors are trying to discredit Admiral Kirk through us. Maybe they're planning to manufacture evidence that he put us up to the thefts, or maybe they just planned to let rumor and innuendo do the dirty work after we'd been tried and convicted. Either way, the admiral's career is ruined along with ours."

"But how could the traitors have counted on you both being assigned to projects this sensitive?" Uhura objected. "I mean, *you* were already assigned as executive officer on the *Resolution* before the *Enterprise* even got back into port."

"True, but I turned down that assignment as soon as I was offered the spot on the Wraith project. Someone had to have submitted my name to the project planners, then monitored whether or not I accepted."

"But Dr. Piper didn't invite me onto the disruptor project until the last minute," Chekov pointed out. "They couldn't have known he would do that."

"They probably planned on blaming Dr. Piper in the beginning," Uhura said. "You were just a more convenient scapegoat once you signed onto the research team."

Sulu gave a snort of laughter and poked at Chekov. "What she's saying is, if you'd gone off to Command

School like you were supposed to, you wouldn't be in this mess right now."

Chekov pulled his arm away from Sulu's prodding, suddenly disgusted with the whole discussion. "And if you'd taken the assignment on board the *Resolution,* you wouldn't be in this mess, either." It came out more harshly than he'd intended, and that only made him feel worse. "Don't criticize my decisions."

"Hey, Pavel . . ." Sulu pulled his feet down to straighten himself in his chair. "It was just a joke. I'm sorry."

"Well, it's a joke I'm tired of hearing. What difference does it make to you what division I go into?" He stacked the empty dishes into uneven towers at the center of the table. "Can't I make this one decision on my own, without everyone feeling they have to second-guess me?"

"It's just . . ." Sulu tried to help, but aborted his cleanup when Chekov snatched the small stack of dishes from his hands. "Command School was all you talked about for the last three months of our mission. I guess we all just assumed that's where you'd be while we were in dock."

"Well, I'm not! All right?" He swept their debris into an armload and stood to stalk away from the table.

"They turned down your application."

He froze, staring at Uhura in an agony of betrayal, wishing none of this had ever come up, wishing he could just turn around and walk away. Apology sparkled in her wide, regretful eyes, but she'd clapped a hand over her mouth an instant too late to stop the damning sentence. No one had told her, Chekov realized. She'd simply guessed, and blurted out what to her seemed an impossible answer. He wasn't surprised to find he couldn't force himself to feel angry about the innocent blunder.

Sulu finally broke the silent impasse. "They didn't let you in?" He turned in his seat to look up at Chekov, and the ensign retreated to the dish recycler to avoid having to meet his friend's gaze. "You've got to be kidding! *Why?*"

"My . . . age," he said carefully as he fed the dishes one by one into the chute. Actually, the rejection had made specific, stinging references to his "maturity." But he couldn't make himself admit that to them out loud. "The command board didn't feel I was ready for the responsibility of Command School. Maybe with a little more 'seasoning,' they said, I might be ready to reapply in another four or five years." Almost a quarter of his lifetime. A frustrating, private eternity.

"It's not as bad as it could be." Uhura meant well, he knew, but her gentle words sounded painfully like condescension. "You *are* awfully young—you've got plenty of time to reapply."

He smiled mirthlessly into the bank of machinery in front of him. "Admiral Kirk was a year younger than I am when he was accepted into Command School."

"Yeah," Sulu agreed. "But we aren't all Admiral Kirk."

Was it worth trying to explain how badly he had wanted to be?

Uhura saved him from having to pursue the question. "But why *security?*" she asked, obviously fighting against whatever private prejudices she held inside. "There are so many other positions that would have made better use of your talents."

He sighed and leaned one shoulder against the recycler. "When I was on the *Enterprise,* I always respected and . . ." He had to think for a moment to excavate the proper English word. ". . . *appreciated* the strength and dedication needed to function in security. In so many ways, a security chief is as responsible for a starship's crew as her captain. I thought maybe . . ." That it would be the next best thing to actually having a command. That it would feel useful and meaningful to a starship's functions, in a way navigating never truly had. That it would reveal something of the maturity the Starfleet review board was so certain he lacked. "I thought the experience of leading a security division might give me the edge I need when I reapply five years from now."

"So you're pretty sure you'll get another starship tour after the Security Academy?" Sulu asked, sounding hopeful.

Chekov smiled in appreciation of his friend's concern, then realized the irony of standing here when he told them this. "I already have another five-year assignment on board the *Enterprise*."

Sulu blinked as though unsure how to process this information, and Uhura blossomed into a radiant smile. "Assuming, of course," Chekov added with a hopeless shrug, "that any of us has a career left by the time this is over."

The distant hiss of the sickbay door woke Uhura the next morning, bringing her from restless slumber to tense wakefulness in a few seconds. She jerked up on the examination table that served as her bed and tried to listen for voices coming around the curve of auxiliary sickbay. After a moment, her sleep-fuzzed brain recognized the soft burr of Commander Scott's voice, answered by Sulu's deeper murmur. Sighing in relief, Uhura hopped down and went to comb her hair and wash her face in their small bathroom.

She emerged into the part of the room where the others had slept, in time to see Mr. Scott knit his face into a familiar expression of beleaguered worry. "But, lad, we've had *thousands* of deliveries over the last few weeks," he told Sulu, pulling a cup of hot coffee from the small food synthesizer. Chekov still lay asleep behind them, tangled like a puppy in his thermal blankets. The engineer kept his voice considerably hushed. "If ye dinna know what kind of shipment it was . . ."

Uhura glanced down at the chronometer on her wrist and her eyebrows shot upward. It was only 4 A.M. Pacific time. No wonder she still felt sleepy.

"Why have we started looking for Dr. Piper's package

so early?" she asked plaintively. The date on her watch reminded her what day it was and she added, "Santa Claus hasn't even come yet."

Sulu glanced over his shoulder at her with a rueful smile. "We were both too tense to sleep," he confessed, then tipped his steaming cup toward her. "Tea or coffee?"

"Hot chocolate." Uhura came to join them beside the food synthesizer, finding it, with the warmth of its waste heat emissions, almost as soothing as a kitchen stove. "If this little monster can manage it, that is."

"I'll make it manage." Scott leaned over the control panel, scowled when he couldn't find an appropriate button, then punched an access code directly into the synthesizer's memory. A moment later, a cup of steaming cocoa emerged from the tiny interior.

"So that's the trick." Uhura accepted the cup with a smile. "You have to know its secret machine language."

"The benefit of being an engineer, lass." Scott drank his coffee thoughtfully. "That, and getting to stay up here on the *Enterprise* while the rest of you get yourselves into trouble down on Earth."

Sulu made a wry face, then turned to Uhura. "Did Dr. McCoy give you any idea at all what kind of package Dr. Piper sent up here?"

"I don't think so." Uhura closed her eyes, trying to recall her hurried conversation with McCoy. The shock of the firebomb had blurred most of her memories. "All I remember him saying was that Piper sent a package with evidence about who the traitors were up to the *Enterprise.* He never said how or from where."

"Well, the one thing I can tell ye is that it didn't come from Johns Hopkins University." Scott took a step down the counter and swung a medical computer terminal around on its revolving pivot. It came to life at the brush of his fingers across the screen, its control menus flickering past as the engineer worked his way into the ship's main network. He finally pulled up what looked like a standard stocking chart, and punched in a brief command. "See? We've had no shipments received here from Johns Hopkins, ever."

"Then it must have come from somewhere else." Sulu laced his fingers around the hot tea, his face taking on the Buddha-like inscrutability that meant he was thinking hard. "The problem is, we don't know what other Starfleet suppliers Piper might have had access to. Have any shipments at all come up from the Baltimore area?"

Mr. Scott punched another command into the computer and grimaced. "No. The closest supplier we've used is in upstate New York."

Uhura blew the steam from her cocoa and sipped at it cautiously. "So much for that."

"All right, let's try a different approach." Sulu hadn't given up yet. "If we could figure out exactly when that package was sent up here—"

"—we could find the list of shipments it might be inside. Aye, that could work." Scott pulled up a different menu. "The computer's already got deliveries sorted out by date and time. All we need is an initial and final bracket, and we can look at what falls inside the window."

Uhura frowned. "Well, I guess the final bracket would be when Piper died. That would have been about noon last Friday."

Scott lifted a bushy eyebrow at them. "And the initial bracket?"

"That's harder." Uhura exchanged thoughtful looks with Sulu. "Maybe when we met him at Harborplace? Surely he wouldn't have asked Chekov to come work for him if he'd known there was something wrong at the lab—"

A snort from the examination table behind them stopped Uhura. "That's exactly why he asked me to come," Chekov informed them gruffly. He managed to untangle himself from the thermal blankets and sat up on the edge of the bed, steadying himself with his good arm.

"He wanted me to help him prove that Peter Broad was a spy."

Uhura rubbed at the frown line she could feel forming between her eyebrows. "Then he could have sent the evidence up to the *Enterprise* anytime this month!"

"Possible, but unlikely." Chekov maneuvered himself off the medical bed with care. "Can I have some coffee?"

"Not if you're going to talk like Mr. Spock," Sulu complained, but he punched the coffee button obediently. "Why's it so unlikely?"

"Because I don't think Piper thought there was much of a threat, at least not before the day he got killed." Chekov came over and accepted the cup Sulu handed him. "My guess is that he sent the evidence up here early that morning. As a sort of . . . insurance."

Uhura glanced at Scott, waiting patiently at the computer. "That would have been Friday, December twenty-first," she told him. "Sometime between zero hundred hours and twelve hundred hours, Eastern Standard Time."

Scott punched in the appropriate codes and waited while the computer compiled its list. Even from her place by the food synthesizer, Uhura could see that the final menu produced was mostly blank. The engineer looked up at them with somber eyes.

"Sorry, gentlemen," he said. "There was nothing at all shipped up to the *Enterprise* on that date."

Chekov frowned. "Try the day before."

Scott queried the computer, then shook his head again. "All that came up that day were the segments of the new Jeffries tubes. In fact, now that I remember it, that was about all that came up that whole week."

They sat in silence over their cooling drinks, faces grim with frustration. After several long minutes, Scott sighed and tapped up another menu. "May as well check the refitting schedule while we think," he said glumly.

"Or don't think. I'm out of ideas." With his usual restless curiosity, Sulu leaned to read over the engineer's shoulder. "'Replace shielding circuits in the primary hull'? But I thought the primary was getting refitted down on Earth."

"Aye, so it is," Scott agreed. "But I'm still the chief supervising engineer, so all the scheduling and completion packets get transmitted up to me every day—"

"Packets!" The word broke from Chekov's and Uhura's lips at the same moment. They exchanged looks of growing understanding, but Chekov put it into words first. "What if Piper told McCoy he sent a *packet* of evidence—"

"—and McCoy translated that into *package,* because he got a package from Piper—" Uhura continued.

"—so we assumed it had to be a physical object, rather than a subspace mail message!" Sulu finished for them both.

Chekov looked a question at Mr. Scott. "Now that the main computer's engaged, could anyone on Earth send subspace mail up to it?"

"Anyone who could get through to the Starfleet net," Scott confirmed. "Could your Dr. Piper do that?"

"I'm sure he could," Uhura said when Chekov hesitated. "After all, he was working on a Starfleet research project."

"But the Starfleet net is monitored by Starfleet Security," Sulu pointed out, frowning. "They'd have seen whatever Piper sent."

Chekov let out a vehement Russian curse. "In which case, his transmission probably never even got here!"

"No." Uhura shook her head. "Dr. McCoy said Piper *had* sent his message, which means he must have gotten confirmation of its arrival—"

"Dr. McCoy also said it was a package," Chekov pointed out gloomily.

"Yes, but there are other nets Piper could have used." Uhura had a sudden brilliant memory of Christine Chapel and Admiral Kirk sitting in her office, Chapel saying, "So he sent the message on the medical net, coded as a confidential patient file," and Kirk saying, "Good work, Bones!"

"Mr. Scott—" Uhura swung around with such fierce intensity that the engineer's eyebrows beetled upward. "Can you call up medical files on this computer?"

"I should hope so, lass. It's the sickbay computer, after all."

"Then check to see if there were any data packets received through the medical net on December twenty-first."

Scott's fingers drummed against the screen, tapping through a cascade of menus. He grunted, finally arriving at the one he wanted. "Well, I'll be a Welshman's uncle!" He grinned and pointed at the screen.

For the date of December 21, the medical net log read, "One data packet received, contents encoded patient file for James Tiberius Kirk."

"That's it!" Sulu crowed with laughter. "That's got to be it!"

"But can we access it?" Chekov demanded.

Scott tapped at the screen, then growled as the file stayed stubbornly closed. "Not until we convince this damned computer that I'm the chief physician of the *Enterprise.* Wait a minute." He tapped back to the main menu and typed in some arcane code, then flicked back to the medical net. The file labeled "James Tiberius Kirk" was now flashing its accessibility.

"Open it," said Uhura, Chekov, and Sulu in unison.

Scott tapped the screen a final time, and the file blossomed out into a scroll of words. All of them leaned close around the engineer's broad shoulders, reading in tense silence.

Piper's written message was blunt and to the point. It read: "Peter Broad came with attached security clearance and technical certification from project backer UniMed, Inc. Certification is provably false, but the signature and thumbprint of chief operating officer verified as authentic. I think UniMed wants the disruptor."

Sulu groaned. "Some evidence! Now we know a company name, but not who at the company is responsible."

"Wait, there's more." Scott paged down to an electronic replica of a Starfleet security clearance, and then once more to what looked like some sort of technical certificate.

"There's a name." Uhura pointed. "The name of UniMed's chief operating—" Her voice broke off abruptly.

For at the bottom, below the impressed seals and fancy Latinate writing, was the strong, straightforward signature of Jackson Kahle.

Chapter Seventeen

U.S.S. Enterprise
Earth Sector, Standard Earth Orbit
Terrestrial Date: December 25, 2269
0700 hours shiptime

"Jackson Kahle?" Chekov blurted, and realized Uhura had echoed him when Sulu and Scott fixed them both with questioning frowns.

"You know him?" Sulu asked.

"He's a former starship captain," Uhura explained with a dumbfounded nod. "The one who founded UniPhase Incorporated. He—he audited my class at the Academy this semester." She lifted her eyes from the screen at last. "But I can't believe he'd ever betray Starfleet!"

"The man who practically invented starship phaser banks?" Scott snorted a noise of utter skepticism, then peered again at the signature on the technical certificate. "You're right, lass. It canna be him behind all this!"

Chekov glanced above the signature and felt his heart fall into his stomach. "Yes, it can." He pointed to the company name at the top of the brief document. "UniMed. That's obviously some sort of subsidiary of UniPhase Incorporated. If it's also the company that was funding Dr. Piper's disruptor research program, as it says here—"

"Kahle could have set the whole project up just to get

his hands on the Klingon disruptor!" Sulu clapped both hands to the top of his head, as though overwhelmed by the thoughts whirling around inside. "But why would he want it? What good would it do him?"

Uhura brought one hand to her mouth in shocked realization. "He plans to sell it to the Romulans." She glanced up at the startled looks around her. "Admiral Kirk told me Jackson Kahle had been instrumental in arranging the Romulan Territorial Conference that's taking place at Annapolis tomorrow. If he really is responsible for stealing the disruptor, the timing is too close to be a coincidence. He must be planning to give it to them there."

"But why would anyone turn over technology like that to enemies of the Federation?" Chekov protested.

"Because he wants them to use it on other enemies of the Federation." Scott stated the suggestion with grim certainty. "You wouldna know," he explained in answer to Chekov's questioning frown, "being stationed down below like you are, but there's been a lot of talk in the space nets about hostilities between the Klingons and the Romulans. There's already been a handful of skirmishes along their border. I'll bet your Mr. Kahle's hoping to help that war along."

"By giving the Romulans the Klingons' greatest weapon?" Another piece of information snapped into place with almost supernatural clarity. "Oh, my God!" Chekov gasped, spinning on Sulu. "You realize what this means?"

"Kahle sold the cloaking device to the Klingons." The helmsman swore in a chain of Orion vile enough to blister the walls. "How the hell did he get the plans away from White Sands?"

"I'm afraid I know that." Uhura sighed. "Admiral Kirk told me weeks ago that Kahle was known for seducing Starfleet officers to work for him. If he promised high-paying positions in his company to people still in service . . ."

Bitter flashes reminded Chekov unpleasantly of Leong.

"Some of them would be willing to betray their oaths for that kind of reward." The disgust he felt toward the treacherous security lieutenant sickened him.

"Well, all I—" A high, frantic beeping interrupted Scott and rocketed Chekov's adrenaline straight into his head. He paced a tight circle to wear off the worst of the jitters while Scott consulted the notepad on his belt and grunted. "Now, that's not the sort of thing I was hoping to see."

"What is it?" Sulu asked.

Scott switched off the notepad's signal and pursed his lips around a scowl. "It says here we've got three people moving around on the orbital platform." He raised a meaningful look to his companions. "And none of them are us."

Chekov prowled back and forth outside the catwalk's open airlock. "Why won't you let me come with you?"

"Because it's most likely one of the repair crews come back early," Scott said from the doorway of the airlock. He'd carefully collected enough tools and random equipment to make it seem reasonable he'd spent so much time on the *Enterprise*. "We can't afford to let 'em see any of you if it is."

"And if it's not?" Chekov protested. He halted his pacing long enough to lean between Sulu and Uhura and appeal to Scott. "What if the traitors have managed to follow us up here? What are you going to do then?"

"Chekov," Scott interrupted with a sigh. "Going into security doesn't mean you've gotta expect the worst out of every situation you come across. *Nor*"—he raised a stern finger to cut off the ensign's objection—"does it mean you outrank me and can willfully disobey my orders. I'm tellin' you all to stay here and wait for me until I come back. Do you understand me?"

Sulu reached back to clamp a warning hand on Chekov's arm, nodding obediently to Scott. "We'll be here, sir. You just be careful."

The engineer clapped both younger men on the shoulder before signaling the lock to shut behind him. "Don't you worry about me."

But worry was all Chekov seemed able to do.

"We have to get this information about Mr. Kahle down to the Territorial Conference." He paced to one side of the half-finished hallway, fidgeted impatiently with the bare bulkhead structure, then came back across to join the others.

"Pavel . . ." Uhura clasped his hand as he stalked by. "You've got to stop worrying—everything's going to be fine now."

He pulled gently loose with a shake of his head. "Nothing will be fine until we find someone to trust with that information." They had a very long way to go before fine; he was certain of it.

The deep, breathy hum of atmosphere flooding the long catwalk tube drew all their eyes in an instant to the airlock. "It hasn't even been five minutes," Sulu pointed out, his voice hardly loud enough to be a whisper. Chekov ducked around him without commenting, trotting a short distance down the corridor to find a portal still open to a view of the dry-dock platform outside.

"Well?" Sulu called.

Chekov shook his head, unable to discern either movement or shape through the translucent walls of the catwalk. Then a quick, stealthy figure crept into view, muted into anonymous shadow by the distance, and he felt every nerve ending in his body seize with fear. "It's not Mr. Scott."

Sulu came halfway to meet him as Chekov dashed back to join the others at the airlock. "What?"

"It's not Mr. Scott—it's them!" He slapped at the controls to open the inside lock door, then turned to help Uhura with the bundle of cable she was dragging across the hatchway. "I'll hold them off the ship for as long as I can; you two get that information to Admiral Kirk." The door crunched a deep dent in the cable, but stopped before forming a seal.

"We can't just leave you up here," Uhura began, but Sulu grabbed her arm to silence her.

"Find out what they did with Mr. Scott!" he shouted as he dragged the communications officer down the hall. "We'll send you some help as soon as we're able!"

"Be careful!" Uhura called over her shoulder.

Careful was all he knew how to be anymore. "Don't let anything happen to you!" he shouted in return.

But by then Uhura and Sulu were already gone. Chekov tried to turn his mind from them, to pretend they were already as safe as he could make them. Then the airlock door behind him screamed against the superheated blast of a phaser from outside.

Uhura slammed up against the skeletal framework of a future doorway, and hung there for a moment, gasping. Now that the noise of her own running had subsided, she could hear Sulu's thunderous footsteps chasing down the curving corridor behind her. She wished hopelessly that there was something they could do to lessen the noise of their passage. The *Enterprise*'s gaunt interior amplified every noise they made into an avalanche of sound. It made evading the unknown enemy seem an impossible task.

She pushed herself upright when Sulu swung around the corner, preparing to run again. But the pilot caught her arm and pulled her to a stop.

"Are we safe?"

Sulu nodded, too winded to speak. "No echoes," he gasped after a moment, and Uhura, listening, realized he was right.

"Now where do we go?" She glanced around, disoriented by the faceless metal skeleton of the secondary hull. "Do we even know where we are?"

"Not anymore," Sulu admitted. "But all we have to do is find a viewport and we'll know where we are in relation to the docking bay and the Wraith."

They began to move down the corridor again, this time with cautious steps that made the deck plates chime and quiver beneath them. Now that she wasn't running for her life, Uhura had time to notice how much the unsupported floor swayed under their weight. She edged toward the wall, then froze when the muffled sound of a phaser shot echoed from far behind them.

Sulu paused beside her, head tipped back to listen, but no other sounds followed the first. The silence was worse than any noises could have been, Uhura decided. She glanced worriedly at Sulu. "Could Chekov have found a phaser?"

"Let's hope so," Sulu said grimly. "Come on, I see a portable airlock up ahead. We must be near the hull."

They followed a shaft of pale, shining earthlight to its source: a makeshift airlock plugged into what looked like a torpedo bay door. The transparent aluminum portal yawned over a view of several unfinished torpedo bays gaping along the curve of the secondary hull. Several decks up, Uhura spotted the straight seam of the main docking bay, fringed with tethered workbees and scaffolded with gantries.

"If these guys are as smart as they've been so far," Sulu muttered beside her, "they'll guess we're heading for the Wraith. We'll have to take the sneaky way in."

"'Sneaky way'?" Somehow, Uhura had the feeling that she wasn't going to like this plan. "What does that mean?"

Sulu turned and headed back down the main corridor, scanning the walls as he went. "There's got to be one here somewhere," he said beneath his breath. "They're the first things to go in . . ."

"What are?" Uhura trailed behind him, frowning. "Sulu, what are we looking for?"

"An access panel." The pilot suddenly grunted in satisfaction as he came to a halt in front of a detachable metal plate in the wall. He tugged it free to reveal a narrow vertical opening stapled down its length with metal handholds. "For the repair shafts."

"We're going to climb up *five* decks?"

"No. We're going to climb up six." Sulu turned and grinned at her, the flashing grin that meant he had begun to enjoy the adrenaline edge of their situation. Uhura glowered at him and he said hurriedly, "Because there's no direct exit into the docking bay from the maintenance tunnels, and the one direction they won't be expecting us to come from is above."

The metallic-sharp stench of ozone stung Chekov's eyes as the superheated airlock door expanded with a popping creak.

"Warning," a computerized voice echoed politely from somewhere farther down the hall. "Unshielded use of a phase-shifted optic device in a mooring catwalk could result in a loss of atmosphere."

Chekov had thought of this when the first transparent aluminum seal began to steam. Dragging on the tangle of cable, he cleared the hatchway with two long tugs, then slapped at the airlock controls to slide the door closed across the opening. It mated with the seals on the other side of the hatch with a hollow boom.

"For your safety and the safety of others, please erect appropriate shielding before continuing with your work," the computer suggested with inhuman patience. Then, without so much as a conversational pause, "Inner airlock door engaged."

And unable to open again as long as that outer door was breached. At least, that was the way it was supposed to work. Chekov didn't know if the engineers had actually gotten that far.

If the assailant heard the computer's announcement, the song of his phaser showed no sign. Muted now by the thickness of two airlock hatches, the high-pitched wail drummed flatly against the bare starship superstructure, a peevish reminder of how limited the options really were up here. Chekov stepped against a half-finished slope of wall and scanned quickly around the corridor for inspiration.

"Rule number one in any security engagement," Oberste's voice barked inside his head. "Never enter a combat that you know you can't win." He could still see her sweat-dampened face in the Academy gym, scowling down at him after a particularly humiliating hand-to-hand encounter. "That doesn't mean never fight back against an opponent. That means choose your fights wisely."

Some stubborn remnant of the boy who'd first set foot in the Security Academy all those months before clenched a petulant fist inside his chest, refusing to believe that advice. He didn't want to run away—didn't want to give the enemy the satisfaction of walking onto the *Enterprise* to find an empty corridor and no one left in sight to challenge him.

"Stop thinking like a navigator who wants to impress his commanding officer!" Oberste's voice slapped at him like a lash from his memory. He could almost feel the rough shove of her hands against his chest. "Think like a security officer, dammit! What is your first responsibility to the success of this mission?"

The safe escape of his friends and the information they carried.

"And how will that be served by you throwing yourself against a superiorly armed opponent without even a baseball bat to defend yourself?"

It wouldn't be.

Choose your fights wisely.

He pushed away from the wall, dashing aside the last of his childish resistance. A scaffolding draped with welding hookups screamed across the decking as he dragged it in a circle to block the mouth of the adjoining corridor. He scooped up a few loops of cable, throwing them over the scaffolding's rungs and legs in the hopes it would make the equipment look somehow more permanent—as though it had been there for days or weeks, and not just moved there a few moments before. With luck, the intruder would discount that blocked passage as an avenue of escape and follow Chekov down the only other stretch of hallway, away from the docking bay, and away from Sulu and Uhura.

The *Enterprise's* corridors felt chill and breezy, more

vulnerable to the cold of space than they ever had when Chekov had called this ship his home. He resisted touching the exposed struts when he crouched for shelter beyond a curve in the long, sweeping tunnel. It felt too much like bothering an uneasy sleeper, or handling a corpse's rib cage. Neither image was one he found comforting just now.

A thunderous *clang* rang out through the hallway, and Broad clamored free of the airlock in a wash of cursing and ghostly steam. He jerked first toward the looming hulk of the rearranged scaffolding, leading with his phaser, and Chekov ducked back out of sight. Turning to face away from both assailant and airlock, Chekov clenched his uncasted hand for courage and shouted as though to his companions, "They've gotten through the airlock! Come on—we've got to hurry!" Then he pushed up from his crouch and started to run.

Too much cold, abuse, and tension. Muscles pulled and ached with every step, complaining that he should demand so much from them after so many days of hard living, promising to give out in protest, to cramp. He put his head down and ignored every twist and clench of threatened pain. Stiff muscles loosened up within a hundred meters or so, he told himself; the only way to ease the stiffness was to work it. Besides, the consequence of stopping now would surely be death, and he couldn't very well prove helpful to the others unless he stayed alive.

"Chekov, wait!" Broad's voice ricocheted, ever thinning, from far behind him. "Don't make me chase you—you'll just make things harder!"

At least as hard as Piper and Oberste had made things so far. That was Chekov's promise to both of them.

The round, orange-lit portal of a functioning airlock glowed through the dim internal lighting where the corridor straightened out ahead. Another catwalk, Chekov realized. The mooring tunnels were scattered all up and down this deck, providing service between the orbital platform and the *Enterprise* for the countless engineers who scurried back and forth every day. If he could cycle the airlock and bolt the gap to the platform before Broad caught up to him, he might even be able to lead the technician back off the *Enterprise* again, leaving Sulu and Uhura to make their own way to freedom in the Wraith. It was, at best, a desperate time-killing device, but the thought of even that small a victory nonetheless swelled his heart with hope for the first time since he'd heard Piper die in the Johns Hopkins stairwell.

He skated to a stop with his hands braced against the big round doorway, then cried out in despair when he reached for the controls and saw the reading that was still left blinking on the display.

Someone besides Broad had come across to the *Enterprise* more than seven and a half minutes ago, closing down the airlock and blowing free the catwalk behind them.

Chapter Eighteen

U.S.S. Enterprise
Earth Sector, Standard Earth Orbit
Terrestrial Date: December 25, 2269
0830 hours shiptime

"WELL?" Uhura tried to keep her voice low, but her aching wrists and raw palms made it come out sharper than she intended. "Is there anyone out there?"

For answer, Sulu swung the access hatch open above her and swung himself out onto the deck outside. Uhura stifled a sigh of relief and pulled herself up the last few rungs to join him, trying to ignore the outraged complaints of her newly healed burns as they stretched to accommodate the motion. Compared with the icy draft of the repair tunnels, the clammy air of the deck felt almost warm. She shivered with gratitude and hauled herself out to join Sulu.

"This way." The pilot's voice was hushed nearly soundless, reminding Uhura that for all she knew, one of their assailants could be hiding around the nearest corner. The resulting surge of adrenaline dulled the ache of her burnt wrist and let her follow Sulu on silent, careful feet. They crept down the curving corridor, following it until it intersected with one of the straight, radial hallways that bisected the hull, then following that until they arrived at the central bank of turbolifts.

The shafts loomed dark and empty, waiting for cars

that wouldn't be installed until after structural renovations were complete. Sulu propped a hand on either side of the nearest one and leaned out into the darkness, inspiring Uhura with a surprisingly maternal urge to grab at the back of his tunic. *"There's* the ladderway," the pilot said after a moment, and swung down into the darkness. "The engineers finally got sensible and decided to put it on the front wall instead of the back."

Uhura took a deep breath and followed him. Once they were inside, the passage wasn't quite as dark as she had feared, although her hands and shoulders weren't any happier about climbing down than they had been about climbing up. Fortunately, this time she only had a single deck's worth of rungs to navigate. Unlike the repair tunnels, though, this shaft opened directly onto the deck where the assassins had fired upon them, so it was critical that the climb be slow and silent. Uhura closed her eyes to better concentrate on keeping her hands and feet from making any noise. She knew they'd reached the deck below only when Sulu reached up and squeezed her booted ankle.

This time, Uhura knew better than to ask any questions of the pilot. She watched in breathless silence while his slim shadow slipped out into the passageway and vanished. A moment passed, then another. Uhura quietly began to climb down the last few rungs, unable to bear the wait any longer.

Sulu ghosted back to the turboshaft entrance, holding his thumb up to show Uhura the coast was clear, then helped her out onto the deck. She followed him back down the empty corridor to the main docking bay, its access door exposed and vulnerable in a wide conjunction of halls. Uhura swung back and forth, trying to scan all the corridors simultaneously while Sulu worked at the door's control panel. It took him only a moment to verify that the bay was closed and supporting an atmosphere, but it seemed more like an hour.

"We're clear to go in." Sulu's hushed whisper was almost drowned by the hissing of the docking bay doors as they slid apart. Uhura stepped through the entrance as soon as it was wide enough to admit her, with Sulu treading on her heels.

A quick glance showed Uhura that no one else was inside, and she swung back to the open doors, looking for the control panel on this side. Sulu was already heading for the flightsuits he and Chekov had abandoned on the docking bay floor. He scooped them up and came back to her just as she found the door controls and pressed them. Nothing happened.

"The doors won't close," Uhura said urgently.

"Forget the doors!" Sulu threw a flightsuit at her and began to slide into his own. "Maybe the renovations have messed up their programming."

"Or maybe someone at a security station caught us using them and locked them open." Uhura squirmed into the too-large suit, then reached for the helmet Sulu held out to her.

"Then the best thing we can do is get out of here." The pilot caught Uhura's arm and pulled her toward the Wraith. "Come on. Let's get inside before we—"

Without so much as a footstep of warning, the whistle of a phaser bolt sliced through the silence and chased them toward the shuttle's gaping hatch.

When Chekov heard the buzz of a distant airlock's breach warning from back the way he'd come, he knew with sick certainty what Broad intended to do. A resonant *bang!* confirmed his fears, shuddering through the naked ship structure like a death tremor before plunging into a silence as flat and final as space itself. Chekov didn't even need the benefit of a transparent portal to envision Broad's catwalk curling lazily back toward the orbital platform, blasted free of its ship moorings by a ring of emergency bolts. No one would be leaving the *Enterprise* by that route again today.

Chekov pushed away from the airlock in front of him with a whispered curse. How many catwalks had they flown past on their approach to the *Enterprise's* docking bay? A dozen? Five? He suddenly wished he'd been awake to notice. Whatever the answer, he couldn't afford to lead Broad to them all—not if he intended to make it back to the platform and search for Scott. Once the catwalks were disconnected from the *Enterprise,* Chekov would be trapped on board along with Broad and whoever else had already come over. While he might be able to evade Broad and Stern long enough to wait for help from Earthside, he could never hold off Leong for all the hours it would take to rely on outside intervention.

And where did that leave Sulu and Uhura? Could they even reach the Wraith with a second traitor hunting the passageways for them? How would Chekov even know if they'd succeeded in going for the help he was forced to rely on?

"If you're going to be a security guard, you've got to forget all that abstract crap you did as a navigator and learn to work with what's real and what's known." A frustrating lecture on methodology after he'd failed miserably on a computer modeling assignment. Chekov had claimed there wasn't enough information to extrapolate what kind of answer the test program wanted; Oberste had countered that he didn't know how to keep his mind on the information in front of him. "Don't worry about the variables you can't affect and can't know. Tell me what part of this problem is *real,* in front of you, immediate."

Peter Broad's footsteps echoed from around the curving corridor, in a measured trot that never quite broke into a run. From the overlapping sound of his movements, he'd already covered half the distance between them.

"Take care of *that* element first. Worry about finding yourself more things to deal with once you've got what's in front of you under control."

Chekov started away down the hallway again, more quietly this time, wiping away extraneous thoughts as if from a slate until only Broad and the immediacy of Broad's ringing footsteps remained.

"Chekov?" It was not the call of a man who could hear his quarry. Broad's voice faded into a growl of muted grumbling, receding for a moment, then growing in strength again just before rising into a single sharp curse. Chekov heard the dispirited thump of Broad drumming his fist in frustration against the bulkhead. "Pavel, it's not gonna matter how far you go! Talk to me!"

Struts and equipment clogged the passageway at his next turn. Chekov planted both feet, sliding sideways to break his momentum even as he went down on all fours to keep from toppling into the disorderly stacks of metal. A grunt of pain forced past his clenched teeth as he slammed into a down-powered gravsled, and a crate of loose couplings crashed to the floor from somewhere farther back in the pile. So much for subtlety and finesse. Scrabbling out from under an overhang of bulkhead plating, he squirmed between the gravsled and the unfinished wall, nearly shouting in surprise when the deck beneath him dropped by half a meter. Behind him, Broad's footsteps increased abruptly in volume and speed.

Chekov grabbed for the exposed deck ribs ahead of him, hooking one with his good left hand, another with the elbow above his cast. Nothing of this corridor was finished beyond power conduits and simple framing. He dragged himself past the last of the construction debris, banging knees and elbows on the bare-floor framework as he struggled to climb upright atop a string of girders. Dancing from one to the other made his ankles ache, but he didn't dare try and leap from pit to pit, for fear he would trip or land on something people were not meant to walk on. He would just have to hope his own labored progress through the construction was faster than Broad's, weary legs and aching back notwithstanding.

He was barely ten meters from the original tunnel blockage, heart pounding at the clamor of Broad's clumsy pursuit, when he found the second bulkhead pile and the portable transporter console.

It was a small, automated cargo unit, its control panel

stained with carbon and welding flux, its dais scarred by all the crates and hulls and gravsleds that had been dragged across it through however many years of faithful service. Some engineer had patched the unit directly into the deck's main power grid. Taped and twisted cables snaked from the open wall to the transporter on its makeshift flooring, and the column housing the automatic controls blinked serenely into the chill half dark. The little backlit screen read simply: "STANDBY."

Chekov pounced across the last two girders and threw the activation switch with the side of his hand. Power hummed life into the transporter's atomizing cells, and the controls requested "PLEASE WAIT" while the unit began to sing. "I don't have time to wait!" he informed it in an unhappy whisper.

As if in reply, coordinates appeared on the small control readout, a string of unattributed numbers coupled with some kind of shipping code. Chekov paged down through the list, and a shiver of dread spread like ice through his system. There were fifty-seven codes in all. He stopped reviewing them somewhere around number twenty.

Way back at the beginning of the semester, he'd taken a weekend short-course on Departmental Management Skills. The guest instructor—a specialist on Security Divisions who'd come all the way from Bombay—had walked fifteen students through the vagaries of intership transporting, stressing its incredible dangers as well as its importance in certain high-risk situations. "If you memorize nothing else about your transporter, you should always know the coordinates for your bridge, your brig, and your sickbays," the little man had singsonged. "These are the places most important to the security professional, and the places you must never lose time in reaching." The idea had seemed so sincere and reasonable at the time that Chekov had spent the next week memorizing those four sets of coordinates until he could visualize them in his sleep.

But that had been four months ago.

He started back through the coordinate list from the beginning. The advantage to attempting an intership transport now was the lack of a functioning warp drive. Without a subspace field to warp the beam, assuring materialization at any given coordinates became no more of a challenge than placing a routine landing party. However, without absolute certainty as to which of the dozens of codes locked on to the auxiliary sickbay, he ran the risk of beaming himself into a nonenclosed section of construction, a sealed cargo bay, or even open space itself. The bridge and security holding cells were gone with the primary disk, doing double duty as a tourist attraction at the San Francisco navy yards while she was refitted and rehulled. That left only the auxiliary sickbay to aim for, with its promise of laser scalpels and cutting tools and other potential weapons.

He flashed back and forth between two codes, each different by only the juxtaposition of three digits. *Are you certain enough?* he asked himself when he saw that his hand shook so badly he could barely press the keys. *Can you pick just one and really make yourself step up on that platform and believe you'll come through alive?* Three digits was a lot of meters' difference in result.

The whine of a gravsled's motor sliced across his doubtful silence. Broad's voice shouted something Chekov couldn't hear over the scrape and groan of moving metal, and the question of certainty was suddenly answered for him. *Dead is dead—you might as well go down trying.* He chose between the two codes at random, then set the delay for fifteen seconds and vaulted the last two struts onto the dais. The air buzzed with a building charge as he hurried to pull himself onto the glowing locus.

For the first time he could remember, the itching tingle of the transporter's disassociation almost made him want to scream.

Uhura saw the flash as their assailant's first shot went wide, taking out a section of scaffolding across the docking bay. It must have been fired from far down one of the outside corridors, because another minute had passed before Uhura heard the thud of distant running footsteps, a sinister echo to their own. A second phaser shot seared a long gouge across the docking bay floor, this time only meters away. Uhura gasped and launched herself into a final lunge toward the shuttle, with Sulu a half step ahead of her and hauling her with him while he ran.

The next phaser shot hit the Wraith just in front of them, then shattered back off the shuttle's reflective shielding in a glitter of refracted radiation. Uhura felt more than heard Sulu take the impact in front of her and collapse only a few strides away from the shuttle door. She cried out, bending to try and scoop the pilot up just as a fourth phaser shot screeched over her head. Adrenaline stabbed at Uhura so hard it hurt, but it propelled both her and Sulu into the Wraith in an ungraceful jumble of arms and legs. Sobbing with desperation, Uhura squirmed out from under the pilot's dead weight and slammed the door shut behind them.

Another phaser beam crackled against the shuttle's reflective shielding. Uhura ignored it, bending over Sulu to see how badly he was hurt. Her best defense now was to get the Wraith out of here, and to do that she needed its pilot.

"Sulu, damn you, don't you dare be dead!" She rolled him onto his back and flinched at the burnt-flesh smell that rose from the torn and blackened side of his tunic. Unbidden memories of McCoy swept over her, making her vision blur for a moment. Uhura took a deep breath and blinked the tears away, suddenly aware that Sulu was struggling under her hands.

"Hold still, hold still—" She put both hands on the unburnt side of his uniform. "Is there a medical kit aboard?"

"Lock—door—" Sulu panted, still pushing up at her. "Lock—"

Groaning at her own stupidity, Uhura reached up to

dog the hatch just as hands scrabbled across its outer latch. The Wraith rocked under the fierce tug on its door, but the lock held firm. She turned back to Sulu, to find him now squirming out from under her. Uhura made a wordless cry of protest and leapt up to steady the pilot as he staggered to his feet.

"Sulu, you need medical treatment—"

"No time—" Sulu's voice came out thinned by gritted teeth. "Have to get—out of here."

He reeled unsteadily toward the pilot's seat while Uhura scanned the walls of the tiny cockpit, searching for the emergency medical kit she knew had to be aboard. The familiar gleam of the communications panel caught her eye instead, just as a long bombardment of phaser fire sizzled against the hatch. The inside of the lock began to glow cherry bright.

"We can't let them burn through—" Sulu glanced over his shoulder, fingers racing across the control panel to start the sequence that warmed the thrusters. "If we get breached, we won't be able to leave the bay!"

"I know." Uhura slid into the copilot's seat beside him and bent over the Wraith's communicator, scanning all its channels in a frantic attempt to find one that could make contact with the *Enterprise's* on-board computer. The phaser blast outside cut off, and she sighed in relief. "They've stopped."

"And they're coming around the side." Even over the rumble of the impulse engines, ominous footsteps echoed outside the Wraith. Sulu slapped at his obstinate thruster controls. "Hurry up, damn you—one shot through the viewscreen will breach us for sure!"

As if his words had summoned her, a big-boned woman in a nondescript medical tunic materialized in the corner of their viewscreen, phaser raised. Sulu shouted a warning and slammed in the half-warmed thrusters. The Wraith skated itself around in a dragging half circle, just enough to deflect the phaser bolt harmlessly off their radiation shielding.

A moment later, Uhura found her computer channel

and punched in an emergency command she had never used before. A hurricane-fierce roar of wind tore past them in response, skittering the Wraith across the docking bay floor before it.

"What the hell—" Sulu engaged the thrusters again, sliding the Wraith to a stop just before they'd have slammed into the docking bay doors. Those shell doors were slowly pulling apart, just as they'd been ordered to, letting out a giant's breath of rushing air and ice crystals and one tumbling, person-sized object. Uhura caught a brief glimpse of the expression of sudden horror now frozen forever on their attacker's face, and then she spun out into the blackness of space.

Silence fell inside the shuttle, the silence of mingled relief and regret. "How—" Sulu demanded hoarsely, then paused to swallow and try again. "Uhura, how the *hell* did you get the doors to open with someone still inside the docking bay?"

Uhura took a deep breath, scrubbing the dampness off her cheeks. "Emergency procedure code one ninety-three," she told him quietly. "Evacuation of crew on shuttles during a hostile takeover of the ship."

She could see the pilot's eyebrows jerk upward. The docking bay doors were fully open now, revealing the Earth's turquoise disk below them, framed in a receding crescent of night. "And you had that code *memorized?*"

"I had to." Uhura made an ironic noise, not quite a laugh and not quite a sigh. "It was the answer to the last question on the final exam I just gave."

Chapter Nineteen

U.S.S. Enterprise
Earth Sector, Standard Earth Orbit
Terrestrial Date: December 25, 2269
0900 hours shiptime

AWARENESS FLASHED OVER CHEKOV on the fading chime of the transporter effect. He knew the instant his body solidified and his nerve pathways fired their first impulse that he was in free-fall—that there was no deck under him and no immediate pull of gravity to equalize his perceptions. That he had chosen the wrong transporter coordinates, and he was doomed.

Then his feet struck the deck hard enough to buckle his knees, and he recognized the shelves and carts and tables of medical equipment just before landing on his bottom in the middle of the sickbay's diagnostic center. Obviously, no one had required transportation to sickbay since that transporter pad was erected. Chekov would have to remind Scott about aligning those codes when this was all over.

Rolling to his knees, he pulled himself upright on one of the nearby equipment carts, pawing through the contents of its trays and medkits as he stood. Antiseptics, new-skin sprays, a pack of sealed laser-burn kits that he shoved aside without opening their sterile casings. The closest thing to a weapon in the whole collection was a pair of angled scissors half-hidden beneath a roll of bandages. Even those were blunt-tipped and short, though, useless for anything but conventional cutting. He rolled both cart and scissors off to one side between exam tables, and dashed to the wall of pharmaceutical cabinets, with their array of hyposprays and medicines.

Trazadone hydrochloride, dextromethrophan, loperamide, sodium salicylate . . . Vial after vial sported labels that wrapped almost completely around their little cylinders to accommodate the long strings of letters. Chekov groaned, digging farther back in the cabinet to grab another random handful. He didn't even know that any of what he was reading was English, much less what it was good for or how it was used. All hope of finding anything useful among the medical jumble evaporated like a hypospray's discharge. He swept another shelf onto the worktable, praying for something more straightforward than chemicals.

Shimmers of fusion discharge spattered the room with brightness, and the hypersonic whine of a transporter in close quarters yanked Chekov around with a heart-clenching gasp. Peter Broad coalesced into an outline of coruscating energy, then washed dark and solid with a flash and dropped the same three feet Chekov had fallen only a few moments before. He caught himself after only a heavy stumble, though. Phaser still outthrust, Broad flailed one hand to catch at an exam table and keep himself from falling. *Choose your fights wisely,* Chekov reminded himself when Broad jerked upright and steadied his aim once again. The phaser blinked to warn of a lowered charge, but still carried enough power to kill him. *As long as you're living, you still haven't lost.*

"I don't have a weapon," Chekov said aloud. He tightened his hand around one of the useless vials, wishing it were at least big enough to be worth throwing. "You don't have to kill me."

As though surprised by Chekov's civil tone, Broad eased into a more relaxed stance. He kept one hand on the exam table, though, and didn't lower the phaser. "I'm not supposed to kill you," he admitted, sounding almost apologetic. "Leong just wanted me to bring you back to him—said he'd kill your engineer friend if you didn't agree to come." A flush of color up his cheeks darkened the bruises along his still-swollen jaw. "I'm really sorry about this."

Chekov set down the vial behind himself, standing away from the wall. "Then why are you doing it?"

"I told you." Broad twitched the phaser a little higher, not even seeming to realize he did so. Chekov made himself stand very still again. "He's got your friend hostage. Leong swears he's going to kill him, and I just didn't want to see anyone else get hurt."

"Even though Leong is planning to kill me, too."

Broad said nothing, only darting his gaze to one side as though unable to face the private monster he'd created. A curdle of dread twisted in Chekov's stomach. It was real, then. There would be no arrest, no charade for the media, no trial. He'd been meant for swift removal all along.

Rubbing at his bruises with one hand, Broad leaned forward over the exam table and dragged a shaky sigh. "I want you to know, I don't *do* things like this. Not for money, not for anything." The tech was getting good at holding the phaser straight and steady, so Chekov resisted making a move against him. Broad laced his hands together around the phaser and raised fretful brows to Chekov. "I steal stuff—stuff from corporations, not stuff from people or anything. I never hurt anybody."

Chekov wondered how many beings would be hurt with the spread of the Klingon disruptor, but decided this might not be the best time to bring the subject up.

"When Mr. Kahle asked me about the job at Johns Hopkins, I only took it to keep from going to prison. See, he found out I was selling UniPhase specs to Earth corporations off-planet. He said he had friends in the judicial system who could make sure I'd never get parole, and that no amount of money was worth that." Broad shrugged helplessly, eyes wetly bright. "He was right." He sounded immeasurably ashamed of that fact. "Mr.

Kahle said he just wanted the plans. That's all—just the disruptor plans."

"And is that worth going to jail over?" Chekov asked. *As long as you're alive . . .* "Peter, I know you haven't killed anyone. I heard what happened to Dr. Piper; I *saw* what happened to Commander Oberste. If Leong has forced you to help him, you need me to protect yourself." He risked taking one earnest step forward. "I'm your witness, Peter. We can speak for each other—you about Kahle's involvement in the technology thefts, me about the murders and your unwillingness to participate. You don't have to go to jail," he promised solemnly. *"We* don't have to die."

Eyes focused thoughtfully on nothing, Broad nodded faintly and bobbed the phaser. "Yeah, that's the salient point." A tart wryness livened his otherwise dull tone. "I've never been able to figure out how Mr. Kahle was going to justify keeping me alive once he had all the other loose ends tied up. It just didn't make good business sense." He looked up at Chekov again, and something that was almost a smile quirked at the edges of his lips. "I think we're really screwed, you and me."

"Not necessarily." Chekov held one hand out expectantly. Broad blinked as though not sure how to take the gesture, then seemed to come to himself and stretched across the exam table to drop the phaser into Chekov's palm. The reassuring weight of the pistol swept Chekov with a relief that made him giddy. He stepped back away from Broad, the phaser tucked discreetly out of sight. "Do you know anything that we could use against him? Anything that might help me get him away from my friend?"

"Sure." Looking suddenly tired without the threat of death to support him, Broad motioned past Chekov with a weary lift of one shoulder. "For starters, I can tell you what's in those vials in the medical cabinet behind you."

A long time ago, Sulu had read a study proving that human beings, unlike the rest of the animal kingdom, felt more pain when they were under stress than when they were at rest. It seemed vastly unfair. Given the vital need to pilot Uhura and her packet of evidence safely down to Annapolis through the tattered but still-treacherous remnants of Hurricane Kevin, Sulu considered that the least his burnt arm and side could do was cooperate in keeping their owner alive long enough to heal them.

But logic didn't work on scorched nerves, unless maybe you were part Vulcan. The ache in Sulu's side got worse with every breath and every motion, despite Uhura's best attempts at dressing it with topical analgesics. Piloting rules forbid the use of anything stronger, unless the pilot's life was in danger. And unfortunately, the emergency medical kit's diagnostic sensor had pronounced Sulu's burns to be "minor surface damage." Sulu had a suspicious feeling that the intensity of the pain he felt might be due more to the subspace radiation that the rent in his suit was letting in than to the wounds themselves.

For the umpteenth time since they'd left the *Enterprise,* Sulu put that thought out of his mind and tried to concentrate on his viewscreen display. Hurricane Kevin was plotting as a spidery gray mass in the West Atlantic now, just north of New York City, the storm, having skipped across the coast at Assateague and veered back out to sea overnight. The original flight plan spit out by the on-board computer had carefully skirted the hurricane's outspread arms, taking them to Annapolis by way of Ohio and Virginia. Sulu had considered how many Starfleet bases existed in those states, and decided to risk flying through the hurricane fringe instead.

Uhura stirred in the copilot's seat, pointing a gloved finger at the weather display on the screen. "Won't Starfleet be able to track us because you're receiving that?"

"No." Sulu's gaze moved from the map to the view of Earth slowly enlarging below them. "That's just a general piloting screen, broadcast from satellite along with the global positioning signals for any interatmosphere ship to monitor. I haven't tuned in to any of the ship-specific Starfleet channels. They don't know we're here." He felt the first tickle of atmosphere along the sides of the Wraith and added, honestly, "Yet."

"But they might?" Uhura demanded. "Even with the cloaking device on?"

Sulu started to shrug, then felt the anguished protest of his side and stopped at once. "Only if someone's lucky and catches visual sight of our turbulence inside the atmosphere. Once we're inside the hurricane, we should be safe."

"Somehow, the words 'safe' and 'hurricane' don't really go together," Uhura said wryly. "I hope you know what you're doing."

Me, too, Sulu thought, but he didn't say it aloud. He watched the wrinkled old mountains of the Appalachians come into view through the hurricane's outspread fingers, bleached white with early-winter snow across the highest peaks. Sulu oriented himself by the abrupt bend of the chain in Pennsylvania and cut the Wraith's altitude, heading south and east. The thrum of atmospheric friction increased along the shuttle's ribbed sides.

"Do you think we should contact Starfleet and tell them to send security guards up to the *Enterprise?*" Uhura asked suddenly. "I've been racking my brain trying to think what we could do to help Chekov . . ."

"Me, too." A gray wall of storm clouds loomed ahead of them, torn ragged along its lower edge by slicing rain. Sulu gritted his teeth and let the Wraith descend into the maelstrom. The sudden increase in turbulence felt like torture on his scorched side. "But we can't do that without giving our own position away. And even if we could, Kahle's people would intercept the transmission and run for cover before we'd have had the chance to catch them."

Uhura fell silent. "I still can't believe it was him," she said at last. "He was so nice."

Sulu let out an involuntary bark of laughter that sent a

ripple of pain down his rib cage. "So was Kodos the Executioner."

The communications officer sighed. "Yes, that's true. I guess I should say that I don't *want* it to be him." She paused, and then her soft voice turned unusually cold. "But if it is, I want him caught and punished."

Sulu grunted agreement. "We'll have Admiral Kirk send Chekov a squadron of security guards as soon as we get Kahle arrested."

Navigation beacons began to flare on the Wraith's viewscreen when they descended into the lower levels of Earth's atmosphere. The circling radar probes showed very few ships in their vicinity. Air traffic control must have routed most of the commercial flights farther south and west, just as Sulu had hoped when he took this route. The two or three blips that did show up wore standard codes identifying them as armed Starfleet vessels. Sulu fervently hoped they were there to escort the Romulan delegation to the Territorial Conference, and not to erect any kind of defense screen over the Security Academy.

The small Annapolis navigation beacon came in at last, fainter and less precise than those of the major cities around it. Sulu got a fix on it, then tapped a final course correction into the computer. They were flying low enough that the haze around them now was made of driving rain instead of clouds, allowing an occasional glimpse of the Maryland landscape below. The sharply pinched ridges of the Appalachians softened into the rolling winter pastures of the Frederick Valley, then rose to the broad, snowcapped crest of the Blue Ridge. All downhill from here, Sulu thought in grim amusement, and began to ready the antigravs for landing.

"Almost there?" Uhura sat very still against the hurricane's buffeting, but her voice was edged with stifled anxiety.

"Passing over Baltimore now." Sulu could feel his own tension rise in a beating rush, drowning out the pain of his side at last. They swung out over Chesapeake Bay, its gray waters almost invisible beneath the sweeping veils of rain that thickened as they neared the coast. "Thirty kilometers . . . twenty . . ." If there was a defense screen set up, this was about where they should encounter it, he knew. A brief jolt of lightning on the horizon made Sulu's heart leap into his throat, but the Wraith's placid sensors told him it was only a natural part of the hurricane. "Ten kilometers . . . five . . ."

He caught sight of the military sprawl of red brick and slate roofs that was the old Naval Academy, familiar to him from many previous visits to Chekov. The Wraith's antigravs pulsed as he cut them in and gradually throttled the impulse engines down, searching for a good spot to land on the wet grass of the school's central quad.

"There!" This time, Uhura's pointing finger showed him the ripple of the Romulan and Earth flags through the driving rain. The flags flew over an ancient red-brick building, ornate with porticos and balustrades, that wrapped around a central stone-flagged courtyard. "That must be where they're meeting."

"All right." Sulu maneuvered the ship over the heads of two security cadets scurrying through the rain, then cursed when he saw their heads jerk up in wide-eyed amazement. He'd been depending so much on the utter silence of the antigrav drive, he'd forgotten that the Wraith itself would tear the air it passed through. "We've been spotted, Uhura. Get ready to run."

She scrambled out from between the seats, tumbling over the cloaking device on her way to the hatch. "What will you do?"

"Stay here and get arrested." Sulu brought the Wraith down right in the center of the stone-flagged courtyard, where its weight could not indent the ground. "Okay, go!"

Uhura slammed at the door control, then cursed when nothing happened. "I can't! The door's stuck shut." She beat on it with futile fists. "That woman aboard the *Enterprise* must have fused the latch with her phaser."

Sulu began to swing around without thinking, then

gasped when his ribs protested. "Blow the emergency bolts."

"Where—" Uhura's voice cut off when she found the emergency controls, and a moment later a dull thud rocked the Wraith and let the door come crashing down. She dove out through the hatch before the smoke of the explosion had time to clear. Sulu heard the echo of her running footsteps vanish beneath the roar of the rain.

Somewhere across campus, an alarm began to howl. Sulu grinned and settled himself back in his seat, waiting for the security guards to arrive. By the time the first ones poked the business ends of their phasers cautiously through the open hatch, he had already lifted his hands in surrender.

"Lieutenant Commander Hikaru Sulu," he told them gravely. "And you're arresting me for unauthorized flight and trespass."

"No, Commander." The guards parted to let a taller, darker man through, one whose deep voice echoed resonantly inside the shuttle. Sulu stared up at Commodore Adam Willis in amazement. "We're arresting you for theft of restricted Starfleet technology. And treason."

Chapter Twenty

SHEETING RAIN drove Uhura across the courtyard and into
the shelter of the nearest portico she could find. She cut
through a hedge of neatly landscaped yews to reach it,
then pulled herself up and huddled behind the stone-
carved railing, wiping the rain from her eyes and taking
her bearings.

The first thing she saw was how lucky she'd been. The
Territorial Conference flags were flying over the other
wing of the building, and it looked like Starfleet Security
had concentrated its guard posts there. This side stood
dark and silent, the old leaded panes of the windows
revealing dim shadows of beds and desks and dressers. A
cadet dormitory wing, Uhura realized, deserted for the
holidays.

She began to scurry along the portico on hands and
knees, hoping the heavy rain would keep her movements
hidden from watchful eyes across the courtyard. Her
caution was rewarded a moment later when the gloved
hand she'd been running along the wall for balance
suddenly met a slick and yielding surface. Uhura glanced
over at the line of windows in surprise and saw that one
had been left slightly ajar.

244

Blessing Starfleet's reluctance to tamper with the architectural integrity of historic buildings by installing automated windows, Uhura pushed the opening wider and squirmed her way into the room's shadowed interior. The rain followed her in, dampening a dark swath of the room's worn carpet in the brief moment it took her to close the window again. She waited, but no alarms went off to betray her presence to the authorities. A dim wash of light filtered through the open door from the hallway, but the utter quiet that came with it told Uhura that the entire wing was deserted.

She sighed in relief and ghosted to the door, closing it, more for her own sense of security than for any actual protection. Then she stripped out of her conspicuous silver flightsuit and stuffed it into the room's old-fashioned wastebasket. A quick search of the room's dresser drawers revealed only large-sized security jumpers. Uhura bit her lip and ventured cautiously down to the next room, thanking God for the cadet discipline that kept all doors open so superior officers could see at a glance if the rooms were clean.

It took three more room searches before she turned up a cadet uniform small enough to fit her. Uhura made the change quickly, then scrubbed her face and hands and dumped all her jewelry and rank pins into the wastebasket, along with her borrowed medical uniform. None of the boots she'd found had fit, so Uhura finally contented herself with just polishing the ones she had on. Then she stepped over to the room's small utilitarian mirror and regarded the result.

Clad in Security red and black, she looked almost like a cadet, but not quite, and it took a long, frowning moment to figure out why: No Starfleet cadet in the world had the time to wind her hair into the polished and interwoven braids Uhura wore. She winced, then took a deep breath and went to fetch a pair of scissors from the desk.

Ten minutes later, a security cadet with a cropped military haircut and an armful of computer notebooks and data readers approached the security guard station at the entrance to the conference hall. "I heard there were spectator seats at the conference," she said with polite respect to the middle-aged security guard who rose to meet her. "Is that right?"

It was the usual Starfleet procedure when conducting low-level negotiations to allow cadets and ensigns to observe from behind a curtaining forcefield. Uhura had heard Admiral Kirk say that it not only showed the junior officers how to negotiate, it also kept the senior officers who *were* negotiating on their toes. Uhura wasn't sure that standard procedures would be followed for a meeting as sensitive as the Romulan Territorial Conference, but she figured it couldn't hurt to ask.

"Only for the opening ceremonies this morning," the security guard warned her, then pointed at the staircase that led up from the building's main entrance. "It's up on the second-floor balcony."

"Thanks." Uhura bounded up the stairs with what she hoped looked like a cadet's eager energy. She didn't let herself collapse into gasps until she'd reached the second floor. She waited several more minutes to be sure her breath had steadied before she ventured out onto the balcony itself.

The narrow, oak-paneled parapet wrapped around three sides of what looked like an old dining hall or gymnasium, now fitted out as a negotiating chamber. There weren't many seats, and most of those were unoccupied. The same holiday break that had vacated the dormitory had left only a handful of cadets here to view the opening ceremonies, Uhura guessed.

She began to walk the balcony's perimeter, pausing several times as if searching for a good vantage point of the room below. In actuality, she was looking for the forcefield generator. The protective field threw an almost invisible shimmer over the scene below, although Uhura knew that from the other side it would look like an opaque white wall. She spared one quick glance down at the milling clusters of Romulan and Vulcan diplomats,

Starfleet officers, and civilians, whose rich velvet tunics wore the star-cluster symbol of Jackson Kahle's Peace Foundation. Admiral Kirk was nowhere in sight, but it looked like the conference was just getting started.

"Gentlebeings, please take your places at the table." The familiar snap of Jackson Kahle's voice sent a ripple of adrenaline racing through Uhura. She paused again, shaken by one last spasm of doubt as she stared down at the octogenarian billionaire who had seemed so entirely trustworthy in her class. Could this former starship captain really be behind all the horrible events of the last two weeks? Then she watched Kahle scan the still-scattered crowd and saw the way his eyes lit with impatient steel-blue fire. "Gentlebeings, I said *sit down.*"

That whiplash voice broke through the milling, and started the diplomats moving toward their places at the circular negotiating table. It also broke through Uhura's indecision, for some reason reminding her of the ruthless and draconic way McCoy had been attacked at Stanford. With a deep, renewing breath, she pushed herself into motion, circling the rest of the balcony.

She found the field generator midway along the back section, where it could generate two symmetrical wings of force. With a sigh of relief, Uhura sank down into a chair next to it, putting her data readers and notebooks down on the chair beside her. The two or three cadets on the other side of the balcony had begun to give her curious looks, but now they turned their attention back to the floor below.

A portly man in the uniform of a security commodore stood and cleared his throat, obviously waiting for the last few stragglers to sit. Uhura's heart leaped when she recognized the dynamic strides of the final figure to enter in Starfleet gold and black. Admiral Kirk *was* back, along with a hooded figure in Vulcan robes who she guessed must be Ambassador Sarek. Uhura waited expectantly for them to denounce the conspirators, but they merely took their places at the table in silence. Her heart sank briefly, but she reassured herself that she still had all the proof they needed, safely riding on the computer datacard in her pocket.

The portly commodore was speaking now, at first hesitantly in Romulan and then more confidently in Vulcan and English. Uhura recognized the formal greetings of the other planets and sat impatiently through the English equivalent, waiting for an appropriate time to take action. Her damp palm itched, and she scrubbed it down her pant leg, then fished the datacard out. Her other hand crept toward the field generator.

"Gentlebeings of Vulcan, Romulus, and Earth." The officer straightened himself to his full height. "I'm Commodore Keith deCandido, and on behalf of Starfleet I'd like to welcome you to the Security Academy, to Annapolis, and to Earth. There is no better person to open our conference today than the man who inspired this unprecedented first step in communication between warring species. Gentlebeings, I give you the founder of the Peace Foundation—Jackson B. Kahle II."

A polite splatter of applause from the human delegates and a respectful silence from the Romulans and Vulcans greeted the billionaire when he rose from his seat. Uhura sat forward to watch him, her fingers blindly searching out and finding the field generator's power control.

Kahle nodded in curt response to the applause, but typically dispensed with any other preliminaries in his speech. "Gentlebeings, we have gathered here today to heal some long-festering sores along the Federation and Romulan Neutral Zone." Disembodied voices accompanied him as he spoke, translating his words into simultaneous Vulcan and Romulan. Uhura heard a closer second echo, and glanced down the balcony to see moving lips and microphones among the group she had taken for cadets. Translators, she thought with satisfaction, so engaged with their work that they wouldn't even notice when she made her move.

"—in this way, we can try to overcome our mutual prejudices, move past our hostilities, and create a climate of hope," Kahle concluded. "Even if all we can accomplish now is to resolve a few border disputes, we will be setting a precedent for the future. A precedent for peace."

Uhura knew a cue when she heard one. The applause that followed Kahle's speech completely masked the whine of the field generator turning off. As soon as the shimmer died away in front of her, Uhura stood up and tossed the computer datacard down to clang and skitter across the negotiating table.

With an explosion of angry voices, all heads below turned up toward the balcony, seeking the source of the projectile. Uhura stood with both hands clenched on the rail, praying that none of the security guards below would feel threatened enough to stun her with their phasers. She knew she had only a few minutes to make her stand against Jackson Kahle.

Uhura took a deep breath, pitching her trained voice so it would carry to the far corners of the room below. "What kind of precedent for peace did you establish by selling the Romulan cloaking device to the Klingons, Mr. Kahle?"

Her question dropped like a stone into the roar below and silenced it. Uhura watched the human expressions change from incensed to incredulous, while the Romulans turned glaring scowls of suspicion all around them and the Vulcans raised a host of impassive eyebrows. If nothing else, Uhura thought wryly, she had given the participants at the conference something interesting to talk about over lunch.

"Commander Uhura." Kirk's ringing tones broke through the silence. The admiral stood up in his place, her datacard prominently displayed in his lifted hand. "Do you have proof of this accusation?"

He knows, too, Uhura realized, hearing the intensity behind her former captain's measured words. *He must not have gotten the evidence he needs to prove it, but he knows.* She nodded, then realized that the nonhumans below might not recognize that head signal. "Yes, I do, Admiral. That datacard holds a replica of a security certificate, signed by Jackson Kahle, that sent a traitor into the Klingon disruptor lab at Johns Hopkins. The signature and thumbprint are verified to be authentic."

Kahle glared up at her. "But what the hell does that have to do with the Romulan cloaking device?"

"It—it was all part of the same plan." *Don't let him rattle you,* Uhura told herself desperately. The aura of Starfleet authority projected in Kahle's steely gaze made her want to stammer out an ensign's quick apology. "You've already sold the cloaking device to the Klingons, and now you'll sell the disruptor to the Romulans, to—to arm both sides for interplanetary war." Footsteps thundered down the balcony behind her, but she refused to be distracted. "The people who stole the disruptor came from one of your subsidiary companies, and that security certificate proves it."

Kahle barked out a snort of laughter. "The people who stole the disruptor came from Admiral Kirk's old starship, and you, Commander Uhura, are one of them!" He stabbed a finger across the table at Kirk, grimly silent at his place. "I told Nogura you were too young to be kicked up to admiral, Kirk. Other men command ships for decades and never get promoted. You pull off a few flashy missions, get some commendations, and leave boot prints on everyone else's forehead. Just not enough seasoning, not enough years in the field to be sure you could be trusted. And this debacle proves it!"

Rough hands seized Uhura from behind as a security squad converged on her. She didn't try to struggle with them. "Commodore deCandido, what do you want us to do with her?" one of the guards called down over the balcony.

The commander of the Security Academy hesitated, glancing first at Admiral Kirk and then at Jackson Kahle. Neither man spoke, although they exchanged a look that crackled between them like an electric arc.

Commodore deCandido sighed. "Arrest her," he said.

* * *

Having finally braved the darkness of the orbital platform, Broad exploded the mooring bolts on the final catwalk while Chekov stood by and fingered the resin on his newly casted arm. The lightweight sheath hadn't hardened as neatly as before; the angle of his wrist and palm made his forearm ache with vague discomfort, and the edge below his elbow gripped just a little too tightly against the muscles there. Maybe the break had started swelling again, he thought. Whatever the cause, he couldn't keep from tugging at the opening the way he would have a constrictive tunic collar. And just like the collar would have, his cast refused all attempts at after-the-fact resizing.

"That's it." Broad turned his back to the lock the moment his hands finished freeing the catwalk. It was as if he couldn't stand to witness the destruction he'd set in motion, as if ignoring the consequences made what he'd done not count. "That's the last one I know about, at least."

Chekov nodded and stepped forward to watch the catwalk's retreat through the airlock window. "And what were you supposed to do after cutting the last escape route free?" The sinuous tube of cable, glass, and polycarbon curled back on itself like a length of burning plastic, flashing in the space-cold touch of the distant sun.

"I was supposed to take you back to Leong at the dry-dock transporter platform."

Chekov cocked a frown over one shoulder, pulling again at the edges of his cast. "What about Stern?"

Broad only looked at him. His capacity to answer uncomfortable questions had been steadily deteriorating.

"She went over to the *Enterprise*, didn't she?"

Broad nodded.

"And Leong ordered you to abandon her there?" Not that Chekov minded having her cut off from the rest of the platform while they went to meet Leong. The lieutenant's duplicity toward his own comrades just shocked Chekov, even after everything else he'd seen Leong do.

As if having heard Chekov's thoughts in the empty corridor, Broad smiled weakly and offered the ensign a little shrug. "This had something to do with my growing conviction that Leong didn't have my best interests at heart."

But you were still going to do it, Chekov thought soberly. It occurred to him that he'd do well to remember how many sides Broad had already been on in this conflict; it wasn't as if Chekov had recruited the most trustworthy ally ever.

"Stick with the problem in front of you," Oberste's voice reminded him, and Chekov nodded impatiently as he moved away from the airlock, with Broad following hastily behind.

While warmer and slightly better ventilated due to a network of completed atmosphere ducts, the dry-dock orbital platform was just as empty and silent as the vacant ship had been. Chekov threaded a trail as far away from the airlock passage as he dared go, stopping at every intersection to wave Broad forward and to check his bearings. It wasn't the same dry-dock layout he remembered from Academy tours as a cadet; at least, he didn't think it was the same. But Broad had confirmed that the transporter platform still sprawled between the first deck's central support pylons, and that the construction crew's quarters still occupied most of the third through seventh levels.

They'd blown the airlocks one by one in a line leading away from the dry dock's central spine, finishing as far from the platform's transporter facility as Chekov could possibly contrive. Still, he hated the loud clanging of their footsteps on the grated floor, hated the long halls of openness stretching from one end of the dry dock to the other. He detoured into the second maintenance tunnel they passed, unable to stand the exposure anymore.

"Where are we going?" Broad hitched to a stop inside

the tunnel entrance, his voice echoing up the tall ladderway.

Chekov, already three rungs up, squatted to scowl a hush down at him. "I'm taking you to the crew billets," he whispered. He reached out to hook Broad's sleeve with the fingers poking out of his cast and urged the tech two steps farther into the tunnel. "It's only two decks up, and this will be faster than following the normal pedestrian routes. We need to be quick and we need to be careful." *Swift, Silent, and Deadly.* He didn't remember who at the Security Academy had first told him that unofficial motto, but it chilled him to realize how appropriate it had become.

"But if we don't go to Leong . . ."

Chekov straightened, climbing another few rungs to give Broad room to grab hold of the ladder below him. "*I'll* go to Leong," he promised, starting upward with a deliberateness he hoped he could make Broad believe in. "You're going to contact Starfleet Command from one of the billet radios and get someone to send help. I'll give you the correct priority codes and show you how to reply to them." An uncertain murmur from somewhere beneath his feet made Chekov peek past his elbow at the bruised and frightened face below. "Remember—we need each other as witnesses. I can't afford to let *you* die, either."

Broad ducked his head in what might have been an unsteady nod, then continued climbing in silence.

By the time they could see the deck three access above them, Chekov's legs had reached the point of leaden numbness that had been lurking just on the other side of fatigue. He crawled out into the corridor on hands and knees, then used the closest billet door to drag himself ungracefully to his feet. Even so, he wasted three minutes of their precious time with his casted arm braced against the bulkhead and his ankle gripped behind his back, trying to stretch some feeling back into his thighs. Broad paced in tiny, nervous circles, unable to conceal his unhappiness about the delay or about Chekov's slow progress, before the ensign finally limped the last dozen meters to the entrance of Scott's waiting quarters.

"If we were this close," Broad whispered peevishly, "why didn't you just tell me?"

Chekov opened the door without volunteering a reply.

Once inside, Chekov dropped into the com terminal's desk chair and rubbed at his thigh while punching one-fingered codes into the keyboard as fast as his injured hand would allow. The delicious swell of pleasure offered up by his muscles the moment he relieved them of work nearly pulled a groan from him. He fought it back for the sake of his own dignity; besides, both Broad and he had enough to worry about without him admitting how shallow the reserves were he was running on. Abandoning his efforts at self-massage, he lifted both hands to the keyboard and tucked his legs underneath his chair to bring back a little of the discomfort.

"Give me twenty minutes before you start transmitting." A crisp blue screen scattered with stars and the ovoid Starfleet logo welcomed him into the communications net. Chekov pushed back from the terminal and carefully stood. His calf muscles felt two inches shorter than they had only three days before. "I'm assuming Leong has communications monitored, so you have to give me time to distract him or he'll know the minute you open the call."

Broad sank into a chair without looking at Chekov, staring at the waiting screen and running both hands through his hair as though preparing to take on the worst Academy simulation ever devised. "Is twenty minutes going to be long enough? I mean, what happens to me if you *haven't* got him distracted before I start the signal?"

The technician's blatant self-interest seemed oddly amusing against the backdrop of multiple murders and interstellar intrigue. "If I haven't managed to do something with Leong by twenty minutes from now," Chekov said with a weary smile, "then he's probably already killed me and started looking for you. I'd suggest you ask

Starfleet Command to hurry, because they'll be the only ones who can help you then."

"Great." Broad took a deep breath and poised his hands beside the keyboard, ready to pounce as soon as the chronometer gave him permission. "Just great."

Chekov left him that way, fearing only that Broad would frighten himself into transmitting too early and thus ruin everybody's chances for survival. Still, it wasn't as if they had any other options open, so he tried to anticipate Oberste's advice and wiped Broad and the radio from his thinking as he moved on to the second part of the plan.

It took him only seven minutes to reach central sector.

Easing down the ladder proved harder than climbing up. With each rung, his knees refused to support him beyond a ninety-degree bend; he dropped heavily each time he stepped down to the next foothold, always sure he wasn't positioned correctly to keep from plunging the full three stories, always finding the rung squarely with his arch before he lost his balance. His hands trembled from seizing tightly over and over again the rods of chilly metal, and his jaw ached from clenching. It was all he could do to slip quietly off the last two rungs onto the decking, then pad out into the open hall without stumbling about like a bear.

Sneaking up on anyone in this echo chamber was impossible; the very attempt would be made conspicuous by its futility. So he tried to keep his walk firm and confident, crossing the final distance to the transporter room doorway as though he had nothing to fear from it. He was supposed to be Peter Broad, after all, returning triumphant with his prisoner and his weapon. Let Leong think Broad was stupid enough to walk into his own murder without questioning. It was Chekov who approached now with the phaser in his grip, and he could use every haughty assumption Leong could possibly spare.

He didn't mean to slow down just before the open doorway, but he did it anyway, flexing his casted hand into a fist and bringing that arm down tight to his side. As he tipped back the phaser to verify the setting and dispersal, a light, teasing voice called out, "Come on in, Chekov. I've been waiting to see if I'd hear two sets of footsteps, or one. If I don't see you in the next thirty seconds, I'll blow his brains right through this wall."

"Don't worry about me, lad!" Scott shouted. The engineer sounded defiant and angry, and Chekov felt a pang of bitter guilt at the Scotsman's brave words.

Chekov stepped around the doorway with the phaser held stubbornly in front of him. It wouldn't save him— he knew that. All it would grant him was the right to die with a gun in his hand. Still, that was a right he wasn't about to let Leong take away, not after the traitor had already stolen so much else that mattered to him. "All right, I'm here, damn you." Chekov jerked a stiff nod across the room at Scott, too angry to even meet the Scotsman's eyes. "Now let him go."

Feigning a look of hurt surprise, Leong quirked a brittle smile and kept his phaser pressed to Scott's temple with easy malice. "And have you shoot me the minute you've got him out of our way? I don't think so." Hatred glittered brightly from deep inside his cold black eyes. "It's my call this time, Ensign. Throw down your phaser, or the engineer dies."

Chapter Twenty-one

SINCE THEY'D LEFT the *Enterprise,* the one thing Uhura hadn't permitted herself to think about was the possibility of defeat. Now that it loomed in front of her, she felt more stunned than anguished. She'd been so sure that Dr. Piper's evidence would be enough to convict Jackson Kahle of treason. Instead, the billionaire had managed to twist her accusations and hurl them back against the *Enterprise* crew. Uhura wasn't sure what she'd expected after she'd dropped her datacard into the conference, but it certainly wasn't being hustled unceremoniously out to whatever served as the Security Academy's equivalent of the brig.

At the foot of the stairs, the security squad that walled her in was met by a second group of guards, coming in wet-shouldered and dripping from the downpour outside. A handcuffed figure in a scorched silver flightsuit walked in the center of this squad, setting their pace with his painfully slow strides. Uhura opened her mouth on an indignant protest, then caught sight of the plas-skin bandages beneath the torn suit edges and subsided. At least the guards who'd arrested Sulu had been considerate enough to get him some emergency medical care before they'd dragged him out into the rain.

The pilot's eyes met hers through the swarm of silent guards, and his strides lengthened noticeably. "Any luck?"

Uhura held up her wrists to show him her own handcuffs. "I showed them the data-record," she said hurriedly while their groups converged at the foot of the stairs. "Kahle just accused us of stealing the disruptor and shrugged it off. If they take you in, see if you can—"

"Prisoners will refrain from speaking." The canyon-deep voice came from the tall, dark-skinned man who had followed Sulu's guards into the building. He wore the rank of commodore on his sleeves, along with the golden sun and mountain badge of the White Sands Experimental Flight Center. Uhura's eyebrows arched in silent surprise. What on earth was the White Sands base commander doing here in Annapolis? She threw Sulu a questioning look and got only a shrug in reply.

The doors to the conference room burst open, and a figure in Starfleet gold strode out, sweeping the entrance with a commanding hazel gaze. "Bring both those prisoners in for questioning," Admiral Kirk ordered when he saw them, in a tone that brooked neither uncertainty nor delay. The security guards snapped into motion obediently, then paused in confusion when the tall commodore pushed in front and stopped them.

"I really don't think we should disrupt the conference," he advised. "Admiral, if you could just ask Commodore deCandido to come out—"

"I said, bring the prisoners in." The quiet chill in Kirk's voice told Uhura he was furious. "That was a direct order from a superior officer, Commodore Willis. Are you going to disobey it?"

The White Sands base commander locked stares with Kirk for a moment, but his dark eyes were the first to drop. "No," he said stiffly. "Sir."

Kirk grunted acknowledgment and waved the security guards into the conference room. Uhura turned and climbed the three polished oak steps, only to be greeted by a roar of angry voices when she stepped through the heavy, carved doors. Thinking that these accusations were directed at her, Uhura froze on the threshold. The security guard at her shoulder tugged at her, clearing the way for Sulu to enter behind them. By the time Kirk had followed, with Commodore Willis at his heels, Uhura had begun to realize that the shouting wasn't directed at any of them. She could also see why Kirk hadn't been worried about disrupting the conference.

The Romulans had left the negotiating table, gathering into a solid wall of outrage at the far end of the room. Most of the Peace Foundation officials and a few of the Vulcan diplomats seemed to be trying to open a discussion with them, but the sheer volume of Romulan indignation made it an almost impossible task. The remaining Vulcans and the Starfleet officers had gathered into a quieter but equally tense knot in front of the door. Several of them looked up when Kirk entered, with expressions ranging from suspicion to relief.

"All right, gentlemen." Kirk hauled Uhura and Sulu out of their squads of security guards and brought them with him toward the table. "Let's see if we can make some sense of—"

"No!" One of the strident Romulan voices finally outroared the others and won a relative stretch of silence in which to speak. "We will not negotiate with you. We refuse to stay on a planet of such shame!"

"Praetor, we don't know that these accusations are true!" one of the Peace Foundation officials protested.

"But *we* know." The stocky Praetor stepped forward, drawing his metal-studded cloak around himself. "Over the last seven Earth days, we have detected the ion trails of a shielded vessel not our own, probing from our Klingon Neutral Zone. We assumed it to be merely some Romulan outlaw, hiding in the bosom of our enemies. Now we know"—a thick finger pointed wrathfully across at the group of Starfleet officers, centering on Admiral Kirk—"the same treacherous human dogs who stole our cloaking device have sold it to the bloodiest of our enemies!"

Kirk gave the Romulan leader a cold and mirthless smile. "With your permission, Praetor, I'd like to prove that it was not exactly the *same* treacherous human dogs. Feel free to walk out, unless you'd like to find out who your real enemies are."

The Romulan glowered, but made a gesture that halted his second-in-command when the younger man growled and tried to push past. "We'll stay," he said curtly, making another gesture that turned the wing of officers behind him ominously silent. "Do your inquisition, Kirk."

The admiral nodded, then swung around to face Uhura. "Commander, I'd like you to summarize the sequence of events leading up to your acquisition of this evidence against Mr. Kahle."

"Unnecessary." It was a new voice, and although it came from the hooded figure who'd entered with Admiral Kirk, it was *not* the voice of Sarek. Uhura's eyes widened as the hood was thrust back to reveal a scowling Klingon face beneath it.

"Kang!" Uhura shuddered as she recognized the Klingon commander who had once tried to take over the *Enterprise.* A hiss of indrawn breath went through the group of Starfleet officers, and a distinct space widened around the robed figure. Kang replied with a contemptuous snort, striding forward until he stood directly in front of Sulu's security squad.

"There, Kirk." Kang spat the English words out as if they tasted bad on his tongue. "There is the traitor you brought me here to identify." Uhura's heart leaped into her throat as the Klingon commander took another step closer to Sulu and the security guards closed their ranks in response. "We bought the Romulan cloaking device directly from *him.*"

There was no warning. Motion exploded from the back of the security squad, as if someone had broken to run. The attempt didn't succeed. With one powerful Klingon lunge, Kang reached into the tightly packed knot of men, and dragged out Commodore Willis.

"You heard me, Chekov. Throw away your phaser."

Even though he'd expected this ultimatum from Leong —had counted on it, in fact—Chekov still found himself clenching his jaw in anger at being forced into such a heartless decision. "I heard you." He nodded toward Scott, bound with wire and patching tape to some jumble of equipment awaiting the end of the holidays for transport to the *Enterprise*. Leong had just slapped another length of patching tape across the engineer's mouth, effectively excluding Scott from any further discussion. "What's to keep you from killing him the moment you have me unarmed?"

Leong shrugged. "Nothing."

A chain of Russian invectives flashed untranslated into Chekov's mind, and he realized with a twist of disgust exactly what it felt like to want another living creature's death. No guilt, no pleasure—just a dull, aching hatred. "Weren't you the one who told me that a security officer should never surrender his weapon, no matter who the enemy, no matter what the threat?"

"That's a rule for guards who honestly earned their ranks." The loathing in the older officer's voice was savage and bitter. "Not for command school dropouts who only got their assignment because they had a captain in Starfleet Headquarters to pull for them." He motioned with his phaser, more sharply than before, and Scott recoiled almost unconsciously from the movement. "I'm getting tired of saying this—throw down your gun."

Oberste's voice loomed up inside Chekov, as sharp and insistent as if the commander was standing firmly at his right shoulder. "Choose your fights wisely," she warned him with a scowl.

That only works if you get to choose your battles. He was being as wise as the situation would let him. *When this is all over, you can grade me on the outcome.*

His phaser clattered against the foot of the transporter

console, then skated off at an angle to spin to a stop halfway across the deck from Leong. The lieutenant flicked a snake-quick look at the sacrificed weapon, and caustic laughter rippled through him. "Predictable," he declared, as though pronouncing the name of a mineral specimen.

Chekov kept his anger focused tightly on Leong. "So are you."

"We'll see about that." Stepping neatly away from Scott and the clutter of equipment, Leong displayed his own phaser grandly on the flat of one open palm. Then, with a twist, he pitched the gun behind him onto the transporter platform, where it slid behind the dais and disappeared from sight. "Now we get to see who's right about procedure and who's wrong. Go ahead." He jerked his chin at the phaser between them and grinned wickedly. "Pick it up and kill me before I break your neck."

Scott struggled suddenly against the wiring that bound his hands, his eyes wide with warning as he tried to call out from behind the strip of patching tape. But Chekov didn't dare break concentration long enough to look at the engineer. Concern would be too much of a distraction, fear too much like believing Leong had already won. Chekov had to ease himself into the timeless clarity of a weapon—had to absorb every breath and blink and movement of his opponent until some microscopic shift of weight registered in the wordless depths of instinct and his body leapt into action.

Chekov didn't even get to within arm's length of the waiting phaser. Leong darted forward with the playful grace of a dancer, slapping the gun into another skittering slide with one foot and cracking his heel against Chekov's shoulder to throw the ensign backward. Rolling, knowing that distance was his only protection against Leong, Chekov tried to spring to his feet without pressing any weight against his casted right arm. The loss of balance brought him up irregularly, though, and he was forced into taking a single wide step to one side before gathering himself into a proper defense. Leong all but materialized in front of him. Pain exploded, blindingly bright, inside his skull, and some distant, intellectual part of him recognized that Leong must have hit him, although he never actually saw the swing or felt the blow. Chekov backed up hard into the bulkhead behind him, and would have slid straight to the floor if Leong hadn't caught him under the jaw to pin him upright.

"Well, I'm disappointed." The older lieutenant tipped his head as though considering, and Chekov noted, almost absently, that the back of Leong's hand was spattered with drops of fresh blood. "I really thought we'd go a bit longer than this."

Uncomfortably aware of the slimy drizzle of blood down the back of his throat, Chekov thought blearily, *I didn't even want it to go* this *long.* He wondered if his nose was broken, or if Leong had done something even worse.

"I told you, Chekov—you just don't understand what it takes to survive in security. Between the two of us, who would you rather have leading a dangerous landing mission?"

In answer, Chekov uncurled the fist of his right hand and swung as hard as he could for Leong's exposed throat. He didn't really expect to connect with anything vital—Chekov wasn't fast even without the cast to weigh him down, much less with a half kilo of resin to restrict his speed. But he hadn't expected Leong's keen reflexes, either. In a blur of gold and red, the lieutenant's arm shot up between them and caught Chekov's hand palm-to-palm as though he were planning to offer a robust handshake. It was better than Chekov could have possibly hoped for; he closed his eyes in relief and dropped his head back against the bulkhead with a sigh.

Leong seemed more surprised by Chekov's sudden submission than he did by the hiss of the hypospray. Peeling his hand away with dull disbelief, he stared at the palm as though amazed by something he saw there. He never did move to inspect the hypospray embedded in the palm of Chekov's cast, or even raise his eyes in question of what had just been done to him. He only folded slowly down to his knees, then toppled over backward like an overweighted mannequin.

"I meant it for the best."

Uhura looked up from rubbing at her loosened wrists in time to see Admiral Kirk and Sulu exchange an ironic look over Commodore Willis's bent head. The White Sands base commander sat dejected and handcuffed, surrounded by a brace of hostile admirals in lieu of security guards. The other admirals and commodores had closed an equally tight knot around Jackson Kahle, although so far Willis had refused to implicate him.

The proof that Sulu had not been involved in the cloaking device theft had swung the tide in favor of the *Enterprise* crew. Uhura had been freed by a quiet word from Commodore deCandido, who had also sent for a medical team to treat Sulu's burns. The pilot had steadfastly refused to leave the negotiating chamber, in case he was needed to testify against Willis.

"Mr. Willis." It was the highest-ranking admiral who spoke, the short and deceptively placid-looking Hajime Shoji. Uhura noticed he hadn't given Willis the title of his rank. "Are you really trying to tell us that you thought the Federation would benefit from giving the Klingons the Romulans' greatest tactical weapon?"

"Yes!" Willis's resonant voice lifted in defiance. "It will give them the ammunition they need to take on the Romulans at their own game."

"And then turn the cloaking device on us when they're done!" Kirk snapped. Across the room, a growl of angry whispers arose from the Romulan delegation, but Uhura noticed no one made any attempt to leave. Kang stood off to one side, his intense dark eyes never leaving Willis's face. Uhura wasn't sure how Admiral Kirk had convinced the Klingon commander to identify the man who'd sold him the cloaking device, but it was obvious Kang was angry at Willis, too.

The base commander flinched away from the murmur of agreement that followed Kirk's words. "No! Armed with the same weapons, the Romulans and Klingons will tear themselves apart fighting each other." He looked up at the circle of stern faces surrounding him, clearly searching for support. "All we did was give them a level playing field to fight on."

"And the motivation to blame us when they lost," Shoji pointed out relentlessly. "Not to mention the other negative impacts of having half the galaxy immersed in a bloody interspecies war."

Uhura took a deep breath. "There's one impact that won't be negative for some people. Thousands of war contracts will go out through neutral planets, for phaser banks and torpedoes and planetary defense shields."

"But *we* won't be making any of that money," Willis protested, then jerked up in his seat as he realized what he'd just said. "I meant to say—"

"We know what you meant, Mr. Willis." Kirk's voice had turned ice-cold. "You're due to retire next year, and it's common knowledge that you've been offered a top management spot at UniPhase Incorporated."

"That—that may be." Willis swallowed and recovered his poise with an obvious effort. "But what I said is still true. UniPhase is not going to make any money from this exchange of military technology."

"Oh, no?" Kirk turned away from the commodore to pin Jackson Kahle with his cold gaze. The billionaire stared back, clamping his age-spotted hands together to still their tremors. Uhura would have put the quivering down to fear, if she hadn't seen the arctic glare of rage in Kahle's pale eyes. "Then why," Kirk said slowly, "has UniPhase just built forty thousand torpedo drives at their Orion plant?"

Willis's handcuffs racketed up the arm of his chair as he sprang to his feet. "Is that true?" he demanded.

Kirk nodded grimly, but Uhura knew the question hadn't been directed at him. The White Sands base commander was staring at Jackson Kahle. Uhura wasn't sure what he read on the elderly billionaire's face, but she saw the moment the surprise in Willis's gaze became a feeling of betrayal.

"You promised me—" Willis's deep voice faltered for a moment under Kahle's whipping look, then rose with anger. "You promised me you were only doing this for the good of the Federation. You swore you weren't going to make any profit off it yourself!"

Kahle spoke at last, his once steel-sharp voice grating with failure like a rusty knife. "I won't. Personally, I won't. If UniPhase does make money, all the excess profits will go into the Peace Foundation and its work—"

"And that's supposed to justify the deaths of millions of beings in the galaxy?" Sulu demanded hotly.

Kahle shrugged. "Less of 'em for us to fight." His icy eyes swept the furious Romulans and Kang with one dismissive glance. "There's no way those savages will ever come to terms with the civilized galaxy. Every starship captain in the fleet knows it. We'll have to fight them, sooner or later. All I did was tip the odds in our favor."

"At the expense," Admiral Shoji said dryly, "of destroying the reputations and careers of some of the best officers—and future starship captains—in Starfleet."

Kahle looked over at Uhura and sighed. "Necessary evil," he said gruffly. "Someone had to take the blame, and it seemed as good an opportunity as any to leverage Kirk out of Starfleet." His bushy eyebrows lowered slightly, in what was either remorse or the simple acknowledgment of a miscalculation. "I wasn't counting on the whole damn *Enterprise* crew pitching in to help out a couple of their former bridge officers."

"Or on old enemies working together to discover who was manipulating them into a war." Kirk nodded at Kang, who snorted some kind of Klingon reply back at him.

Admiral Shoji shook his head. "But most of all, Mr. Kahle, you didn't count on the fact that Starfleet is full of honorable men and women, who will not let injustice be done to anyone if they can help it." He gestured to the security guards at the doors and they came forward in a rush. "Admiral Kirk, I believe I'll let you give this order. It seems only fitting."

"Thank you, Admiral." Kirk drew himself up to his full height, hazel eyes gleaming. "Jackson Kahle and Adam Willis, you are hereby placed under arrest for murder, attempted murder, conspiracy, theft of restricted technology, and"—Kirk paused to let his final words echo in the waiting silence—"high treason. Take them away."

Chekov stumbled away from Leong's prostrate body, his head swimming in thick, dizzy circles. Right now, he wanted nothing so much as to find someplace to sit down.

A muffled complaint from near the transporter pad caught his attention before he'd made it very far from the wall. Detouring somewhat groggily, he stumbled across to fumble with Scott's bindings while the engineer grumbled and pulled and generally got in the way. Chekov was almost ready to give up and leave him there by the time Scott finally wormed one hand free to yank the tape off his lips.

"Good God, lad!" He stood and half-turned to squirm his other hand out of the bindings. "Are you all right? You're bleeding all over the place!"

Chekov thought about nodding, but even envisioning such a movement made his head clog up with pain. "Trazadone hydrochloride," he said, very carefully and slowly.

Scott looked up from disentangling the kinked-up wire from the equipment. "What's that?"

"Trazadone hydrochloride," Chekov said again. He helped himself to a seat on the steps to the transporter and rested his forehead in his hand. "I don't know how many cc's. I knew Leong would never kill me without giving me the chance to humiliate myself. All I had to do was let him do it." He rotated his cast palm up and fingered the hypospray nozzle that Broad had so carefully placed there after loading it with the anesthetic of choice. Abruptly, a swell of nausea rocked his stomach, and he closed up his hand to lean back against the edge of the transporter pad with a groan.

"Mr. Scott, could you restrain Mr. Leong for me, please? I don't think I'll be able to stand up and help you right now."

Before Scott could even respond, Chekov's adrenaline released its days-long hold on his system and dropped him down into blessed darkness.

Chapter Twenty-two

New Harborplace
Baltimore, North America
Terrestrial Date: January 1, 2270
0000 hours EST

PHOSPHORESCENT FIRE exploded in the night over Baltimore's Inner Harbor, throwing gold and crimson shimmers across the dark water below. From her seat near the window of a downtown tower restaurant, Uhura watched spangles of afterglow cascade past in a shower of glowing ruby and topaz embers. She sighed into her cupped hands.

"If someone had told me a week ago that I'd be watching fireworks here with you at midnight on New Year's Eve," she informed her table-mate, "I wouldn't have believed them."

Sulu grinned at her over the elegant dinner candles. A few days of antiradiation treatments had brought the pilot's face back to its usual smoothness, and his subsequent "recuperation" at a Colorado ski resort had wind-burned the color back into his cheeks. Out of respect for the four-star restaurant they'd selected for their New Year's celebration, he'd exchanged his silver flightsuit for a more formal gold Starfleet tunic, but the recent barrage of press attention still made the other restaurant patrons glance at him and whisper. The attention didn't seem to bother Sulu, although it made Uhura want to go check herself in the mirror and make sure she didn't have a smudge on her nose.

"And what if they'd told you we'd be here celebrating our reassignment to the *Enterprise?*" the helmsman asked while he scanned the wine list. "What would you have done then?"

"Pinched myself and woken up!" Uhura retorted, laughing. "What are you going to order for us to celebrate with?"

"Altairean champagne." At her startled gasp, Sulu grinned again. "Hey, I've got a week's worth of hazardous-duty pay to spend. Not to mention our special service bonuses for catching Kahle and Willis. Speaking of which . . ." He reached in one pocket and pulled out a bracelet, casually tossing it across the table to her. Turquoise glowed, lustrous as evening clouds, inside squash blossoms made of authentic Navajo hammered silver. "Here. I picked this up in Alamogordo—at the suggestion of a friend."

"Sulu! It's beautiful." Uhura draped the heavy silver appreciatively over her wrist, then looked up when a new wash of whispers swept through the quiet restaurant. A figure in distinctive Security red threaded his way through the candlelit dimness toward them, his smile of greeting made only a little crooked by the recognition he was getting. "Chekov! You got your cast off!"

The Russian nodded and took the seat beside Uhura. Another firework painted the sky bright teal and azure behind him. "And that's not all." He held out his sleeve for her to see the new rank stripes on it, laughing a little at her amazed look. "Admiral Kirk just told me today."

"You made lieutenant!" Uhura reached over to give him a quick, happy hug. "Oh, Pavel, that's wonderful!"

"*Two* bottles of Altairean champagne," Sulu told the hovering waiter.

"And food!" Uhura interjected. "I haven't eaten—"

"—since you left California," Chekov and Sulu finished in unison for her.

She made a face across the table at them. "Well, it's true. I want the vegetarian stuffed grape leaves, the tabouleh salad, and the lobster couscous." She gave her companions a laughing look. "*And* dates and nuts baked in phyllo for dessert."

The waiter nodded, jotting the order down on his tastefully old-fashioned notepad. "And for the gentlemen?"

Sulu never hesitated. "I want the muhjadra appetizer, the dandelions with fried onions, the okra and lamb stew, and zalabee for dessert." He glanced over at Chekov with a wicked grin. "The same for you, Pavel?"

"No." Chekov leaned over the menu scrolling down the tabletop. "I want a meat pie, some shish kebab, and kibbe."

"Kibbe?" Uhura exchanged startled looks with Sulu while the waiter discreetly vanished. "Chekov, do you know what kibbe is?"

He gave her a surprised look. "Lamb, onions, and bulgur wheat, all ground together. Why?"

"Do you know how they cook it?" Sulu demanded.

"They don't." Chekov grinned at their dumbfounded faces. "I *like* it raw."

Sulu whistled in amazement. "Will wonders never cease? He eats strange ethnic food, and he's a lieutenant, too." The pilot leaned over to punch at his friend's shoulder in elation. "God, you're not even out of security school yet and already you've gotten a promotion! How did you manage that?"

Chekov's grin widened until it almost matched Sulu's. "By getting assigned to be the next security chief on the *Enterprise*," he said modestly, then sat back and enjoyed their whoops of delight. "Admiral Kirk put in a good word for me with the assignment board. He said he was impressed by the way I handled the situation up on the orbital platform." The young Russian's dark eyes shone with pride. "He said I demonstrated a lot more maturity than the average ensign."

Sulu snorted with laughter. "By the time we came up

to rescue you, all I noticed you demonstrating was your ability to snore."

Uhura swatted the pilot in exasperation. "Admiral Kirk was right," she told Chekov. "You not only rescued Mr. Scott and protected us, but you did it with minimal casualties."

"That's what the assignment board said when they accepted the admiral's recommendation." Chekov's face turned sober. "But it's not true. I probably would have killed Leong if I could have thought of any safe way to do it. I just couldn't."

Sulu snorted again, this time more seriously. "Oh, yeah? You mean you couldn't have found a vial of synthetic adrenaline in one of those medical cabinets? All you would have had to do was put that in your cast instead of a tranquilizer, and Leong would be dead now." He poked a stern finger at Chekov. "You may have *felt* like killing him, but you didn't *want* to kill him. There's a big difference, and the assignment board knows it."

Uhura nodded. "That's why they picked you, Chekov. Because you didn't have to stop and decide to save lives—your instincts simply worked that way."

The Russian's cheeks darkened, but the arrival of the Altairean champagne, jasmine-sweet and fizzing pearlescently in its fluted goblets, saved him from further embarrassment. Uhura smiled and reached for the first ruby-red glassful, then held it high above the table.

"To us," Uhura said. A gold and silver firework blossomed in the night outside, throwing sparkling shadows across the glasses Sulu and Chekov lifted to meet hers. "And to another five years together on the *Enterprise.*"

Epilogue

THE *ENTERPRISE*'S SECONDARY HULL glinted silver-blue in the rising earthlight, a distant angel whose wings were wrapped in a tinsel glitter of scaffolding and wires. Kirk gazed at her through the porthole of the diplomatic courier, almost unconsciously assessing the newly integrated lines of her pylon and struts, the radically redesigned warp drive that would let her attain cruising speeds he'd only dreamed of in his days as her captain.

A snort misted the porthole and obscured the view. "Your ship out there?" Kang demanded, leaning across Kirk's shoulder with the blunt curiosity that passed for politeness in a Klingon.

Kirk sighed and hitched his attention back to the task at hand: escorting his unruly temporary ally out to his waiting ship. "The *Enterprise,* yes. She's being refitted."

Under shaggy brows, Kang's eyes gleamed with the dark intelligence Kirk kept reminding himself not to underrate. "No longer under your command?"

273

L. A. Graf

"No." At least he didn't need to worry about how curt that might sound. The Klingon would consider it normal conversation. "I've been . . . promoted."

"Battle leader?" Kang demanded, the deepening growl of his voice betraying aroused military instincts. "Strategist?"

Kirk's lips twisted. "Diplomatic envoy." He didn't try to hide the frustration coiling through his voice. "In charge of conferences like the one we just had with the Romulans."

A more contemptuous Klingon snort feathered hot breath across the courier's windows. "Wars fought with words instead of valor. They are beneath a warrior's dignity, Kirk."

"That didn't stop you from taking part in this one," Kirk pointed out ironically.

Kang grunted. "It was the lesser dishonor to barter a few worthless star systems to the Romulans than to fight them at some human traitor's bidding." He pointed a scornful fist at Kirk. "But I will never put aside my disruptor and surrender my ship to another commander."

Kirk strangled the first, angry retort that rose to his lips, letting his tension out with a grunt of mirthless laughter. "Become famous for solving intergalactic problems, Kang, and see if you can still say that."

The Klingon regarded him in stymied silence. "I had hoped to face you one more time on the battlefield, Kirk," he said at last. "You and that ship—" Kang jerked his chin at the silhouette of the *Enterprise,* now dwindling to a distant silver glimmer behind them. "Together, you would have made me a worthy opponent."

Together. Kirk shrugged away the unwelcome longing as that word shivered through him, like waves from a carelessly thrown stone. *Together* was a word for someone else to savor now, some young captain at the beginning of his Starfleet career. It was not a word that fit in an admiral's vocabulary.

"Another time, Commander Kang." Kirk tried to keep his voice even, but a last phantom glint of the *Enterprise,* orbiting high above the blue and white skirl of Earth, turned his words jagged with regret. "Another life."